HE WAS, UNDOUBTEDLY,
THE WORLD'S OLDEST MALE VIRGIN.

The oldest male virgin *vampire,* he amended.

He had been turned on his thirty-ninth birthday. He recalled the event as clearly as if it had happened only last night instead of centuries ago.

He had been on his way back to the rectory after giving last rites to an aged nun when he was attacked. It had happened so fast, he'd had no chance to defend himself, although he knew now that would have been impossible. He was floating, drifting away into darkness, when the vampire suddenly reared back. Giovanni remembered staring up into a pair of blood-red eyes that somehow managed to look surprised.

"You're a priest!" the creature hissed. "I can't kill a priest! Heaven forgive me," he murmured, and sinking his fangs into his own wrist, he held the bleeding wound to Giovanni's lips. "Drink!"

Giovanni wanted to refuse but something in the monster's voice compelled him to obey.

NIGHT'S ILLUSION

AMANDA ASHLEY

ZEBRA BOOKS
KENSINGTON PUBLISHING CORP.
www.kensingtonbooks.com

ZEBRA BOOKS are published by

Kensington Publishing Corp.
119 West 40th Street
New York, NY 10018

All Kensington titles, imprints, and distributed lines are available at special quantity discounts for bulk purchases for sales promotion, premiums, fund-raising, educational, or institutional use.

Special book excerpts or customized printings can also be created to fit specific needs. For details, write or phone the office of the Kensington Sales Manager: Attn.: Sales Department. Kensington Publishing Corp., 119 West 40th Street, New York, NY 10018. Phone: 1-800-221-2647.

Zebra and the Z logo Reg. U.S. Pat. & TM Off.

First Printing: September 2021
ISBN-13: 978-1-4201-5161-9
ISBN-10: 1-4201-5161-4

ISBN-13: 978-1-4201-5162-6 (eBook)
ISBN-10: 1-4201-5162-2 (eBook)

10 9 8 7 6 5 4 3 2 1

Printed in the United States of America

To my grandson, Luke,
for his inspiration.
Love you.

Prologue

Father Giovanni Lanzoni strolled through the city park's narrow, deserted, twisting paths. A brilliant yellow moon hung low in the sky, illuminating his way, though he needed no light to guide his feet. He was Nosferatu, one of the oldest of his kind. As such, he was blessed—or cursed—with supernatural senses and preternatural strength.

Like all vampires who had survived more than a century or two, he had grown to love and appreciate the quiet beauty of the night. He enjoyed being able to see clearly in the dark, to hear the flutter of a moth's wings, to move from place to place with astonishing speed, to think himself across great distances, to move faster than mortal eyes could follow, to dissolve into mist. So many amazing supernatural powers, all his to command.

He had never expected to survive so long. He had always been a pacifist—given to contemplation rather than conflict. As a child, he had dreamed of dedicating his life to the Church. It had proved to be all he had hoped for and more. He had loved the discipline, the interior silence, the sense of inner peace born of service and self-sacrifice. Hearing confessions . . .

He grinned inwardly. His most recent confession—heard only a few years ago—had come from Nick Desanto. Nick had been born a slave in Egypt and had been turned by the infamous Queen of the Vampires—Mara, herself.

Giovanni had known Mara for centuries. They had met when he was still mortal. He had been a young priest at the time, hoping to render aid and comfort on a battlefield in Tuscany. She had been in search of prey. The only thing that had saved him that night had been her surprising reluctance to harm a man of the cloth—or perhaps it had been some ancient superstition regarding priests.

They had met again when he was a young vampire in the streets of Paris. He had been badly injured and close to death when she found him. She had generously offered him a little of her ancient blood and it had revived him. And then, for reasons unknown, she had tasted his. They had both undergone some amazing changes since that long-ago night.

In the years since then, he had made a few friends and an enemy or two—both mortal and immortal—in countries around the globe. As a priest, he had willingly given up all thought of home and family. But now, having lived like a monk for so long, he thought he would gladly give up immortality to know the simple joys of one mortal lifetime. To experience a woman's love. To father a child. To watch his sons and daughters grow and have children of their own. What good was endless life when you had no one to share it with?

Leaving the park, he ambled down the street toward his lair.

The DeLongpre/Cordova coven was the closest thing he

had to a family. He considered himself blessed indeed to be a part of their lives and to have officiated at their weddings.

His steps slowed as he gazed at the vast expanse of the sky. Worlds without end, he mused. Times changed, the world itself changed, but he remained forever the same. In mortality, he had been an ordained priest. As such, he had made vows of chastity, poverty, and obedience. He had been celibate in mortality.

And in death.

Lately, he had begun to rethink his vow to remain chaste. Though he was, at least in his own eyes, still a priest, he was no longer recognized as such by the Church that doubtless thought him dead long ago. He had no parish, no superior. Why did he cling to a vow that, after so many centuries, was very likely no longer binding? He had broken the others without a second thought.

Why now, after so many centuries, did he suddenly feel so alone? So lonely?

He thought of Mara again. She had spent centuries refusing to be tied down. Yet she had been married twice—once to a mortal, and now to Logan Blackwood, the man she had loved for centuries. She had been blessed with a son.

Others of his kind had found companions. Roshan DeLongpre. Vince Cordova and his twin sons, Rane and Rafe. Mara's son, Derek. Nick Desanto. Vampires one and all. Yet each had found love. Even feisty ex-vampire hunters Edna Mae Turner and Pearl Jackson—both turned far past their prime—had found life mates.

Why not him? Perhaps it was time to remember that, in addition to being a priest, he was first and foremost a man.

He chuckled softly. He was, undoubtedly, the world's oldest male virgin.

The oldest male virgin *vampire,* he amended.

He had been turned on his thirty-ninth birthday. He recalled the event as clearly as if it had happened only last night instead of centuries ago.

He had been on his way back to the rectory after giving last rites to an aged nun when he was attacked. It had happened so fast, he'd had no chance to defend himself, although he knew now that would have been impossible. He was floating, drifting away into darkness, when the vampire suddenly reared back. Giovanni remembered staring up into a pair of bloodred eyes that somehow managed to look surprised.

"You're a priest!" the creature hissed. "I can't kill a priest! Heaven forgive me," he murmured, and sinking his fangs into his own wrist, he held the bleeding wound to Giovanni's lips. "Drink!"

Giovanni wanted to refuse but something in the monster's voice compelled him to obey. The blood had been thick and hot, unlike anything he had ever tasted. He gagged with the first swallow and then, to his horror, he grabbed hold of the vampire's arm and suckled as if the blood was as sweet as mother's milk.

He had cried out in protest when the vampire jerked his wrist away.

"We have to find you a place to rest," the vampire muttered, yanking Giovanni to his feet. "And there are things you must know before you rise tomorrow night."

The vampire had dragged him to a cave in the Apennine

Mountains and tossed him into it with a warning to stay inside until he returned.

Giovanni had had no intention of doing as he was told, but minutes after entering the cave he had collapsed on the floor. As his vision narrowed and the world went black, he knew he was dying. Sinking into oblivion, he had uttered a prayer begging for mercy and forgiveness with his last breath.

When awareness returned, it was dark again. Lurching to his feet, he had stumbled toward the cave's entrance, his gaze searching for the creature who had warned him to wait for his return.

Hours passed and there was no sign of the vampire.

As time dragged by, what started as discomfort gradually turned to agony.

Afraid he was really dying this time, he staggered out of the cave and made his way to the city in search of a doctor.

Ignorant as he was, he had no idea what was happening to him. He stopped abruptly, nostrils flaring. He didn't recognize the scent, knew only that whatever it was, he needed it. Veering down a narrow alley, he came upon two men engaged in a knife fight.

Giovanni took a deep breath. *Blood,* he thought. The enticing smell was blood.

Hardly aware of what he was doing, he stepped between the two men. It took no effort at all to control them. One was bleeding from a cut on his neck. As though mesmerized, Giovanni leaned forward to lick it up and then, to his horror, he bit the man. Overcome with euphoria at the taste of fresh hot blood, he hadn't stopped to wonder at how effortlessly his teeth had bitten through flesh. It was only later that he discovered he had fangs, and that blood was the only thing that could ease the awful hunger that clawed at his insides.

And later still that he found the courage to admit he was no longer human, but Nosferatu.

The transformation had not been easy. To his shame, he had taken human lives before he learned it wasn't necessary to kill his prey to survive. Stricken with guilt, he had gone to confession time and again in hopes of finding forgiveness for the lives he had taken, but he had found none.

Thrusting his past behind him, Giovanni willed himself to his lair in the bowels of an abandoned church. He had another, more comfortable place where he occasionally passed the daylight hours, but resting here, among the dead, seemed more appropriate for one of his kind.

Stretching out on the cold stone floor between a pair of ancient coffins, he closed his eyes and surrendered to the deathlike sleep that swallowed him whole.

Chapter 1

From his place on the bed, Logan Blackwood watched Mara pace the floor of their Hollywood home. "What's wrong?" he asked.

She shook her head. "You won't believe this, but I'm picking up some sort of weird vibe from Father Lanzoni."

"The old priest? What kind of vibe?"

"Like he's . . . lonely."

Logan sat up. "Wait a minute? How the devil can you know that?"

"I have no idea. We've never exchanged blood. . . ." Her voice trailed off and she frowned. "Wait a minute. I think maybe we did, a few hundred years ago." She shook her head. "Assuming I did, why would I suddenly be able to read his thoughts now, after such a long time?"

"Beats the hell out of me." Logan grabbed her forearm as she passed by the bed, pulled her down on the mattress, and tucked her beneath him. He had known her for centuries, but he never tired of looking at her. Hair as black as ink tumbled over her shoulders. "Think about me instead."

She looked up at him through sultry, emerald-green eyes. "I'm always thinking of you."

"Good." His hand stroked up and down her back.

In a move too quick even for him to follow, she rolled over, carrying him with her, until she was on top. "Later," she said, nipping his earlobe. "I need to call Giovanni."

"Don't you think if he wanted help, *he* would call *you?*"

She scowled at him, then sighed. "You're right. I need to think of a reason to get in touch with him."

"I don't know what it would be," he muttered. "Everybody in the family is already married."

"You're not helping."

"Mara, the man is more than old enough to take care of himself."

"You're right, but he's not just lonely. He's alone."

Logan grunted softly. He knew what that was like. He and Mara had been lovers centuries ago. When she dumped him, he had wandered the earth, feeling lost and lonely for what had seemed like an eternity, until he ran into her again hundreds of years later.

"I think we need to find him a woman."

"A woman! Mara, he's a priest!"

She made a face at him. "He's a man first. And a man needs a woman. Even if he is a priest." She batted his hands away when he tried to caress her. "Stop that! I need to think."

"Making love will relax you and help clear your mind," he said, leering at her.

She glared at him. "Do you ever think of anything else?"

"Not when you're this close."

With a sigh, she stretched out on top of him. It was impossible to ignore Logan when he was looking at her like that, his black eyes hot and heavy-lidded with desire. She had known countless men in the course of her long existence, but she had loved none of them the way she loved this man. As a mortal, he had been arrogant, self-confident, and strong, characteristics that had served him well as a vampire.

"Hektor." She threaded her fingers through his long, dark hair, then claimed his lips with hers.

Logan smiled. Hektor was the name he had worn centuries ago when they met. Rolling her onto her back, he buried himself deep within her sweetness.

The good Father's problem would have to wait one more day.

Finding a companion for her old friend was still on Mara's mind when she woke late the next afternoon. Pulling on a red velvet robe, she kissed her sleeping husband, then went downstairs. One of the perks of being an ancient vampire was the ability to endure the sun's light.

Standing on the balcony of her Hollywood mansion, she gazed into the distance.

The first thing she needed to do was find a woman suitable for Lanzoni. No easy task, she mused, since she had no female friends other than those she considered family. And they were all married.

An ad on the Internet, she decided with a grin. *Wanted, unmarried female, 25-30, preferably a virgin. Must be willing to sleep days. Object: matrimony.*

She could always kidnap some lovely young thing as a last resort.

But before she went that far, maybe she'd get in touch with a few family members and see if they had any ideas.

* * *

Savannah frowned at her husband. "I can't believe Mara wants our help in finding a woman for Father Lanzoni."

"I wouldn't put anything past her," Rane Cordova muttered. "But if she thinks he needs a woman, she'll find him one, whether he wants her to or not. You can bet on that. Pimping for a priest." He threw back his head and laughed. "Now I've heard everything!"

Edna Mae hurried toward Pearl's house, which was located across a narrow swath of grass, only to find her longtime best friend hurrying toward her.

"Did you hear the news?" they said in unison, then broke out laughing.

"I take it you got a phone call from Mara about Father Lanzoni," Edna Mae said.

"Yes, dear! Can you imagine, trying to find a woman for a priest! What is Mara thinking?"

Edna Mae shook her head. "I'm sure I have no idea. She does realize we're in New Mexico, doesn't she?"

"Of course, she does. But when has a little inconvenience ever bothered her?" Pearl laughed again. "I can't wait to tell Monroe! See you later, dear."

Kathy looked askance at her husband as he set his cell phone aside. "What did Mara want? We haven't heard from her in ages."

Rafe Cordova shook his head. "You won't believe this. She thinks our priest is lonely and needs a mate."

"Well, every man needs a woman," Kathy said with a grin.

"I can't argue with that," he said, pulling her into his arms. "But the man's a priest. He's been celibate for centuries. I don't know what makes her think he's looking for female companionship after all this time."

"If you'd been celibate for hundreds of years, you'd be looking, too."

"You got that right!"

She cuffed him on the shoulder, then kissed him. "I'm glad you didn't wait centuries."

"Me, too, darlin'. I hope Lanzoni really wants a woman, 'cause I've never known Mara to fail once she puts her mind to something."

Abbey Marie looked at her husband and laughed. "You've got to be kidding."

Nick shook his head. "She sounded dead serious to me—you'll forgive the pun."

"But a woman? For Father Lanzoni? He's a priest!"

"He made those vows hundreds of years ago when he was mortal. I don't think anyone will hold it against him if he breaks them now."

"I guess not. But surely, he doesn't need any help. I mean, he's a great guy. And not bad-looking, either."

"Well, it's Mara's problem."

"Not really, Mr. Nick Desanto," she exclaimed, arms akimbo. "You said Mara expects the family to help her find—how did she put it?—'the perfect woman.'"

"Well, she's out of luck," Nick said, pulling Abbey into his lap. "Because I've already found her."

* * *

"Your mother called while you were out," Sheree informed her husband. "You won't believe what she wanted to talk about."

Derek Blackwood grunted softly. "When dealing with my mother, nothing would surprise me. What did she want?"

"She asked for our assistance."

Taking his wife in his arms, he kissed her, long and slow and deep, before asking, "What does my mother, the infamous Queen of the Vampires, want from us that she can't get for herself?"

"A wife for Father Lanzoni," Sheree said, stifling a grin. "She's calling everyone in the family for help."

Derek stared at her, then threw back his head and laughed. "Heaven help the poor man. He's as good as married!"

Chapter 2

Giovanni frowned when he checked his phone and saw Mara's name. He hadn't heard from her in a couple of years, he thought as he answered and said hello.

"Giovanni, how are you?"

"Same as always," he replied. "Is something wrong?"

"You tell me."

"Everything's fine here. So, to what do I owe the honor of this call?"

"I've been thinking about you quite a lot lately."

"Oh?" He didn't like the sound of that at all.

"Well, that's not entirely true," she said. "I sensed some of your thoughts a few days ago and . . ."

"You *what?*" he exclaimed. *How the hell was that possible? And why now?*

"You heard me."

"What thoughts?" he asked, wondering what she was talking about. And then he knew.

"We just want to help."

"We?" he exclaimed, wondering how many people she had discussed this with. "Who is *we?*"

"Just the family."

Giovanni groaned as he imagined the whole family laughing at him, making jokes about the poor old priest looking for a woman.

"No one's laughing," Mara said quietly.

Time to start blocking my thoughts, he decided. *Or, more likely, past time.*

"To start things off, I put an ad on the Internet," Mara said.

He groaned softly. "You didn't. Tell me you didn't."

"I already got an inquiry. You're to meet Adella tonight at ten at Club Raven."

"Have you lost your mind? I'm not going to go meet some strange woman in a nightclub."

"What are you afraid of? You're a vampire, not some puny mortal who can't defend himself."

"I'm not afraid," he said, which was a blatant lie. Not that he was scared of being attacked. Hardly. But he was desperately afraid of making a fool of himself. He had never had a date in his life, and he was far too old to start now.

"We'll make it a double date," Mara said cheerfully. "Logan and I will meet you there."

"No, Mara."

"Ten o'clock, Giovanni. Don't be late."

Shoulders slumped in defeat, he tossed his cell phone on the sofa, then leaned back in his chair.

Adella. What was she like? Tall or short? Pretty or plain? He shook his head. Probably some lonely female as pathetic as he was. Who else would answer an ad on the Internet and agree to meet a complete stranger in a bar at ten o'clock at night?

* * *

In spite of his trepidation about meeting the woman, Giovanni arrived at Club Raven promptly at ten. He found Mara and Logan seated at a table near the door. They were alone.

Relief washed through him. *Stood up,* he thought. *Thank the Lord.*

He slid into the seat across from Mara's. "From now on, stay out of my love life," he growled. "If I want a woman, I'll find my own."

"I have the whole family looking," she said with an airy wave of her hand.

"Did you hear what I said?"

"Of course. You're tired of being alone."

And likely to stay that way, he thought, scowling, as the minutes ticked by.

At ten-thirty, he stood. "Looks like she's not coming. Let's not do this again." Head high, he left the club.

Mara stared after him, her expression pensive. "I guess I'll just have to keep trying."

"You heard the man," Logan said. "Leave him alone."

"Have you ever known me to quit?"

"First time for everything, love. Come on, let's go home," he said with a wink. "I've got an itch that only you can scratch."

Giovanni strolled down the street, his hands shoved in his pockets. If he was honest with himself, he was both disappointed and relieved that his date hadn't shown up. It might have been nice to spend an evening with a woman. Any woman. Then again, he would likely have made a complete fool of himself.

He'd never been good at small talk, wasn't really up-to-date on the latest movies or music.

The whole idea of finding a significant other had been ridiculous. He didn't know anything about the female of the species—at least not the human ones. He'd had little contact with humanity since becoming a vampire. Like most male vampires, he preferred to feed on the opposite sex, but mesmerizing a female so he could satisfy his thirst was hardly the same as engaging in flirtation. Or anything more intimate.

It had been a bad idea from the start, and when he saw Mara again, he'd tell he so, he thought. And then he scowled into the darkness. Mara had said the whole family was involved in finding him a date. Maybe he should just make himself scarce for a while. The more he thought about it, the better it sounded. He had gone this long without a woman. Why look for one now?

Maybe he should go to ground for a decade or two.

Maybe by then Mara would forget about him.

"What about Angelica?" Mara asked, propping another pillow behind her head.

"That vampire medium you introduced me to a few months ago? *That* Angelica?" Logan asked, frowning.

"Why not? She's pretty and smart and single."

"I don't know." He shook his head. "Maybe you should start with someone a little more . . . you know."

"More what? I think she's perfect. She's been a vampire for a good long time, so she knows the ropes. She's independent and very feminine. I'm going to call her."

* * *

"You want to set me up with a fortune-telling vampire witch?" Giovanni exclaimed. "Are you serious? What could we possibly have in common? I'm a priest and she's a . . . a . . . charlatan." He stared at Mara, thinking he never should have accepted her invitation to meet for drinks.

"I happen to know she's the real thing," Mara said with asperity. "Not every medium is a fake."

"Did you tell her about me?"

"Yes."

Darn. "And?"

Mara picked up her wineglass, took a sip, and grinned at him over the rim. "She said she would *love* to meet you."

He was about to tell her he wasn't interested in the least, but he couldn't help asking, "What's she like?"

"Very pretty."

"That's not what I meant."

"Of course, it is." She slid a piece of paper across the table. "Here's her name and phone number. She's expecting your call."

Giovanni shook his head. "Forget it. I'm not interested."

"Don't you dare wimp out on me now! You're going to call her and ask her out. I went to a lot of trouble to set this up! She's a good friend of mine, so you be nice."

"I didn't know you had any friends," he muttered.

"One or two," she said dryly. "I met Angelica a long time ago in a Gypsy camp. She told my fortune. Everything she predicted has come true, which is how I know she's the genuine article."

Giovanni picked up the paper, folded it in half, and slid it into his shirt pocket. "I'll think about it."

Mara smiled at him, a knowing look in her eye. And then she was gone.

* * *

Angelica drummed her fingers on the arm of her chair, her brow furrowed as she pondered Mara's request that she go out with Father Lanzoni. *A priest!*

She laughed softly, genuinely amused. In her day, the clergy had burned witches at the stake. They hadn't dated them.

Still, it was an incredibly intriguing idea. All the ancient ones knew about Father Giovanni Lanzoni, the vampire priest who had clung to his vows for over a thousand years. What had changed, she wondered, that he was ready to abandon them now?

Giovanni picked up his cell phone. Put it down. Picked it up again. He had no idea what to say to Mara's friend once he got past "Hello." He had never had a date, didn't know how to make small talk with a woman who wasn't in need of comfort or spiritual help. The only female friends he had were all married women.

Who also happened to be vampires.

He drew in a deep breath, blew it out in a long, shuddering sigh, and made the call.

She answered on the second ring. "Hello, Father."

"Angelica?"

"Yes. Mara said I might hear from you."

He cleared his throat. "I . . . uh . . . thought we might . . . um . . . meet for drinks some night."

"I'm free tonight."

"Oh. I, um . . ."

"Shall we say nine at Florentine's? Do you know it?"

"Yes. That would be . . . ah, splendid."

"Until nine, then."

Giovanni ended the call, then stood there, too stunned to move.

He had a date.

Giovanni stood outside Florentine's. It was a high-end club that catered to the rich and famous. He straightened his tie, rubbed his hands on his thighs, took a deep breath, and opened the door. One drink and he would tell her good-bye.

He spied Angelica immediately. She was seated at the bar, looking like a rose in a patch of weeds. Her hair was the color of flame, her eyes the same deep shade of gray as a stormy sky. She wore a slim blue skirt and matching V-neck sweater that outlined every voluptuous curve. A slow smile spread over her face as he strode toward her. Just one look and he knew he was outclassed. She was self-assured, poised, and completely at ease.

She held out her hand. "Giovanni, I'm so pleased to meet you."

He smiled faintly. "And I you." Her skin was cool, her grip firm.

"Mara's told me so much about you," she went on in a well-modulated voice. He could easily imagine her bent over a crystal ball, he mused, spinning fortunes for the unwary. Without meaning to, he blurted, "She didn't tell me enough about you."

Her laughter washed over him as she handed him a glass of red wine, picked up her own drink, and led him to a table for two in a secluded corner.

He held her chair for her, then took the one opposite. He couldn't stop looking at her, couldn't believe he was sitting across from the most beautiful woman he had ever seen. She was way out of his league, he thought, with a sigh. This was obviously a pity date.

"Talk to me, Giovanni. I'm curious about your life. We all are. Only Mara really knows anything about your past. And even that is sketchy at best."

He shrugged. "There's little to tell. I was a priest for many years. I said Mass and united people in holy wedlock. I heard confessions, I administered last rites to the dying. Occasionally, I cast out evil spirits."

"But that was only a small part of your life."

Giovanni nodded. It had been less than five percent, yet it had left an indelible mark on everything that came after.

"Who turned you?" Angelica sipped her wine, her expression genuinely curious as she waited for him to go on.

"I never knew his name or saw him again after he sired me."

"And yet you survived with no one to guide you. Few fledglings make it past their first year on their own."

"I was lucky."

"Do you remember nothing of the one who turned you?"

"He looked like a gladiator," Giovanni recalled.

Angelica stared at him. "A gladiator?"

"He was tall and muscular, with short black hair and hell-black eyes." He shook his head. "That's all I remember."

"Did he have a tattoo of a viper on the left side of his neck?"

"How did you know that?" Giovanni asked sharply.

A look of wonder crossed her face. "You were sired by one of the ancients. His name is Alric. Before being turned, he fought in the arena. He was never defeated and won his freedom."

"He still exists?"

"As far as I know, although no one has seen him for maybe two hundred years."

There was a longing in her voice that made him ask, "Do you know him?"

A strange expression flitted across her face. "I did. A long time ago."

They'd been lovers sometime in the distant past, Giovanni thought. "Alric . . ." He murmured the name. It made no difference in the grand scheme of things, but it was nice to finally know the identity of the vampire who had sired him. "Hard to believe he's existed for so long. I wonder if he knows Mara?"

"Everyone knows Mara. She's the oldest of our kind. Even older than Alric." Angelica laughed softly. "I feel like a fledgling compared to the rest of you."

"How long ago were you turned?"

"Almost four hundred years."

"Just a babe," Giovanni agreed. He picked up his glass and let the contents slide down his throat. The wine was delightfully full-bodied, like the woman across from him. "Why did you agree to meet me?"

"I was curious, of course. I've always had a weakness for vampires, and Mara speaks very highly of you." Angelica's gaze moved over him, bold as brass. Mara had claimed he was handsome, and she was right. Warm hazel eyes, olive skin, wavy black hair heavily laced with silver at his temples. Was he truly a virgin after all this time? It didn't seem possible that some woman hadn't seduced him centuries ago. She smiled inwardly. Maybe she was the right woman for the job.

Had he been able, Giovanni would have blushed under

her scrutiny. And yet, it was oddly flattering. Clearing his throat, he asked, "Who sired you?"

She smiled with the memory. "A delightful man. We were lovers before he turned me. We stayed together for almost a century." Her smile faded. "He was destroyed by a pack of hunters."

"I'm sorry."

"So were they, when I found them."

He didn't have to ask what she meant, though it was hard to imagine the woman sitting across from him doling out blood and death.

"There hasn't been anyone in my life since Rudolfo. Well," she amended, "no one serious. And you? Is it true what they say?"

"It depends on what *they* say."

"I think you know."

Looking away, he said, "It's true."

"All this time?" She shook her head. "Vampires are notoriously sensual creatures. Are you . . . Let me phrase this as delicately as I can. Are you unable to please a woman?"

"I'm perfectly capable!" he exclaimed indignantly. And then he frowned. How was he to know when he had never even tried? Was Angelica the woman who would unleash his passion? "You claim to be a medium," he said thoughtfully. "Do you see the two of us together?"

Frowning, she took his hand in hers and closed her eyes. A minute passed. Two, before she met his gaze. "No," she said with some regret. "We are not meant to be. But there is a woman for you out there somewhere. I cannot see her clearly. But you will find her."

* * *

Giovanni thought of nothing else after bidding Angelica good night. She had claimed he would find someone. But what if he did and he *couldn't* perform? What if centuries of abstinence had left him both mentally and physically unable to please a woman?

As a young man, he'd had fantasies just like every other male. But he had never done any experimenting, never done more than kiss one of the village girls. Once he had spied on a neighbor's daughter while she bathed. He had felt guilty for weeks afterward. Even after he went to confession for absolution, her image continually popped into his mind at the most inopportune moments.

And then he had entered the priesthood and done his best to forget such things. Until he met Maria Elena. He had loved her desperately, but he had been a young priest who had just taken his final vows and she had been betrothed to another. The first time he'd met her had been in the confessional, a moment he would never forget.

She had poured her heart out to him, sobbing because her father was forcing her to marry a man she didn't love. A man more than twice her age. She had come to confession frequently, though after the first few times, their conversations had been less about repentance and of a more personal nature. And as the weeks passed, they had fallen in love.

Maria Elena had continued to come to confession every couple of days; they had few other chances to be alone. Things changed after her marriage. As an unmarried woman, it was unseemly for her to go anywhere unchaperoned, but once wed, she had a little more freedom.

Unhappy with her husband and her life, she had begged Giovanni to take her away, and when he refused, she had pleaded with him to make love to her. There had been times when he was sorely tempted to turn his back on his faith, to renounce his vows and take what she so willingly offered. And then, when he was about to turn his back on the priesthood and yield to temptation, Maria Elena told him she was pregnant. It was like being splashed with cold water. He loved her, he wanted her, but he could not steal another man's wife, or make love to her while she was carrying another man's child.

To his regret and relief, a few weeks later he had been transferred to another parish.

He had never seen Maria Elena again.

With the coming of dawn, he sought refuge in his lair. It was with a sense of peace that he closed his eyes. There would be no dreams in the Dark Sleep, no sense of loss or regret for a love affair that had never been.

Chapter 3

Deep in the earth, the ancient vampire known as Alric stirred. Bored with his existence, he had gone to ground two hundred years ago. He might have slept another two hundred had he not heard someone mention his name—someone he knew from long ago. And with it a name he had never thought to hear again—Giovanni Lanzoni.

Curious, he propelled himself upward, through tons of earth, until he reached the surface. He shook away the bits of dirt that clung to his clothing

Lifting his face to the midnight sky, he drew a deep breath. Scents he had never experienced before flooded his nostrils. But one scent remained ever the same.

The enticing aroma of fresh, warm blood.

He smiled as he explored his surroundings. Rising after two hundred years in the earth was like being born again, he mused, as he sped through the night. A kaleidoscope of colors and sounds. Things he had never seen before—multi-hued lights brighter than a thousand wax candles. Streets covered in a black substance he didn't recognize.

He paused when he saw a couple strolling down the street, his eyes narrowing as he studied their clothing. The dress the woman wore would have been considered scandalous in his time. The man wore short pants and a short-sleeved shirt with BLACK IS MY HAPPY COLOR printed on the front.

With a shake of his head, he continued on.

Strange-looking conveyances shot past him, spewing noxious fumes. Buildings made of some shiny material rose higher than the hills back home. Had he been a young vampire, he might have been frightened by so much that was unfamiliar. But he relished the chance to explore this new world. He was Nosferatu. He learned and adapted quickly and had nothing to fear from mere mortals.

A thrill of excitement skittered through him as he looked forward to discovering and mastering all of mankind's latest inventions.

A thrill of a different kind filled him as he contemplated revisiting old friends.

And old enemies.

But first he needed to feed.

After two centuries of abstinence, he had a prodigious thirst!

Chapter 4

Giovanni woke to the insistent ring of his cell phone. Eyes still closed, he fumbled for the phone, murmured an irritable "Hello?"

"So," Mara asked cheerfully, "how was your date?"

Scowling, he sat up, his back propped against the wall. "Is nothing private?"

"Not when I'm the one who arranged it," she replied with asperity. "Did you like her?"

An image of Angelica flitted through his mind. A wealth of red hair. Beguiling gray eyes. A figure to make a saint weep. "She seems nice enough." And yet she had stirred nothing within him. Had he truly lost the ability to feel desire?

Mara snorted. "Did she like you?"

"Why don't you ask *her?*"

The sound of throaty laughter rang in his ear. "I did. She found you handsome and thoroughly charming."

"She said that?"

"Word for word."

"And did she tell you that we are not fated to be together?"

There was a pause before Mara said, "Yes. I'm sorry. I

thought you would be a good fit. But never fear. I'll keep looking."

"No," he said firmly. "I've changed my mind about abandoning my vows. I'm just not cut out for the whole dating scene."

"It was just one date. Give yourself a chance."

"It was a bad idea. I was uncomfortable the whole time. I don't know how to make small talk with a woman. If I ever knew how to flirt, I've forgotten it long since. Give Logan my best."

"Hey! Don't you dare hang up on me."

He heaved a sigh of impatience. "Now what?"

"I think you're giving up too soon."

"I appreciate your concern, Mara, truly. But my mind is made up."

Her sigh of resignation came through the line loud and clear. "I hope you know what you're doing," she said, and ended the call.

"Well?" One brow raised, Logan looked at his wife. "Are they going to crown you Matchmaker of the Century, or throw you out on your ear?"

She glared at him. "He says he's not ready. I don't know what else to do."

"How about leaving the poor man alone?"

"Tomorrow, I'll tell the family to stop looking for possible dates," she said glumly. "At least for the time being."

Giovanni dropped his phone on the bed. Had he made a mistake? Should he have agreed to let Mara keep looking? Sure, Angelica had said there was a woman somewhere out there for him, but it might take years—decades, centuries—for him to find her. Maybe she hadn't even been born yet!

Shucking his clothes, he stepped into the shower in his secondary lair. Though he usually preferred to take his rest in the bowels of the old church, he made his home here. It was a large, old house with five bedrooms. Built for a growing family, it had far more space than he needed. He had bought it furnished some years ago.

He closed his eyes as the water sluiced down his back. In the old days, people had bathed in the river. Running water and electricity were conveniences he very much appreciated. A washer and dryer were far more convenient than scrubbing clothes in a stream and drying them on a rock. A closet was far better than storing his garments in a wicker basket, as he'd once done.

After stepping out of the shower, he dried off quickly. Maybe he would take a trip, he thought as he dressed. Go visit Italy. It had been a long time since he'd seen his homeland. Of course, his family and everyone he had once known were all long dead.

He ran a comb through his hair, turned out the lights, and left the house. He hadn't hunted in a while. It was, he thought with a wry grin, one way to get a woman in his arms.

Chapter 5

Cassie ran headlong through the darkness. Heart pounding with terror, lungs burning, she plunged through the thick hedge that bordered the east side of the park. She whimpered as sharp thorns raked her arms and tore at her clothing.

She never should have let Darla talk her into attending that party. Something had warned her not to go, but she hadn't listened. It was Friday night, after all. Time to forget about her boring life. Time to stop wondering if she was going to get fired. Time to have a little fun for a change.

She darted a glance over her shoulder. Had she lost her pursuers?

But no, she could hear them clamoring through the hedges, hear their drunken laughter as they called back and forth, boasting about what they would do to her when they caught her.

Her legs were trembling when she reached the concrete walkway that meandered through the gardens.

Gasping for breath, sides heaving, she glanced over her shoulder again. They were gaining on her.

She was doomed.

A startled cry erupted from her throat when she slammed into something solid. Only it wasn't some*thing*, but some*one*.

The man took a step back, his arms darting out to grab hold of her to keep her from falling.

Cassie stared up at him, but it was too dark to see his face clearly. Had she run away from one predator only to fall into the arms of another?

And then Lynx and four of his buddies were there, circling her and the stranger. Moonlight glinted on the wicked-looking knife Lynx held in front of him.

The stranger's arms tightened around her waist. "Easy, there," he murmured. "There's no need to be afraid."

No need to be afraid, she thought. Was he blind? Didn't he see Lynx and the others surrounding them like hungry wolves around a wounded animal? The knife blades glinting in their hands?

"Give us the chick, old man," Lynx demanded. "And we might let you go."

Cassie closed her eyes and buried her face against the stranger's side. She felt an odd tremor in the air. It made the fine hairs at her nape stand at attention. Gathering her courage, she dared to open her eyes to see what was happening, only to find that Lynx and his buddies were nowhere in sight. "What? Where . . . ?"

"They've gone." Her rescuer's voice rumbled in her ear, deep and kind. "What are you doing out here, child, wandering in the park alone at this time of the night?"

Child? She was over twenty-one. "It wasn't my idea," she said, taking a step away. "My girlfriend took me to a party. I didn't know what I was getting into. When I said I was leaving, Lynx said I couldn't go until I . . . until I'd paid the toll."

It took him a moment to comprehend her meaning. "He's a friend of yours?"

"No! I just met him tonight." He had seemed so nice when she was first introduced to him.

"If he's smart, he won't bother you again." Feeling suddenly protective of her, he asked, "Where do you live? I'll walk you home."

"That's not necessary."

"Maybe not, but I'm still taking you home."

Shoulders slumped, Cassie muttered, "Whatever," and started walking.

"What's your name?" Giovanni asked, falling into step beside her.

"Why?"

"Suspicious, much?" he asked.

She glanced up at him. In the glow of a nearby streetlight, she saw his face clearly for the first time. His eyes were light—hazel, perhaps—his shoulder-length hair black and wavy and edged with silver. He seemed awfully young to have gray hair. "Sorry, but you *are* a stranger."

He nodded, a faint smile lifting the corners of his mouth. It was, she thought, a very nice mouth.

"Perhaps I should introduce myself first. My name is Giovanni Lanzoni, but please, call me Johnny." It was what his mother had called him, though he'd given the girl the English translation of his name.

"Hi, Johnny."

"I'm very pleased to meet you, Miss . . . ?"

"Douglas. Cassandra, but everyone calls me Cassie." She frowned, thinking she had never known a man with such nice manners. Not that she'd known that many men.

They walked in silence for a time. Cassie was acutely aware of the man beside her. Though he was not big and bulky and stood only a few inches taller than she, there was an air of power and authority about him that was both comforting and unsettling. With a shake of her head, she dismissed it as nothing more than the aftereffect of the night's events.

She felt drawn to him in a way she didn't understand. But what was even stranger, she felt safe with him, and that was really odd, because she hadn't trusted anyone since her parents had abandoned her when she was fifteen.

"What happened back there?" she asked as they left the park. "Why did they leave without a fight?"

"I merely advised them that it would be in their best interest to leave you alone."

Cassie frowned. "I didn't hear you say anything."

He shrugged. "Perhaps you were too frightened to notice."

Cassie shook her head. She had been scared, sure, but too scared to hear whatever threat had sent Lynx and the others hurrying away without an argument? She didn't think so. She shook her head again. Why was she always drawn to the wrong guys? First her ex, and then Lynx? Not that she ever wanted to see *him* again.

She felt a sudden spark of attraction when Johnny's hand accidentally brushed her fingers.

His gaze jumped to hers, leaving Cassie to wonder if he had felt it, too. She stopped at the end of the concrete path that led to the door of her apartment complex. "We're here."

Giovani glanced at the run-down building. It was in desperate need of a coat of paint. Some of the roof tiles were missing. A few of the windows were patched with tape. "You live here?"

She bit down on her lower lip, suddenly embarrassed

as she looked at the place through his eyes. "It's a dump, I know, but it's all I can afford."

"What is it you do?"

"I serve drinks at the Winchester Lounge five nights a week." The place was a dive. Her salary was nothing to brag about, but with tips, she made enough to pay the rent. Barely. "Do you know it?"

"Yeah." He had gone hunting there a time or two. "I live alone," he said, weighing each word carefully. "In a rather large house with five bedrooms. It's nothing fancy, but certainly better than this. And in a safer neighborhood."

She blinked up at him. "Are you asking me to move in with you?" she exclaimed. "Are you crazy? I've only known you, what? Ten minutes?"

"I'm not suggesting anything immoral," he said, obviously insulted that she would think otherwise. "I'm gone all day, and a good deal of the night, so you would have the place to yourself most of the time. The house is paid for, so there's no need to pay rent. I've been alone a very long time and I've grown weary of my own company. I merely thought . . . Forgive my impertinence. It was a bad idea."

Cassie shrugged it off. Had she known him better, she might have jumped at the chance to live rent-free in a decent house. "Thanks for walking me home."

"Please accept my apology," he said stiffly. "I didn't mean to offend you. I was merely trying to help. Good evening."

She stared at him a moment. Perhaps she *had* misjudged his intentions, she thought as she walked swiftly up the stairs to the front door. She paused, her hand on the latch. Maybe she owed him an apology. She turned to tell him she was sorry, but he had already gone.

What a strange man. He had seemed harmless enough. A gentleman. And yet. . . She shivered as her mind replayed what had happened in the park. There was something about him, although she couldn't put her finger on it. Something she'd felt on some primal level but couldn't explain.

With a shake of her head, she went inside and closed the door behind her, thinking that perhaps she had escaped two predators that night, even though one had rescued her from the other.

She laughed softly as she went into the bedroom, bemused by her fanciful thoughts.

Chapter 6

Giovanni's first thought when the sun went down was of the young, golden-haired, brown-eyed woman he had met the night before. Cassie Douglas. No woman had ever affected him quite the way she had. Even now, hours later, he clearly remembered the flowery fragrance of her hair. The warmth of her skin.

The tantalizing aroma of her life's blood.

When she'd looked at him, his whole body had responded. That, too, was unusual. He was, after all, a priest. Years of abstinence and rigid self-discipline had left him immune to the temptations of the fair sex.

Or so he'd thought.

Her scent, the sound of her voice, had awakened feelings and desires he'd not known since Maria Elena.

Leaving his lair, he went to his lonely house, where he showered, dressed, and ran a comb through his hair. And all the while, the memory of his meeting with the young woman played in the forefront of his mind. He told himself he was centuries too old for her. She was barely more than a child. But try as he might, he couldn't stop thinking about her.

Cassie. She worked five nights a week at the Winchester Lounge, he thought. Was tonight one of those nights? Before he could talk himself out of it, he was on his way out the door.

Cassie glanced at the clock, willing the hands to move more quickly. It never worked, of course. Tonight, more than usual, she hated her job. Hated the lustful stares of the men, their furtive snickers, their lewd attempts at humor. She was tired of fighting off their unwanted advances, tired of forcing herself to laugh at their vulgar jokes. Heck, she was just plain tired.

Waiting at the bar for an order to be filled, she found herself thinking of the man who had come to her rescue the night before. What was his name? Johnny something. A real gentleman, he was. Then again, maybe he wasn't. After knowing her for only a few minutes, he had hinted that she should move in with him. Though he seemed nice enough, she could only imagine what might have happened if she had agreed. No doubt she would have become one of those women you read about in the paper who vanished without a trace, never to be seen or heard from again. *Suspicious, much?* She grinned inwardly as his words from the night before replayed in her mind. *Always,* she thought.

And with good reason.

She slapped the hand of one of the regular patrons when he tried to pat her behind as she passed by, more annoyed than usual. She needed a vacation from this place, but that wasn't going to happen anytime soon. Not if she wanted to continue eating.

Maybe she should have taken Johnny what's-his-name up on his offer, she thought, then shook her head. Definitely not a good idea. She was just tired and edgy. She tensed every time a new customer arrived, always afraid Lynx and his buddies might come swaggering through the door. Where had Darla found a loser like that anyway? Cassie wondered. And why was she always attracted to the wrong kind of guy? Maybe it was in her blood. Her mother had certainly picked a bad apple.

She felt a startling sizzle of awareness when the door opened and Johnny stepped inside. Had he come looking for her? Filled with a nervous sense of excitement and apprehension, she licked her lips and ran her fingers through her hair.

He smiled when he saw her.

She lifted her hand in acknowledgment, then delivered her drink order to a booth in the back. When she turned around, Johnny was sitting at one of the small tables near the front window. One of her tables.

"I didn't expect to see *you* here tonight," she said, her order pad at the ready. He looked quite handsome in a pair of dark slacks, a white shirt, and a thigh-length black coat.

"I was out for a walk and . . ." He shrugged. "I thought I'd stop by for a drink. I hope you don't mind."

"It's a free country. What can I get you?"

"A glass of red wine, please."

Nodding, she made her way to the bar, conscious of his gaze on her back.

Giovanni glanced around the room. He rarely frequented bars, preferring to hunt in less crowded venues.

He had spent far too much of his existence alone, he thought ruefully. Perhaps it was time to change that.

He murmured his thanks when she returned with his drink.

"I didn't think I'd ever see you again," Cassie remarked.

"I was hoping I might walk you home."

She hesitated a moment, then said, "I get off at two A.M."

"I'll meet you at the door."

With a nod, she moved to another table.

Giovanni sipped his wine, content to sit and watch her as she took orders and served drinks. Twice, he was tempted to interfere—once when a man tried to place his hands on her and a second time when another man made a lewd suggestion—but she seemed capable of fending off both of them without causing a scene.

When he finished his drink, he left her a hefty tip, lifted his hand in farewell, and took his leave. He had plenty of time to hunt before he was to meet her.

Cassie applied fresh lipstick, tucked a lock of hair behind her ear, took a deep breath, and stepped outside, wondering if Johnny would really show up. Most people, working or otherwise, were in bed by now, she thought, but maybe he didn't work. Maybe he was a bored, retired millionaire who'd grown weary of dating wealthy socialites and had decided to go slumming. She shook her head. He didn't seem like the millionaire type, but then, how was she to know? She had certainly never met one, nor was she likely to.

She smiled shyly when she saw him waiting for her. "Hope I didn't keep you waiting."

"Not at all." Drawing his hand from behind his back, he offered her a bouquet of red roses.

Cassie stared at the bouquet, momentarily speechless. "Why?"

"Why not?"

"No one's ever given me flowers before."

"Then I'm glad to be the first."

"They're beautiful."

As are you, he thought, but he lacked the courage to say the words out loud.

"How was your day?" she asked.

"Long," he murmured. "And quiet."

"Oh? Are you retired?"

"In a manner of speaking," he said, stifling a grin.

"What did you do before you quit?"

"I was a priest."

She stared at him, eyes wide. "A priest!"

"Guilty as charged."

"I didn't know priests left the Church. I thought it was a lifetime calling. You know, like being a Supreme Court justice."

He shrugged. "It happens."

"You seem awfully young to be retired. How old are you, if you don't mind me asking?"

"I was thirty-nine on my last birthday. Might I ask how old you are?"

"Twenty-six. You're not married or anything, are you?"

"Of course not!" he exclaimed, obviously offended by the question. "Would I be here with you now if I were?"

She shrugged. "I don't know. Lots of men cheat on their wives."

"Well, *I* would never!"

She laughed at the horrified expression on his face. "I believe you."

Suddenly at a loss for words, he slowed his steps. What was he doing here with her? In mortal years, he was thirteen years her senior. But as a vampire, he had existed hundreds of years longer. Yet he feared she was far more worldly-wise than was he. He knew nothing of women, of intimacy—sexual or otherwise. Of dating. Or marriage.

He was relieved when her apartment building came into view.

She paused at the foot of the stairs. "Thanks for walking me home."

"I was happy to. You shouldn't be walking the streets at this hour."

Frowning, Cassie looked up at him. *Walking the streets!*
"Is something wrong?"

"Are you implying that I'm a whore?"

"What? No, of course not! What makes you think that?"

"You practically called me a streetwalker."

He stared at her in confusion for a moment, then with growing horror as he realized what he had unthinkingly implied. *Streetwalker. Doxy. Light-skirt.* "Cassie, please forgive me. That's not what I meant at all."

She found herself grinning at his stricken expression, and then she laughed. "Don't worry about it. I've been called that and worse at the Winchester."

He was surprised to find himself laughing with her. And even more surprised when she went up on her tiptoes and kissed his cheek.

Murmuring, "Good night, Johnny," she ran up the stairs. She stopped at the door and glanced over her shoulder.

"Thank you again for the flowers," she called before going inside and closing the door behind her.

Whistling softly, Giovanni strolled down the sidewalk. Maybe she would agree to let him walk her home again tomorrow night.

Chapter 7

Giovanni groaned as he checked his caller ID. Mara. Again. He let the phone ring several more times, then sighed. If he didn't answer, she would just keep calling. Or worse, show up at his house. The woman had the tenacity of a pit bull.

"What?" he growled.

"Get up on the wrong side of the casket tonight?" she asked dryly.

"Very funny. What do you want?"

"I wondered if you were ready for a little more matchmaking."

He frowned at the hint of laughter in her voice. "You know, don't you?"

"Know what?" she asked innocently.

"That I met a woman."

At that, she burst out laughing. "I don't know why I'm getting your thoughts so clearly, Father," she said, "but you really need to block them."

"I thought I was." Although he had to admit, it was something he rarely thought about. But he would certainly make more of an effort from now on.

"So, is it serious?"

"No. I'm too old for her. And she's far too young for me."

"She'll catch up in a few years."

He grunted softly but said nothing.

With an aggrieved sigh, Mara muttered good-bye and ended the call.

Giovanni shook his head. He knew she meant well, but sometimes she took her Queen of the Vampires title a little too far.

Suddenly restless, he wandered through the house, trying to imagine the lives of the people who had previously lived here. Had they been happy? Wealthy? Had the walls echoed with the laughter of children? His own childhood had been harsh, his father barely able to support his wife and six children. They had often gone to bed hungry. He and his older brother had done what they could, frequently begging for handouts in the city streets. Sometimes they were rewarded; sometimes they were whipped and beaten for their efforts.

It wasn't until he entered the priesthood that he had a warm bed to sleep in, clothes that weren't patched, and enough to eat.

In the bedroom, he sat on the edge of the mattress. What would it be like to fall in love? To share his life with a woman? To take his rest at her side? To hold her in his arms? It would be a rare creature who would agree to share a vampire's life. And yet those he considered family had all found mates willing to do so. Granted, they had endured some rough times, yet their love had been strong enough to see them through.

He had been looking forward to seeing Cassie again but now, thinking about the differences between them, he wondered if it was wise. He had so little worldly experience, so little to offer. In time, no doubt she would grow bored with him. If he continued to see her, she would start to question why he couldn't share a meal with her, why she only saw him after dark, why he was never sick, why his injuries healed rapidly—his aversion to silver. And if their relationship lasted years, she would wonder why he never aged.

Better to end it now, he thought, even though it had never really begun.

Determined never to see her again, he left the house, intending to go in search of prey.

Instead, within minutes, he found himself seated at one of her tables in the Winchester Lounge, the glass in his hand still warm from her touch.

Cassie found herself smiling as she served drinks, cleared tables, endured the usual flirtations and suggestive humor, the invitations to walk her home, the leers. Tonight, nothing bothered her. And it was all because of Johnny. What was it about him that his mere presence made her so happy inside? He was unlike any man she had ever met— shy yet self-assured, quiet yet capable of defending her, outwardly calm, and yet she sensed a kind of power in him that she didn't understand.

She thought he would have a drink or two and then leave, but he stayed until closing and then offered to walk her home again.

"This is getting to be a habit," she remarked as they left the lounge.

"Would you rather I stayed away?"

"What? Oh, no!" She smiled up at him. "I don't work tomorrow night. Maybe we could . . . never mind."

"Could what?"

"Nothing."

Even in the dark, he could see the flush that warmed her cheeks. Had she been about to ask if he would like to spend the day with her and then thought better of it? Did *he* dare ask *her*? He hesitated, fearful of being rejected, then blurted, "Cassie, would you like to go out with me tomorrow night?"

"I'd love to."

"Wonderful! Where would you like to go?"

"Dinner? Dancing? A movie? A walk in the park. I don't care."

"How about a movie?" That seemed safe enough. He could sit beside her in the dark, inhale her warm, womanly fragrance, the scent of her blood, look at her to his heart's content and she would be none the wiser.

"Great! I've been wanting to see that new dinosaur flick."

"Sounds good. I'll pick you up at seven. Is that okay?"

"Perfect."

Cassie was still smiling when they reached her place. She stopped at the stairs, wishing she could invite him in. But her place was small and ugly, and she didn't want him to see it. Or hear the fighting and cussing that went on nightly in the apartment next door. Or have to listen to the crying baby on the other side. "Thanks for seeing me safely home once again."

He nodded, wondering if he dared kiss her good night.

He was still trying to make up his mind when she went up on her tiptoes and pressed her lips to his.

Shocked, he simply stood there. Then, summoning his courage, he slid his arm around her waist and kissed her back. It had been centuries since he'd kissed a woman. He had forgotten how soft a woman's lips were, how sweet and mysterious.

When he lifted his head, Cassie murmured, "Wow. Where did you learn to kiss like that?"

Was she complaining? But no, she was reaching for him again. Filled with a sudden, unexpected sense of—he wasn't sure what, confidence or exhilaration—he took her in his arms and claimed her lips a second time. She leaned into him, her breasts warm and supple against his chest. And ever so slowly, desire unfolded deep within him. He had held many women in his arms, but they had been prey, nothing more than a means to satisfy his hellish thirst. None had ever aroused his senses like this.

When they parted this time, he was no longer worried about his ability to please a woman.

Cassie stared after Johnny as he walked briskly down the street. My, oh my, that man could kiss! She ran her fingertips over lips that were still tingling. Tomorrow, she would take a little of the cash she had saved and buy herself a new outfit. She would curl her hair and paint her nails and pretend she was Cinderella going to the ball instead of a lowly waitress serving drinks in a second-rate bar.

And maybe, if she was lucky, she thought with a sigh, the handsome prince would kiss her again.

Giovanni paced the living room floor, willing the minutes to pass. He hadn't been this nervous since the morning he'd heard his first confession. That had been a day he would never forget. He smiled inwardly. With luck, this might turn out to be a night he would never forget. He had been a mortal man the last time he'd been with a woman. He and Maria Elena had never really gone out together. Forced by circumstances to meet on the sly, they had rarely spent more than a few stolen moments in each other's company.

Unable to wait any longer, Giovanni went out the back door into the garage. He rarely drove the Mustang parked inside, but there were times when it came in handy, and this was one of them, he mused as he slid behind the wheel. He had formed attachments to few things in his life, but he loved this car; cherry red with white racing stripes, it was considered a classic.

He backed out of the garage, felt a rush of nerves as he drove to Cassie's apartment.

Cassie stood in front of the cracked mirror in her bedroom, turning from side to side. Did she look all right? She had spent the day shopping for a new dress. She had settled on a simple dark green sheath with long sleeves and a modest slit on one side. She had splurged on a new pair of heels, too, and a new lipstick. Good thing she had paid her rent in advance, she thought.

Earlier, she had taken a long shower, shaved her legs, washed and curled her hair, and now she was ready to go, thirty minutes before her date was to arrive.

She couldn't help smiling when Johnny called to say he was sorry for being early, but he was waiting downstairs.

Cassie came to an abrupt halt when she saw him standing in front of a gorgeous red Mustang with racing stripes. "Is that yours?"

"Like it?"

"It's a beaut!" she exclaimed as he opened her door. Never in all her life had she ridden in such an amazing car. "It must have cost a fortune."

"It's a 1967," he said, a note of pride in his voice. "I bought it used, but it's in top condition. Last time I looked, it was worth around thirty grand. Of course I didn't pay that much."

She ran her fingertips over the edge of the leather seat. "It still looks brand-new."

"I don't drive it very often," he said, pulling away from the curb. "I'm glad you like it."

All too aware of the woman sitting beside him, Giovanni paid little attention to the movie. He was captivated by the scent of her skin, her perfume, her hair. Her blood. It called to him as no other. Halfway through the movie, he found the courage to take her hand, his fingers twining with hers.

His heart swelled when she didn't pull away.

He studied her profile—the tilt of her nose, the dimple in her cheek, the way her hair fell over her shoulders. He smiled ruefully. He had known her only a few days and he was already totally smitten. She was his first thought on waking from the Dark Sleep and his last thought before falling into oblivion.

And now she was here, beside him, her hand small and warm in his.

"What a great movie!" Cassie exclaimed as they left the theater. "It had everything! Action. Adventure. Dinosaurs. Romance. A happy ending. I loved it. Didn't you?"

Nodding, Giovanni said, "It was awesome."

"The dinosaurs looked so real. I've been fascinated by them ever since I was a little girl. I don't know why."

"Well, they were incredible creatures. It's amazing how Hollywood makes them look so believable."

"I know. I think I saw the first *Jurassic Park* five or six times. So," she asked when they reached his car, "what shall we do now?"

"What would you like to do?"

"I'd love some ice cream."

"All right."

He held the car door for her, closed it when she was seated.

Cassie watched him walk around to the driver's side. She loved looking at him. He moved with such effortless grace, she wondered if he'd ever been a dancer. Sometimes it seemed as though his feet weren't touching the ground.

"This really is a great car," she remarked as he slid behind the wheel.

"It's my one vanity." He pulled out of the theater parking lot and headed for Pop's Ice Cream Shoppe. He'd often wondered what the treat tasted like.

He parked the car and followed her inside.

"What kind do you like?" Cassie asked as they took their place in line.

"I'm allergic to dairy."

"Really? Why didn't you say something? We could have gone somewhere else."

"My lady wants ice cream," he said gallantly. "My lady gets ice cream." Though he wondered how one decided which flavor to choose. Neapolitan. Pistachio. Chocolate Fudge Ripple. Moose Tracks. Cherry Garcia. Chocolate Chip Cookie Dough. They all sounded quite exotic.

Cassie grinned at him, thinking again that she'd never before met a man like him. "Maybe we could go get a nightcap later."

"Anything you want."

At the moment, she wanted a hot fudge sundae with extra whipped cream and three cherries. They found a table for two near the window. Giovanni couldn't help smiling at the look of enjoyment that spread over her face as she licked a bit of chocolate from her lips. He couldn't help wondering if he would ever be able to arouse a similar look of pleasure.

"Would you still like to go out for a drink?" he asked as they left the ice cream shop.

"Sure."

Giovanni had been worried that she would quickly tire of his company. After all, he wasn't known for his wit. He wasn't much of a storyteller. But she didn't seem to be in any hurry to go home.

He drove to a small, out-of-the-way nightclub he sometimes frequented when prey was scarce. The bartender, Rick, was a vampire who kept a ready supply of red wine liberally laced with blood for a few of his customers.

"Nice place," Cassie said as they stepped inside. "I've never been here."

"I like it. It's never too crowded."

He was right about that, she thought, glancing around. The lights were low, the music soft and slow with a mysterious, dark undercurrent. The décor was reminiscent of New Orleans during Mardi Gras. Lots of colorful masks and beads.

At the bar, Cassie ordered a mimosa. Johnny asked for a glass of the house special.

"I'm so glad you asked me out," Cassie said as they

made their way to a booth. "I don't remember when I've had such a good time."

"Me, either."

"So, you said you're retired. What do you do with your time these days?"

He should have expected a question like that, he guessed, but he was totally unprepared with a reply. "I've been look-ing for something to do," he lied. "But there's not a lot of call for retired priests."

"No, I guess not."

"What about you?" Johnny asked. "Please don't take this the wrong way, but why do you work in that dreadful place?"

"I don't have much education and I didn't have any experience when I took the job. I thought maybe, after a few months, I could find something better. But"—she shrugged—"nothing better ever came along. And with tips, the pay's not too bad."

"I guess we do what we have to do to survive," he said quietly.

"Exactly." Cassie sipped her drink. He was hiding something, she thought, though she had no idea what it might be. He didn't seem like the criminal type, nor could she imagine him doing anything cruel or illegal. But his voice had been laced with regret.

Johnny glanced at the band. "Would you like to dance?"

"Sure."

Leading her onto the small dance floor, he took her in his arms.

Cassie had always been self-conscious about dancing. She didn't feel that she was very good at it and it made her uncomfortable, which tended to make her somewhat clumsy. But it was different with Johnny. She felt at ease in his arms. He moved so effortlessly that somehow his confidence spread to her. When she closed her eyes, it felt as if they were floating above the floor.

Giovanni held her as close as he dared. She fit in his embrace as if she were part of him. Her nearness, her warmth, filled him with desire and he wished he dared carry her home and make love to her all night long.

The very idea brought him up short. A pimply-faced teenage boy had more experience than he did. No doubt Cassie would laugh at his clumsy attempts to seduce her. The thought cooled his ardor and when the music stopped, he led her back to their table. "It's late," he said abruptly. "I should probably take you home."

Cassie stared at him. Had she offended him somehow? She'd been having such a good time; she'd thought he was, too. She wanted to ask him what was wrong. Instead, she said, "Yes, it is late."

When they reached her apartment, she bade him a quick good night, opened the car door, and ran up the stairs.

Giovanni stared after her, wondering why she was so upset.

Chapter 8

Cassie tossed and turned all night long as she replayed her evening with Johnny. Had she been too forward? Asked too many questions? Said something to make him mad? Try as she might, she couldn't solve the riddle. She had been hoping for another dance or two. And maybe a good-night kiss.

Like a dog with a bone, she worried it all the next day but came no closer to finding an answer. He'd seemed to be having a good time. Had she been mistaken?

For once, she looked forward to going to work, hoping that being busy would keep her from fretting about the night before. Serving drinks and talking to customers helped, but every time the door opened, she looked up, hoping to see Johnny striding toward her.

But he didn't show up that night, or the next.

And then, just when she'd given up hope, he appeared at one of her tables. She couldn't smother the excitement she felt when she saw him, or her heart's leap of joy at seeing him again. It was all she could do not to run toward him and ask what she'd done wrong.

She forced herself to finish serving the people at another table before approaching him. "Hi," she said. "What can I get for you this evening?"

"Your forgiveness," he said contritely. "Can I walk you home? I feel I need to apologize for the other night."

"You don't have to . . ."

"Yes," he said quietly. "I do."

"If you insist. Would you like a drink?"

"Not tonight. I have something to do. I'll see you when you get off. We need to talk."

Nodding, she watched him thread his way through the tables to the door. *We need to talk.* Everyone knew what meant.

He was going to tell her good-bye.

Giovanni willed himself to the next town. Ever since meeting Cassie, his hunger had grown stronger. He wasn't sure why. Perhaps because he so badly wanted to taste her sweetness. All he knew was that he had to feed each night before he saw her for fear that he might lose his hard-won self-control.

He stalked the dark streets, his presence shielded from those around him as he searched for prey.

It had taken him a long time to accept what he was. Being a vampire, preying on humankind, went against everything he believed. And yet, it was necessary for his survival. He could feed on animal blood. He could exist on blood stolen from blood banks. Both would sustain him, but they didn't strengthen him, nor did they ease his hunger for long. Neither was particularly satisfying. It was like drinking water when you wanted wine or eating salad when you craved meat.

Entering a dive in a seedy part of the city, he found a

middle-aged woman sitting alone at the bar. He slid onto the stool beside her. Bought her a drink. He eased his arm around her shoulders to draw her closer, and then spoke to her mind, his will overshadowing hers. And then, as if he was nuzzling her neck, he bit her. It took only moments to feed.

When he lifted his head, he released her from his thrall, bade her good night, and left the bar with no one suspecting what he had done.

When Cassie stepped outside after work, she found Johnny waiting for her. She smiled tentatively, not sure what to say.

"Would you like to take a walk?" he asked.

"Sure, if you want."

"You don't sound too certain."

"Well." She glanced up and down the deserted street. "It *is* kind of late, don't you think?"

Giovanni nodded, but he couldn't help wondering if she was suddenly afraid of him. Some mortals sensed the otherworldliness about him, the danger that lurked beneath the surface, without knowing what it was that troubled them. "Would you rather go out for a drink?" Most of the bars were closed, but Rick's Place stayed open until dawn.

"Why don't we go to my place?" She didn't really want him to see where she lived, but it was too cold for a walk, although the chill in the air didn't seem to bother him a bit.

"Are you sure?"

She blew out a sigh. "Not really, but let's go."

Wishing he dared take her hand, he strolled down the

street at her side, keenly aware of her presence, of his desire for her.

Ten minutes later, Cassie invited him into her apartment. She was immediately sorry. Seeing it through his eyes made her realize just how ugly and dilapidated it really was. The couch sagged in the middle. The overstuffed chair was faded, the rug practically threadbare. "Can I get you a drink? The place won't look so bad after you've had a couple."

"I've seen worse," he said, with a crooked grin. "Hell, I've lived in worse."

"So, would you like a drink?"

"Some red wine, if you've got it."

"I do, although I'm not sure how good it is. A friend of mine gave me a bottle of Merlot for Christmas, but I'm not much of a wine drinker. Please, sit down. I'll be right back."

Giovanni looked at the sofa and the chair, uncertain which to take. In the end, he settled in the chair, guessing she might feel better with some space between them. He glanced around the room, thinking she deserved something much better. Did she know a man had been murdered here? The scent of old, violent death lingered in the air.

He stood when she entered the room.

Cassie smiled, thinking none of the other men she had ever dated had shown her such respect.

She handed him a glass, then settled on the sofa and took a sip of the soda she had poured for herself. "So, what did you want to talk about?"

"I have a confession to make."

"You're a priest," she said, grinning. "And you want to confess to *me?*"

"In a manner of speaking." He took several sips of wine, then set the glass on the low table beside the chair. "This isn't easy for me to say, but you need to know. I don't have any experience with women. Or with dating. I've only been on one date in my whole life and that only recently. I've never been intimate with a woman and . . ."

She stared at him, wide-eyed. "You're a . . . a *virgin? Seriously?* This isn't just some kind of come-on to make me feel sorry for you and take you to bed, is it?"

"No!" He stared at her, aghast. "How could you even think such a thing?"

"I'm sorry." She set her glass aside. "I should have known better. You're not a jerk like most of the guys I've dated."

"I left the other night because I wanted to hold you, kiss you, and I was ashamed because I didn't know how to . . ." He huffed a sigh. "I'm an idiot."

Cassie laughed softly. "No, you're not. But . . . are you saying that even after you left the Church, you never . . . weren't you even curious?"

"You have no idea! You probably won't believe this, but until I met you, I never really felt . . . felt . . ."

"What?"

"Physical desire."

Speechless, Cassie stared at him. And then she smiled. "I think I'm flattered." She patted the cushion beside her. "Come here, Johnny."

He blinked at her. Slowly gained his feet. And then sat beside her, but not too close.

"You didn't have any trouble kissing me the other night," she murmured. And then she frowned. "Where *did* you learn to kiss like that?"

"I knew a girl once. A long time ago."

"Oh?"

"Maria Elena. We were both very young. She was betrothed to someone she did not love, and she came to confession. . . ."

"You were a priest then?"

"Yes."

"Wow. Did you do it in the confessional?"

"Good Lord, no! We were never intimate!" he exclaimed. "We never exchanged more than a few chaste kisses. And then she got married and . . ."

"You loved her?"

"Yes. But it was never meant to be."

"I'm sorry. But I'm so glad you're here now, with me."

"Cassie."

Cupping his cheeks in her palms, she kissed him.

At the touch of her lips on his, Giovanni's arms went around her. Holding her close, he kissed her as if he was suffocating and she was his next breath. Cassie clung to him, and for a time, nothing else mattered but the taste of her, the funny little sighs she made, the way she moaned his name. He was drowning, he thought, overwhelmed by feelings and emotions he had never felt before, not even with Maria Elena. It was exhilarating and a little frightening because, as his desire heightened, so did the urge to bury his fangs in her sweet flesh. The musky scent of her skin was almost his undoing.

Alarmed when the need became almost overpowering, he took a deep breath and pulled away. Afraid his eyes had gone red, he stood and turned his back toward her.

"Johnny?" she asked breathlessly. "Are you all right?"

He nodded. "Fine. I just think we'd better slow down."

"You're probably right." She smoothed a hand over her hair, straightened her short uniform skirt. "Are we good?"

Turning, he winked at her. "Better than good." Reaching for her hand, he pulled her to her feet and kissed her gently. "I think I'd better go before this gets out of hand."

"Johnny . . ."

He covered her mouth with his fingertips. "We need to go slow," he said. "There are things about me you don't know. Things I can't tell you now."

"What things?"

"I'd rather not say at the moment."

"You're not wanted by the police, are you?"

"No. Nothing like that," he assured her. "I'm not a fugitive. I don't have a price on my head. I'm not running away from anything. Okay?"

"All right. But you know it's going to drive me crazy trying to figure out what it is, don't you?"

"When the time is right, I'll tell you."

"You promise?"

"I promise. Will I see you tomorrow night?"

"If you want to."

"You know I do." He kissed her again, lightly, then took his leave.

Cassie stared after him. *Damn.*

She hated secrets.

Chapter 9

Giovanni swore under his breath when he opened his eyes and saw Mara standing beside him. "What are you doing here?"

"I think the better question is what are *you* doing here?" She glanced around his lair with distaste. "A cellar in an abandoned church? Is this the best you could find?"

Sitting up, he raked his fingers through his hair. "What do you want?"

With all the grace of a ballerina, she lowered herself to the cement floor beside him. "I was talking to Angelica last night. She asked me about you and about how we met, and, in passing, she mentioned the name of your sire—Alric."

Giovanni frowned. "So?"

"What do you know about him?"

"Nothing. He turned me and abandoned me. I haven't seen him since."

"No contact at all?" she asked, surprise evident in her voice.

He shook his head. "I never even knew his name until Angelica told me. Why?"

"He's here."

"Here? Where?"

"I don't know his exact location. Only that he's in the States, somewhere on the West Coast."

"Do you think he's looking for me?"

"No," she said flatly. "He's most likely looking for me."

"You? Why?"

"There's some history between us."

"Really? You've never mentioned him."

She made a vague gesture. "It was a long time ago."

"I'm getting the feeling it won't be a cordial reunion."

"Hardly."

"So, what's between you?"

"A little over two hundred years ago, I destroyed someone he loved."

Giovanni grunted softly. He knew something of Mara's early life. She had been born in Egypt and raised as a slave in the house of Chuma, one of Pharaoh's advisers. She had been fifteen when Chuma gave her to one of his allies as a gift. Her new master had soon tired of her endless attempts to escape and kept her in chains in a dungeon. She had spent years there until, one night, a vampire known as Dendar appeared in her cell and turned her. She had killed the man who kept her in chains, and she had destroyed the vampire who had sired her.

She had mellowed in the centuries since then, he thought. But he knew she was still capable of dealing death and destruction without a qualm. "I assume you had a good reason."

"Calidora betrayed me to a hunter. She betrayed Alric, too, but he was so smitten with her, he refused to believe it. I killed the hunter. And I killed her. Alric never forgave me. He swore someday he would avenge her." Mara shook her head. "It happened a long time ago, but he never came looking for me, and after a while I thought he must have gone to ground, but certainly not for so long, which made me think someone had destroyed him."

Giovanni shook his head He knew old vampires sometimes went to ground when they grew tired or bored with their existence. But he had never heard of any of his kind who rested in the earth for more than a century.

Mara shrugged. "Time has little meaning to our kind, as you well know. But enough about me. How is your little mortal female?"

"She's wonderful."

A slow smile turned up the corners of her mouth. "I see. Does that mean . . . ?"

"Of course not! I just met the girl."

"But you like her?"

"Very much. Probably more than I should."

"Then what's the problem?"

"I can't just carry her off to my lair."

"Why not? You've broken other vows since you were turned."

There was no accusation in her tone, yet her words cut him to the quick. As a fledgling, he had killed. He remembered his horror the first time he had taken a life. He had considered destroying himself, but suicide was no less a sin than murder.

"You're right," he said quietly. "But defiling her would still be a sin." He held up a hand to silence her. "Besides, how could I do such a thing without telling her the truth of what I am?"

"It's easy," she said with an airy wave of her hand.

"It might have been easy for you," he said irritably.

"Ah, Giovanni, you will be a good boy until the day you die."

"I hope so," he muttered.

She rose in a fluid motion. "If you hear anything of Alric, you will let me know?"

"Yes." Rising, he scrubbed a hand over his jaw. "Do you think I have anything to fear from him?"

She raised a brow. "I shouldn't think so," she said, and then frowned. "I'm surprised you haven't sensed him."

"Should I?"

"He is your sire. Of course, you haven't seen him since you were turned. Perhaps time and distance have weakened the bond."

"Perhaps." He hadn't thought of the man in a century or more until Angelica mentioned his name.

"I've never known a bond to weaken that much," she remarked, "but I suppose it's possible. Well, I'm off."

"Give my best to Logan when you see him."

Mara smiled. "I shall." Kissing his cheek, she said, "I hope your girl brings you the same happiness Logan has brought me."

"So do I," Giovanni murmured as she vanished from his lair. "So do I."

Chapter 10

One brow raised, Logan Blackwood regarded his wife as she materialized in their plush Hollywood living room. "You were with Lanzoni," he remarked mildly. "Why did you go see him? And why did you block me?"

"I didn't want you following me."

"Why? I thought we weren't going to have any more secrets between us." The only reason he knew where she'd gone was because he smelled the priest's scent on her. "What's going on, Mara?"

She settled onto the sofa beside him. "You remember Alric?"

"Not really." He had never met the vampire, though he knew of him.

"I killed someone he loved. I thought he was long dead, since he never came after me. But he's here now."

"In California?"

"I'm not sure, but somewhere on the West Coast. I doubt it's a coincidence."

"You think he's coming after you?"

"Yes."

"Don't tell me you're worried about him?" She was the most powerful vampire in existence.

"Not exactly."

Slipping his arm around her shoulders, he asked, "What, exactly?"

"He's incredibly cunning. And ever since I've known him, he's always had slaves in his thrall to do his dirty work."

"You've got something better than slaves," he said, giving her shoulder a squeeze. "You've got me and the rest of the family behind you."

Mara laughed softly. She wasn't afraid of Alric, but she was afraid of losing the people she loved. Roshan and Brenna. Vince and Cara and her godsons, Rafe and Rane, and their wives. Kathy and Savannah. Abbey Marie and Nick. And her own son, Derek, and his wife, Sheree. She felt responsible for all of them, she mused, as she added Giovanni to her list.

For centuries, she had cared for no one, trusted no one. She had killed those who threatened her without a thought, turned her back on Logan, who continued to adore her no matter how badly she treated him.

He was the only man she had ever loved, though it had taken her hundreds of years to admit it and let him into her life. And yet he had always been there for her, even when she had married another man and given birth to Derek. Motherhood had changed her in ways she had never expected.

"Mara?" Lifting his hand to her nape, he gently massaged her neck.

"I'm all right."

"You're worried about the others."

She nodded. The vampires she called family had faced danger of one kind or another before and had always emerged victorious.

Drawing her into his arms, Logan said, "You've worried enough. I have a sure way to take your mind off Alric."

"I'm certain you do."

"Trust me." Stretching out on the sofa, he pulled her down on top of him, his hands gliding over her slim body as he teased her with his lips and his tongue. He had known her for centuries, yet he never tired of looking at her, holding her. She was the most beautiful, sensual, powerful woman he had ever known and as she poured her love over him, he knew he could ask nothing more of life than to spend the rest of his nights in her arms.

Just as he knew that, should anything happen to her, he would follow her into the Afterlife rather than spend the remainder of his existence without her.

Chapter 11

It had become a habit for Johnny to walk Cassie home. Now, as she removed her apron and slipped on her coat, she found herself smiling in anticipation. He was so easy to be with, to talk to. He made her feel important, as if she mattered. As if she was worth caring for. As if she was somebody.

Humming softly, Cassie left the bar. She felt a rush of disappointment when she didn't see him. After waiting a few minutes, she started walking home. Hearing hurried footsteps behind her, she turned, expecting to find Johnny.

Instead, she saw Lynx and two of his buddies.

"Where are you off to in such an all-fired hurry, sweet cakes?" Lynx asked as he grabbed her arm. "Off to meet that old man you've been hanging out with?"

"Let me go!" she cried, trying to wrest her arm from his grasp. "What I do is none of your business."

"No?" His lip curled in a sneer. "Well, I'm making it my business. I don't like a girl who teases 'yes' and then says 'no.'"

"I never did that!"

"Either way, tonight, you're mine," Lynx said, pulling her down a side alley. "Or should I say ours?"

"No!" Although she doubted there was anyone around to hear her, Cassie opened her mouth to scream for help, only to let out a harsh sob when Lynx slapped her.

Cassie struggled as best she could, but she was no match for three men. Tears of fear and rage burned her eyes as two of them dragged her down on the ground, then pinned her arms to her sides. It was pitch-black in the alley, the night quiet except for her useless struggles. She froze when she heard Lynx unzip his jeans. *Oh, Lord, he was going to do it!* She let out a cry of denial as his weight settled on hers and then, to her surprise, her arms were free. Over the pounding of her own heart, she heard the sound of several muffled blows, followed by a strangled cry, and a garbled plea for mercy.

When someone pulled Lynx off of her, Cassie scrambled to her feet and sprinted toward the mouth of the alley.

She didn't look back.

Giovanni saved Lynx for last. After the would-be rapist's companions were dead, he sank his fangs into the kid's throat even as the words *"Thou shalt not kill"* rose in his mind. But he felt no guilt, only grim satisfaction that these three hoodlums would never terrorize Cassie or any other woman again.

Safe at home, Cassie double-locked her door, made sure the windows were secure, then changed into her sweats and curled up in a corner of the sofa with a cup of hot chocolate, but her hands were shaking so badly she had to set it aside.

What had happened back there? One of the guys had been begging for mercy. It was obvious that someone had attacked them. But who? She blew out a long, shuddering sigh. Whoever her protector had been, she was grateful. She had never been so afraid in her life.

She flinched when someone knocked on the door. Was it Lynx? Had he come to finish what he'd started?

"Cassie? Are you in there? It's me."

"Johnny!" Relief washed through her as she scrambled off the sofa, opened the door, and threw her arms around him. "I'm so glad to see you."

"Is something wrong?" he asked, stroking her hair. "You're shivering."

"I was attacked."

"Are you hurt?"

"No, they just scared the crap out of me." Taking him by the hand, she led him to the sofa, sat, and pulled him down beside her. And then she frowned. "Are you?"

"No. Why do you ask?"

"There's blood on your shirt. And on your lower lip."

Without thinking, he said, "It's not mine."

Her gaze searched his. "Whose is it, then?"

Giovanni wiped his mouth. "Cassie, please let it go."

"It was you, wasn't it? In the alley."

"Yes," he admitted reluctantly.

"What did you do?"

Giovanni groaned. He'd been so anxious to make sure Cassie was all right, he hadn't taken time to check his clothing for telltale stains.

"Johnny? Tell me the truth."

"I should go."

She laid her hand on his arm, staying him when he would have risen. "Is Lynx all right?"

"No."

"And his buddies?"

He shook his head.

"Are they . . . ?" She couldn't say the word, didn't even want to think it.

"They laid their hands on you," he said quietly.

Cassie stared at him, horrified by what he had done. He'd killed them all. Maybe he'd had no other choice. Maybe it was self-defense. She hoped so, because, otherwise, it was murder, and she couldn't condone that. And yet . . . and yet, right or wrong, she couldn't be sorry that Lynx and his friends would never threaten her or anyone else again. She had no doubt all three of them would have raped her, just as she was equally certain that Lynx would have silenced her forever rather than take a chance on leaving her alive to go to the police.

"I should leave," Johnny said again.

"Please stay." She wrapped her arms around her middle. "I don't want to be alone right now."

"Cassie." He shook his head. "I'm afraid I'll only bring you trouble."

"That's a chance I'm willing to take."

"There are things about me you don't know."

"You said that before."

"And if you did know, you'd run away, screaming."

She stared at him, her brow furrowed. Had he done something in the past even worse than killing Lynx and his friends? If so, she couldn't imagine what it might be.

"I don't want to leave you," he admitted. "You're the best thing that's ever happened to me. But I'm afraid if I stay, I'll ruin your life."

"Johnny, we've been seeing each other only a short time, it's true. But I've loved every minute of it. I know what you did tonight was wrong, but you probably saved my life. In fact, I'm sure of it. I . . . I don't care what else you've done."

He shook his head, inhaled a deep breath, and blew it out slowly. Against his better judgment, he was going to tell her the truth. If she couldn't handle it, if he sensed she might betray him, he would wipe the knowledge from her mind and never see her again.

She looked at him expectantly.

"You can never tell anyone else what I'm about to say."

"I won't. I promise."

"I mean it. Sharing this with anyone else could put your life in danger. And mine, too."

Oh, Lord, she thought, he's a convicted felon. Or a terrorist. No, he didn't seem the type. Maybe he was in the witness protection program. Or worse. Maybe he had a wife and five kids. "Just tell me."

He took another deep breath, then said, "I'm a vampire."

Cassie stared at him. She never would have guessed he'd say that. "Yeah, right, and I'm the Little Mermaid," she muttered. "If you don't want to tell me, then just forget it."

"It's true."

She blinked at him, momentarily at a loss for words. Why would he concoct such an outrageous lie? Why would he say it if it wasn't true? And what if it was? She lifted a hand to her throat, trying not to stare at the dried blood on his shirt.

"Cassie, are you all right?" She looked as if she might faint.

"I don't know." She felt suddenly light-headed. It couldn't be true. Vampires didn't exist. And yet, he didn't look like he was joking. "You're really a . . . what you said?"

He nodded, his expression somber.

"Like the ones on TV?"

"Not quite, but basically, yes."

Cassie clenched her hands in her lap to still their trembling. "Are you going to drink *my* blood?"

His gaze slid to the pulse throbbing in the hollow of her throat. "No."

"Isn't that what vampires do?"

"Yes. And I'm not saying I don't want to drink from you, but I won't." He smiled faintly. "Unless you tell me it's all right."

"People give you their permission?"

"No."

She fell silent.

He could see her turning things over in her mind. He drank blood. He wouldn't take hers unless she said it was okay. But he didn't get permission from others. So . . .

He watched comprehension dawn in her eyes.

"You just take it," she said slowly. "Does that mean you . . . kill them?" Silly question, she thought. He had just admitted to killing three guys less than an hour ago. She glanced at the blood on his shirt, remembered the blood on his mouth. She had assumed it came from the fight, but now she wondered if he had taken their blood. She stared up at him. *Vampire.*

"No. I hypnotize my prey, take what little I need, and send them on their way, none the wiser."

Prey. The word conjured images of lions bringing down helpless zebras and gazelles in the wilds of Africa.

Giovanni shook his head. He never should have told her. "Listen," he said, getting to his feet. "Think it over tonight.

If I don't hear from you tomorrow . . ." He shrugged. "I'll understand and I'll never bother you again."

He was out the door before she could think of anything to say.

Giovanni prowled the dark streets, hating what he was, what he might have just lost. In hundreds of years, he had never felt this way about a woman. Not even Maria Elena had touched his heart the way Cassie did. Cassie. She eased his loneliness, made him feel human again. Made him laugh. He never should have told her the truth. He'd been a fool to think he could have any kind of lasting relationship with a mortal woman. Sure, the DeLongpre/Cordova coven had all found mates. But, sooner or later, those mates had become vampires, willing or not.

He was almost home when Mara appeared beside him. He swore under his breath. "What do you want now?" he asked crossly.

"It's nice to see you, too. Are you out of your mind? Why on earth did you tell her the truth?"

"She deserved to know. I doubt if she'll want to see me again after tonight, but how could we have any kind of meaningful relationship when she doesn't know who—or what—I really am?"

Mara nodded thoughtfully and then frowned. "You smell of death."

"I'm a vampire," he said bitterly.

She snorted softly. "You don't kill your prey. What happened?"

In as few words as possible, he told her about Lynx and his companions.

Mara muttered a very unladylike expletive, then said, "You shouldn't feel guilty for taking out the trash."

Giovanni laughed in spite of himself. One thing about the Queen of the Vampires, she always knew what to say to make him feel better.

Chapter 12

Johnny was a vampire. While eating lunch, Cassie tried to reconcile her recollection of the gentle man she had come to care for with her image of a blood-sucking creature of the night, but she just couldn't do it. For one thing, she didn't believe in vampires. For another, he didn't act like one. Vampires were nothing but old wives' tales from centuries ago when people were ruled by myth and superstition, when innocent women were burned as witches, and twins were thought to be evil and shunned or killed. Thank goodness, those days were long gone.

And even if it was true and he *was* a vampire, he was still the nicest man she had ever met. The few men she had dated had only wanted one thing from her and when she said no, she never saw them again. Except for Lynx. Of course, the bar didn't cater to the best clientele and she had little opportunity or means to mingle with the kind of men she'd hoped to date. And then, along came Johnny, sweet and polite, willing to confront Lynx and his buddies to protect her.

She spent the rest of the afternoon doing her laundry

and cleaning her crappy apartment. And all the while, she heard his voice in the back of her mind—*I'm a vampire.*

What if it *was* true? Would she be making the biggest mistake of her life if she saw him again? Perhaps a fatal one?

Finding her cell phone, she selected his number. It rang five times and then a recorded message kicked in: "You've reached Father Lanzoni. Please leave your number and I'll return your call as soon as possible."

Vampires slept during the day.

She shook her head. She was letting her imagination run away with her.

She'd never seen him eat—or drink anything but red wine.

"Stop it, Cassie! Enough is enough."

An hour later, she called him again, and an hour after that, and an hour after that. She heard the same message every time. Well, maybe he'd gone for a walk, or to the supermarket, or a movie or maybe he was . . .

Sleeping in his coffin?

Hoping some fresh air would clear her mind, she put on her running shoes and headed for the park. Next time she called, she would leave a message. One way or another, she had to know the truth.

Giovanni rose with the setting of the sun. As one of the ancient ones, he could be awake during the day if need be. But he didn't deserve to live in the light. He was a creature of darkness and that was where he belonged.

He was surprised to find a message from Cassie on his phone. "Johnny, I hope you'll walk me home tonight. We need to talk."

We need to talk. Even vampires who'd never had a date knew that nothing good ever followed those words.

He transported himself to his house, where he showered and dressed. He had hours to kill—bad choice of words, he thought—until Cassie got off work.

Plenty of time to hunt.

Cassie took a deep breath as she tucked the night's tips into her coat pocket and walked toward the door. Her stomach knotted with trepidation as she stepped out into the night. Would he be waiting for her? If he really was a vampire, was she making a horrendous mistake in seeing him again?

"Cassie." He stepped out of the shadows, silent as a wraith. "I didn't expect to hear from you."

"I had to see you one more time."

When she started walking, he fell in beside her. "You could have told me good-bye over the phone."

"I know. But the thing is"—she shook her head—"I wanted to see you."

"Oh?"

"I have to know if what you told me is true."

"Why would I lie about such a thing?"

"I don't know." Hands clenched at her sides, she took a deep breath, then blurted, "If it's true, I want you to show me."

"Show you what?"

"What you are. What do you think?"

"Ah."

"Will you?"

He huffed a sigh of resignation. "If you're sure that's what you want," he muttered, "although you may not like what you see."

They walked the rest of the way in silence. Cassie's heart was racing by the time they reached her apartment. Had she made a fatal mistake in asking him to prove what he was? What if his true appearance was hidden under some kind of paranormal glamour? What if he really looked like a corpse? What if the only way to prove he was a vampire was to drink from her?

Inside her apartment, she took off her coat and tossed it over the back of the sofa, then sat down, hands clasped tightly in her lap. "Okay," she said. "Show me."

At first, she didn't see anything. Then, gradually, his eyes turned from hazel to red and a change came over him. It was nothing physical, as far as she could see, and yet he was different. Invisible power radiated from him and she realized that she was truly in the presence of something supernatural. The knowledge raised the hair at her nape and made her stomach clench involuntarily.

And then he let her see his fangs. Smaller than she would have thought yet very white. And very sharp.

So, it was true. Shouldn't she be afraid? Repulsed? Horrified? Why wasn't she?

"Satisfied?" he asked. And even his voice sounded different. Deeper, more menacing.

She stared at him, too stunned to speak.

A moment later, he was Johnny again, his eyes the same warm hazel, his fangs gone, along with the aura of invincible power that had surrounded him. The transformation had been frightening and yet oddly fascinating. Fascinating?

She frowned. What was wrong with her? She should be terrified. Revolted. In fear for her life. Was something wrong with her? Was she missing some sense of self-preservation?

"I'll go now," he said. "Take care of yourself."

"Wait! Johnny, wait. I don't want you to go. I . . . I don't care what you are."

He stared at her in disbelief. Did she know what she was saying? What she was getting into? "Cassie . . ."

"I know what I want." Taking his hand, she tugged him down beside her. "And I want you. You're the sweetest guy I've ever met. So, you're a vampire. You don't act like the ones in the movies that go around ripping out people's throats. Besides," she said, stifling a grin, "no relationship is perfect."

He shook his head, not knowing whether to laugh or cry. And then, emboldened by her declaration, he cupped her face in his hands and kissed her lightly, tenderly.

Cassie tensed for a moment and then she leaned into him, her eyelids fluttering down as she slid her arms around his waist. His lips were cool and firm and magical, filling her with a warm sense of belonging that she had never known before—and never wanted to be without again. All her life she'd felt alone, unwanted, and unloved. Until this moment.

Lifting his head, Johnny murmured, "I hope I'm not dreaming," and kissed her again.

When they parted, both a little breathless, Cassie said, "*Do* vampires dream?"

"I never have. I don't know about any of the others."

Others. The thought brought her up short. Of course, if there was one, there were bound to be others. It was a sobering realization. One supernatural creature didn't seem like much of a threat, but what if there were dozens? Hundreds?

"You must have questions," he said.

She made a soft sound of assent. "Do you like being a vampire?"

He thought it over for a moment and then nodded. "I didn't, at first. It was hard, giving up everything I knew. But, in time, I made peace with what I am. I've been lucky to be part of a family."

Cassie frowned. "Vampires have families?"

"Of a sort. A few of those I know have had children. Others have adopted them. And they have generously included me in their circle."

"Wait! I thought vampires couldn't reproduce. At least, they can't in the movies."

"They can't in real life, either."

"Okay, now I'm confused. You just said some of them had kids."

"It's complicated. One of the men, Vince, had been recently turned when he married Cara. Apparently he had enough humanity left in him to father twins."

"Wow, that's weird."

"And it's never been done before or since, as far as I know."

"So, the couples are married?"

He laughed softly. "Yes. And I was blessed to unite each one in holy wedlock and bless their children."

"Vampires marrying vampires," she murmured. "And having babies. Who'd have thought?"

"Well, in each case, the women were human in the beginning."

"So . . ." Her gaze searched his. "What does that mean, exactly?"

"It means that the mortals eventually became vampires."

"Did they want to?" she asked, a note of skepticism in her voice.

"Sometimes."

She digested that a moment. Why would anyone choose to be a creature of the night? And what of those who hadn't wanted it? "Those who didn't choose it . . . Was it forced on them?" Would Johnny do that to her?

"No," he said, and then paused. That wasn't entirely true. "Sometimes the women were turned because it was the only way to save their lives."

"Would you . . . you wouldn't . . . ?"

His gaze slid away from hers. How was he to answer that?

"Johnny?"

"I honestly don't know what I'd do if turning you was the only way to save your life."

"Promise me you won't ever do that."

"Cassie, please don't ask that of me."

"Promise me!"

"All right. I promise."

She breathed a sigh of relief. Vampire or not, he was also a priest. Surely she could trust him to keep his word.

"Being a vampire does have its compensations," he said. "We never get sick or age. We have a great deal of strength. We are nearly immortal. One of the family members I mentioned was alive during the time of Cleopatra."

"Wow! That's unbelievable."

"But true. Her name is Mara. She is the head of the family and a remarkable woman."

"Enough about vampires," Cassie said, a twinkle in her eyes. "Wouldn't you like to kiss me again?"

* * *

Giovanni felt as if he was walking on air when he left Cassie's house an hour later. She knew the truth and she still wanted to be with him. They had kissed and cuddled on the sofa like a couple of randy teenagers. Any doubts he'd had about his libido had been laid to rest. It was a miracle. Lifting his face toward heaven, he murmured a silent prayer of gratitude. And then he frowned. What if she didn't mean anything she'd said? Knowing what he was, why would she want to be with him? Maybe she'd been afraid to rebuff him to his face. And yet, her kisses had seemed genuine. But how was he to know? He'd only kissed one other woman in his life and that had been centuries ago. He shook his head. Tomorrow would tell the tale, one way or the other.

Giovanni was nearing his lair when he felt a jolt, as if someone had just hit him with a live wire. He glanced around when a near-forgotten scent teased his nostrils. His sire. *Alric.* Drawing on his preternatural power, Giovanni looked around again but saw no one.

Giovanni.

The sound of his master's voice raised the hairs on his arms.

He froze as the vampire who had turned him stepped out of the shadows.

His sire looked just as Giovanni remembered him— tall and muscular, with cropped black hair and piercing black eyes.

Alric cocked his head to the side as his gaze moved over the fledgling he had not seen in centuries. "No clerical collar," he said, lifting one hand to his own throat. "Have you given up your calling and your faith?"

Giovanni shook his head.

"You're looking well."

"No thanks to you," Giovanni replied, all the old anger and bitterness rising up within him. "You deserted me."

Alric lifted one shoulder in a casual shrug. "I was detained."

Giovanni grunted. "For thirteen hundred years? What do you want?"

"What makes you think I want something?"

"Why else would you be here?"

"Maybe I just wanted to make sure you were all right."

Giovanni snorted. "You're a few centuries too late for that. Or did you get *detained* again?"

"I don't owe you an explanation," Alric retorted. "I would remind you that I am the one who made you. As your sire, you have no recourse but to do as I wish." As if to prove it, he unleashed his preternatural power.

It burned through Giovanni's veins like molten fire, the pain so intense that it drove him to his knees.

"I *do* want something," Alric said. "I want to know Mara's whereabouts."

Giovanni stared up at his sire, then slowly shook his head. "Do with me what you will. I won't betray her."

He had no sooner spoken the words than he felt an increase in his master's power as Alric sought to take control of his mind. Giovanni summoned his own power in an effort to block him, but Alric was his sire and resistance seemed futile.

The pain of resisting had grown almost unbearable when Giovanni felt another presence in his mind—one he recognized immediately. Mara. He didn't know what she'd done but suddenly Alric released him and vanished into the night, and Giovanni heard Mara's voice in his head: *You're welcome.*

Bewildered by what had just happened and Alric's abrupt disappearance, Giovanni made his way home. When he turned on the lights, he discovered he had an unexpected guest waiting in his living room. Mara.

"What happened back there?" he asked. "How did you do that?"

She looked at him as if he wasn't too bright. "Have you learned nothing these past centuries?"

"Apparently not. Alric is ancient. Why can't he find you? And how did you get him out of my head?"

Looking impatient, she perched on the sofa, long legs crossed at the ankles.

Giovanni sat on the love seat across from her, one brow raised as he waited for her to explain.

"I am the oldest of our kind," she said. "As such, my power is stronger than yours. Stronger than his. No one can find me if I do not want to be found, whereas I can usually locate anyone I wish."

"Don't you need to have taken their blood for that?"

"No. That just makes it easier."

I've been a vampire hundreds of years, he thought. *And I'm still learning about my kind.* "If you can so easily overpower his mind, how is it that he thinks he can destroy you?"

"He's letting his desire for vengeance override his good sense, if he ever had any to begin with. He's no threat to me. But if Alric persists in trying to find me, I'll gladly meet him. Tell Alric that if you see him again."

"Are you really indestructible?"

"No one is," Mara said, her expression sobering. "The things that will destroy you will destroy me, as well. None of us can survive beheading, or fire, or a stake through the heart. As for you, Giovanni, you are stronger than you think. I know you have never had occasion to exert the full extent of your powers. Alric may be older than you are. But you, my friend, you have something he does not." She leaned forward to tap her finger against his chest. "You have my blood in your veins. Next time he threatens you, remember that." She rose with fluid grace. "One more thing. The bond between you and Alric is old and weak. If you do not wish him to find you, I can sever the link between you."

He stared at her in disbelief.

"You doubt me?"

He started to reply, but let out a groan instead as he felt her power inside his mind. It was painful yet oddly pleasurable at the same time, as was her bite.

Lifting her head, she licked a bit of his blood from her lips. "That should do it."

"I don't know what to say."

"'Thank you' will do. Oh, one other thing. You won't be able to find him, either."

Giovanni grunted softly. He hadn't thought of that, but it was too late now. Then again, he couldn't think of a single reason why he would ever want to.

"How are you and your little female getting along?" Mara asked.

"Don't you know?"

"I try not to eavesdrop on you too often."

"Thanks," he said dryly.

"And she does not mind what you are?"

"She doesn't seem to," Giovanni said, grinning. "I think . . . I think I'm falling in love with her."

"She must be something special, indeed."

"She is. I told you I'd find my own woman," he said, smugly.

"So you did," she admitted. "Well, I wish you the best. You are the most decent man I've ever known," she said, eyes twinkling. "And I've known quite a few. Good night."

"Give my best to Logan."

Mara kissed him on the cheek and then she vanished from the room.

Giovanni blew out a sigh. Definitely the most remarkable woman he had ever met.

Logan smiled as Mara appeared on the sofa beside him. "So," he drawled, "what was the emergency that had you flying out of here like a bat out of hell?"

"Giovanni's sire is in town, looking for me. When Giovanni refused to give him my whereabouts, Alric threatened him. I couldn't allow that vile creature to harm my priest, could I?"

"Of course not," Logan said with a wry grin.

"He's found a woman."

Logan grinned at her. "I told you he didn't need your help."

"Be nice," she warned, "or *you'll* be looking for a woman."

"No way," he growled, wrapping his arms around her. "You're the only woman in the world for me."

Laughing softly, she nipped his ear. "I wonder who we'll find to perform the ceremony if Giovanni marries his little mortal?" she murmured.

"He found a woman on his own. I'm sure he can find a priest," Logan said, drawing her down on the sofa beside him. "Stop worrying about Lanzoni and worry about me. I've got an ache only you can cure."

"Tell me where it hurts, baby," she purred, raking her nails down his chest. "And Mama will make it better."

Chapter 13

Alric returned to the abandoned warehouse he had been using for his lair. He had known Mara was strong. Every vampire in existence knew her reputation, knew she was the oldest, most powerful one of their kind on Earth, yet he'd still been stunned by her ability to interfere when she wasn't even present. How the hell had she done that? And how was he going to defeat her if she could thwart him from a distance?

Perhaps he would have to find another way to avenge Calidora's death. There were people Mara cared for. Vampires all, yes, with preternatural powers of one degree or another. Nick Desanto, believed to be almost two thousand years old, and Logan Blackwood, a vampire for over nine centuries, were two of the oldest. Both had been turned by Mara and, as such, possessed much of her strength. But some of the recently turned mates were vulnerable.

There was only one flaw in his plan—he didn't know where to find any of them.

Two flaws, Alric amended, because he was pretty sure his fledgling wouldn't be a damn bit of help. Ungrateful wretch. Lanzoni would be moldering in his grave if not for him. He should have drained the man dry when he'd had the chance. But no, Alric thought irritably. He'd hesitated to kill a priest, an error in judgment he wouldn't make again.

Alric was about to summon Giovanni for another little chat when he felt a searing pain in his mind. Letting out a shriek, he dropped to his knees as the link between himself and his fledgling dissolved. "Mara!"

He hissed an oath as the pain receded. Damned interfering female. She was even more of a threat than he'd thought.

He snorted as he gained his feet. He was nothing if not resourceful. In today's world, with computers and search engines, even the Queen of the Vampires couldn't hide forever. Although he didn't know how the hell he'd destroy her if and when he found her, but what the hell. One thing at a time.

Chapter 14

For Cassie, the next few weeks were the best of her life.
Johnny walked her home every night after work. On her
evenings off, they went to the movies, or for walks in the
park, or dancing. And after every evening out, they spent
an hour or two in her apartment, curled up on her lumpy
old sofa getting to know each other better—in more ways
than one.

Tonight was one of those nights. Wrapped in his arms,
she felt warm and safe and loved.

"Tell me about your childhood," Johnny said.

"Why?"

He lifted one shoulder. "I'm curious, that's all."

She hesitated, embarrassed by her sordid childhood.
Would he think less of her when he knew how she'd lived,
what she had done to survive? Hoping she wasn't making
a mistake, she said, "I was an only child. My father was
a drug dealer, which was nice for my mother, since she
was hooked on meth. I'm not even sure they were married. They fought a lot. I learned early to cook and take

care of myself because neither one of them had much time for me."

She looked down at her hands, remembering how envious she had always been of the kids at school who had caring parents, kids who had good lunches and clean clothes and dreams of a bright future. She'd had dreams, too, of being a beautician with a salon of her own. "One day when I was fifteen, I came home from school and they were both gone." Her dreams had died that day. "I thought they'd just gone out drinking or something, but they never came back." She shrugged, as if it was of no importance. "I never saw either one of them again."

"What did you do?"

"I stayed in the house until the landlord came for the rent. I hocked what little my parents had left behind that was worth anything, but it wasn't enough and he evicted me. I couldn't afford another place and I had nowhere else to go, so late at night, I broke into houses that were for sale. Not nice ones that had alarms and cameras, but the ones in run-down neighborhoods. When my money ran out . . ." She bit down on her lower lip. "Do you want to hear my confession?"

Giovanni frowned. "Is there something you need to confess?"

She nodded, her cheeks heating with embarrassment. "When I ran out of money, I turned to stealing whatever I could—food, cash. Once I stole a car someone had left running and sold it to a dealer who didn't ask any questions. Another time, I found a wallet with some money in it, and I kept it."

"I can't condone what you did," he said, his voice kind. "But I can understand your reasons. You must realize that any forgiveness I offer is only between you and me." Still, he was sure Heaven would understand the why of the sins she had committed and forgive her.

"I know."

He made the sign of the cross on her brow. "I forgive you for your past sins, Cassie, on condition that you don't repeat them."

She smiled up at him. "Thank you. I feel better."

"Good." Cupping her face in his hands, he kissed her gently, and then more deeply.

She wrapped her arms around him, one hand delving under his shirt, sliding up and down his back. His skin was cool and firm beneath her fingertips.

He gasped her name as desire swept through him with the intensity of a forest fire. "Cassie!"

Pulling away from him, she asked, "Do you want me to stop?"

He groaned low in his throat. "No, but . . ."

"I want you," she whispered. "I know you want me."

"Cassie . . . please don't make this any more difficult than it is."

"What do you mean?"

"I do want you, but I'm afraid. . . ."

"Afraid of what?"

Sitting up, he buried his face in his hands. "Cassie, I'm a vampire."

"Yes, I know. But . . . what are *you* afraid of?"

"My desire for you is for more than just for your . . . your body."

"I don't understand."

"I know you don't. I never understood it myself until now. For my kind, desire is closely entwined with our thirst for blood. I'm afraid of . . . of hurting you."

She stared at him a moment, trying to make sense of what he was telling her.

And then he looked up at her, a faint red glow in his eyes, and she knew. "You're afraid that if we make love, you might . . ." She couldn't say the words *feed on me* out loud.

"That's exactly what I'm afraid of. What if I can't control my hunger? What if I take too much?" What if he killed her? He raked his fingers through his hair, then lurched to his feet. "I should go."

"Will I see you tomorrow night?"

"I don't know."

"We can take it slow, like you said. I know you're afraid. But I'm willing to risk it. Are you?"

Was he? After getting to know her, care for her, did he want to go on without her? What if he hurt her? Killed her? What if he didn't? Was he going to let the fear of something that might never happen keep him from the woman he loved? Because he did love her. Deeply. Desperately.

"Johnny?"

"I'll see you tomorrow night," he said.

And hoped she wouldn't live to regret it.

After leaving Cassie, Giovanni wandered the streets for hours, his mind in turmoil. He was haunted by images of taking her in his arms, caressing her, kissing her, until, overcome with lust and hunger, he buried his fangs in her throat and ravished her. He told himself he had more self-control than that. Hadn't he proved it by centuries of abstinence? But what if he was wrong? He shook his head. She might be willing to risk her life, he thought ruefully, but was he? What if loving her, being with her, only made

his lust and his hunger grow stronger? If he hurt her . . .
He groaned low in his throat. How could he give her up
when he'd just found her? But if he truly loved her, how
could he continue to put her life at risk? Best to leave now,
while he still could.

Lost in thought, Cassie sat on the sofa. It was time to
do some serious soul-searching. Was it wise to continue a
relationship with a vampire? Johnny was afraid of hurting
her. If he was afraid, why wasn't she? Was she being foolish? Suicidal? She hadn't trusted anyone in years, and yet
here she was, putting her heart and her life in the hands of
a vampire she'd known only a short time. She grinned inwardly. Talk about walking on the wild side. But then,
she'd grown up taking risks—staying in her parents' house
after they deserted her, stealing food and cash to survive,
breaking into vacant homes to spend the night. She had
always lived life on the edge. Why stop now?

In spite of his fear that seeing Cassie again was a mistake, Giovanni found himself waiting for her outside the
Winchester Lounge the following night.

"I'm surprised to see you," she said, smiling tentatively.
"Even though you said you'd meet me, I didn't think you
meant it."

"I couldn't stay away." He handed her a small velvet box.

"What's this?"

"Open it."

Curious, she lifted the lid. Inside, nestled on a bed of
black velvet, was a beautiful silver crucifix on a thick,

silver chain. She looked at him askance. "So, the rumors are true? Vampires are repelled by crosses?"

"Not exactly. But silver against preternatural flesh burns like the devil and leaves a hell of a scar. Should I ever try to bite you, just slap it against my skin and I'll back off right quick."

"Vampire health insurance," she murmured. "How quaint."

"It's not funny, Cassie."

"I know. Thank you," she said, fastening the chain around her neck. "It's lovely." She couldn't remember the last time anyone had given her a present. And it meant all the more because *he* had given it to her, no matter the reason.

They walked in silence for a moment before she asked, "Penny for your thoughts?"

"I was just thinking that. . . . Never mind."

"What?"

"If we're going to keep seeing each other, why don't you move into my house? It's a lot nicer than your place. It's got a TV and Wi-Fi and you would have your own room. You wouldn't have to pay rent, so you could save some money. You'd have a car at your disposal. I know you said no the last time I asked, but we know each other a little better now, and. . . ."

It made sense, in a way, Cassie thought. And it *would* save her a lot of money.

"You'll have the place all to yourself during the day. I take my rest elsewhere."

"All right," Cassie said. "I guess we can try it for a few weeks and see how it works out."

"You mean it?"

"Yes. I'd love to get out of my place. I found a dead rat in the toilet this morning."

"Are you working tomorrow?" he asked as they reached her building.

"No."

"Okay. Why don't you pack your things and do whatever else you need to do? I'll pick you up at sundown and you can move in tomorrow night."

"Sounds perfect! See you then."

"Okay if I kiss you good night?"

She gazed up at him. "You never have to ask."

Feeling blessed, he took her in his arms and kissed her, wondering what he had ever done to have met such an amazing woman. "Good night, Cassie."

"'Night, Johnny." Humming softly, she ran up the stairs. Who would have thought that meeting a priest would turn out to be the best thing that had ever happened to her? She didn't know what she'd done to deserve him, but she intended to make him the happiest man in the world.

Cassie grinned inwardly. She just might be falling in love with a vampire.

She didn't have much to pack. Her clothes and shoes went in one bag. The Minnie Mouse doll she had loved when she was a little girl went in another bag, along with an old framed photo of her mother, a throw pillow she'd won at a carnival, a fleece blanket, and a few toiletries. She piled what few foodstuffs she had in a cardboard box. She started to pack her dishes, then decided against it. They were old and chipped. She was moving into a new place. It was time for a matching set of dishes and silverware, a couple of new pots and pans.

She gave the apartment a cursory cleaning, took a shower, washed her hair, and she was ready to go when the sun went down.

Johnny arrived five minutes later. "All set?" he asked.

In reply, she gestured at the things piled on the sofa.

"Is that everything?"

She shrugged. "I travel light."

"All right, let's go. I'll carry the box," he said, tucking it under his arm. "You get the rest."

"What are you doing?" she asked when he slipped his free arm around her waist.

"I'm going to take you to my place."

"How?"

"Hard to explain. Just don't make any sudden moves."

Before she could question him further, his arm tightened around her and they were moving, but not in any way she recognized. Before she could even figure out what was happening, the trip was over and she found herself standing in another place.

"Welcome to your new home," Johnny said.

Head still reeling, stomach roiling, Cassie glanced around. There were crosses, large and small, as well as several small clay and porcelain figures, and pictures of the Virgin Mary and other saints. A particularly large crucifix enjoyed a prominent place on the wall above the white-brick fireplace. The room was square, the walls painted a pale green, the floors covered in a darker green carpet. A flowered sofa, flanked by a pair of walnut end tables, stood against one wall. An easy chair and ottoman took up one corner. A small den opened off the living room. Through the door, she could see a leather sofa. A large, flat-screen TV hung on the wall across from the sofa. A small bookcase held books and DVDs.

"Nice," she said, wondering if he had decorated the place himself.

"The bedrooms and baths are down the hall. My bedroom is the last one on the right. Take any of the others you like. The last one on the left is the biggest." He had moved his things out of there last night and switched the beds, thinking she would likely prefer the larger room and closet. "I'll put this stuff in the kitchen."

Cassie nodded, only then remembering that vampires didn't eat. Were there appliances in the kitchen? Why would there be?

As she carried the bags down the hall, she peered into the bedrooms. The first three were painted white and unfurnished. She paused at Johnny's room. The door was open and she looked inside. A cross hung on the wall over the double bed. Beige drapes hung at the single window; the walls were white, the carpet a darker beige than the drapes. A lovely statue of the Virgin Mary stood atop a modest chest of drawers across from the bed.

Crossing the hall, she opened the door to the room that would be hers. It was, indeed, larger than the others and the only one with its own bathroom. She dropped her bags on the foot of the king-sized bed and looked around. The walls were a pale blue; the drapes, heavily lined, a shade darker. A four-drawer chest and a small padded rocking chair were the room's only other furnishings.

Except for religious objects, she hadn't noticed any pictures or knickknacks in the house, she thought as she made her way to the kitchen. But then, guys didn't seem to collect knickknacks the way women did.

"I'm surprised you have a stove and refrigerator," she remarked, standing in the doorway.

He shrugged. "They came with the house. So, what do you think of the place?"

"It's lovely," she said, and then grinned. "No one would ever guess a vampire lives here."

"Why is that?"

"Why?" She cocked her head to the side, a grin playing over her lips. "There's no coffin, no cobwebs, no creepy Renfield eating bugs and hovering in the shadows."

"You've seen way too many horror movies," he said, chuckling.

"I guess. Can I ask you something?"

"Of course."

"Do you . . . I mean, in the movies . . . Do you sleep in a . . . a coffin?"

"No." He was about to tell her he slept on the floor in the bowels of an old church but decided against it. He wasn't sure what she'd think, but he didn't want to freak her out.

At least until she knew him better.

"I need to go to the store and buy a few things," she said. "You know, bread and milk and eggs."

"I'll drive you."

She felt a thrill of anticipation at the thought of riding in the Mustang again. She loved the purr of the engine. The sense of power beneath the hood.

A door at the end of the hallway led to the garage. Johnny punched the button to raise the door. Seeing the look of anticipation on Cassie's face, he said, "Feel free to use it whenever you want."

"Do you mean it? I can drive your Mustang?"

"Sure." He tossed her the keys, then opened the driver's side door for her.

She grinned at him as she slid behind the wheel.

Laughing softly, he shut the door and went around to the passenger side.

He'd barely gotten inside when she peeled out of the garage, leaving a trail of rubber behind. "You do have a driver's license, don't you?" he asked dubiously.

"Of course," she said with a wave of her hand. "Relax."

Relax? He didn't think so. He breathed a sigh of relief when they reached the grocery store.

He was definitely driving home.

Chapter 15

At home, Giovanni helped Cassie put the groceries away. The way food was produced had changed drastically since he was a boy. Even after all this time, he found it quite fascinating. In his day, people grew their own fruits and vegetables, raised their own cattle, sheep, pigs, and chickens. They had spun their own cloth, chopped wood for heating and cooking. But those days were long gone. Now bread came already sliced and wrapped in plastic. It was no longer necessary to butcher your own meat—you could find it already cut, weighed, and packaged. Milk came in handy cartons. There were aisles and aisles of bins containing fruits and vegetables from all over the world. Nuts in handy jars. Pretty much everything and anything people could possibly want available at any season of the year. Truly an amazing age.

He no longer had any real desire for mortal food, save for a good glass of wine, and yet he sometimes wished he could taste a few of the things Cassie had brought home—such as pistachio ice cream and tacos, and maybe a chocolate bar or two. He saw such things advertised on TV and couldn't help wondering what they tasted like.

As if reading his thoughts, Cassie asked, "Do you ever miss eating?"

"Sometimes, like now," he admitted. "In my day, we didn't have so many choices. Food was often scarce. In times of war, the armies came through and carried away everything they could, leaving families to starve."

"That's terrible," she said as she stacked several cans on a shelf. And yet it was happening today, too, she thought. Wars were raging in many foreign countries, tearing families apart, killing young and old alike. "What would happen if you ate something? Say, an apple or a banana?"

"It would be vile," he said with a grimace. "I actually tried eating an orange once. The consequences were not worth repeating."

She grinned at him. "Does it bother you, watching me eat?"

"No."

She quickly put the milk and eggs in the refrigerator, the bread in the cupboard. "How often do you have to . . . ?" She frowned. "Do you call it eating or drinking or . . . ?"

"I can go several days without feeding, perhaps a week." Then, curious to see her reaction, he said, "But I generally feed every day or so, simply because I enjoy it." He grinned as she tried to hide her revulsion. " I only take a little. Going for a long period without feeding weakens us."

Cassie put away the last of the groceries. "Do you mind my asking so many questions?"

"No. I want no secrets between us. You may ask me anything you wish."

Something warm and intimate passed between them as they smiled at each other. Giovanni closed the distance between them and, somewhat tentatively, took her in his arms. She went willingly, lifting her face for his kiss. He gazed into her eyes a moment before claiming her lips with his.

As always, whenever he kissed her, he was surprised by how quickly he wanted more than just kisses. His whole body came alive as she leaned into him, her lips sweet and pliable, her breasts warm against his chest. He felt a rush of embarrassment when he realized she could likely feel his arousal, but she didn't back away.

Cassie moaned softly as he kissed her again, his hand sliding up and down her side, slipping under her sweater to caress her bare flesh.

He was sorely tempted to take her there, on the kitchen floor, but what would she think of him? What would he think of himself if he took her like some rutting stag?

Lifting his head, he blew out a shuddering breath. "We'd better slow down. Don't you think?"

Cassie nodded, even though her body was urging her to take him to bed. Years ago, she had vowed that she wouldn't sleep with a guy unless he married her first, but just now, with her lips still tingling from Johnny's kisses and her body hungry for his touch, keeping that vow suddenly didn't seem so important.

"Close call," Giovanni said, grinning.

And the moment was gone.

"It's still early," he said. "Would you like to go out?"

"I guess so. What did you have in mind?"

"Have you ever been to Hollywood?"

"No."

"Then let's go."

An hour later, they were strolling down the Hollywood Walk of Fame.

"This is amazing," Cassie exclaimed. "I've always wanted to come here. I've never even heard of some of these people. Oh, look! Amy Adams! I love her." Tugging on his hand, she said, "Look. There's the Chinese Theater."

It was crowded with tourists, even at this time of the night.

Giovanni watched, smiling, as Cassie oohed and aahed over the imprints of Tom Cruise and Harrison Ford, Johnny Depp and Hugh Jackman.

"Look, here's Robert Downey, Jr. I love *Iron Man*!"

He grinned as she compared her footprints to those of Cher and Britney Spears.

Moving on, they stopped at a Starbucks, where he bought her a cup of hot chocolate with extra whipped cream.

She sighed as they pulled onto the freeway. "Thank you for tonight. I had a wonderful time!"

"So did I," he said, thinking of the joy he had seen on her face, the sparkle in her eyes. He couldn't remember when he'd had such a good time.

With luck, they would have many more nights like this.

Cassie woke early the next morning after a restless night. She wasn't sure why she'd had so much trouble sleeping. Maybe it was because she was in a new house, in a strange bed.

Swinging her legs over the edge of the mattress, she made a quick trip to the bathroom, then pulled on her robe and went into the kitchen.

While scrambling eggs, she smiled as she thought of the good time she'd had last night. It had been exciting, strolling down the Walk of Fame, reading the names of movie stars, all the while hoping to see a real one.

After breakfast, she wandered through the house. She perused the DVDs on the shelf in the den, noting that Johnny had a preference for superhero movies and that his taste in books leaned toward the paranormal, although there were several Bibles in different languages, as well as several biographies, including one of John Paul II.

She wondered where he spent the day.

Overcome with curiosity, she went into his bedroom and looked in his closet. His taste in clothing ran to dark shirts, pants, and boots. A garment bag held items worn by a priest—a long-sleeved black shirt and trousers, a cassock, a white surplice. A beautiful black rosary was draped over a padded hanger.

Feeling suddenly guilty for snooping, she hurried out of the room, closed the door, and walked down the hall to her own room.

After hanging her clothes in the closet, she stuffed her underwear and socks in the chest of drawers. She carried her toiletries into the bathroom, then filled the tub with hot water and a generous dollop of gardenia-scented bubble bath. Sighing, she stepped into the tub and closed her eyes. What luxury! There had been no bathtub in her apartment, only a tiny shower.

She lingered until the water grew cold.

After dressing, she checked the time. Still hours until she had to go to work.

In the kitchen, she made a turkey sandwich for lunch, added chips and some store-bought potato salad, then went into the den and turned on the TV. And all the while, she wondered where Johnny spent the daylight hours and what it was like to never see the sun. He'd told her he didn't dream. Was it like being dead?

Dismissing her morbid thoughts, she lost herself in an old movie.

Cassie woke with a start to find Johnny looking down at her, a smile tugging at the corners of his mouth.

"What's so funny?"

"Nothing. I was just thinking this is the first time I haven't come home to an empty house. How was your day?"

"Wonderful. I didn't do much of anything."

He laughed softly as she stood and put her arms around him. "Welcome home, Johnny."

"We have a few hours before you have to go to work. What would you like to do?"

"Go out to dinner and maybe take a walk. Just let me change my clothes."

Cassie opted for a burger, fries, and a strawberry shake at her favorite fast-food restaurant. The hamburger was rare and Giovanni licked his lips at the scent of the blood. He was no stranger to feeding on animals, having done so when nothing else was available—a fact he didn't share with Cassie.

They were strolling through the park after dinner when Cassie felt an odd ripple in the air. She let out a gasp and made a grab for Giovanni's arm when a woman suddenly appeared on the path in front of them. A beautiful woman with translucent skin.

Giovanni groaned. "Mara. What the hell are you doing here?"

"Waiting for an introduction to this lovely young lady."

"Cassie, this is Mara, an old friend of mine." He emphasized the word *old* just to annoy the Queen of the Night. "Mara, this is Cassie."

Mara held out her hand. "So pleased to meet you."

Cassie reluctantly took the other woman's hand, felt a jolt of she-didn't-know-what run up her arm.

"Mara, stop it!" Giovanni pulled Cassie closer to his side. He could feel her trembling though she tried to hide it. "You'll have to forgive her, sweetheart. Sometimes she forgets her manners."

Cassie waved off his apology. She couldn't stop staring at the other woman. Her hair, thick and black as ebony, fell over her shoulders in glorious waves. Tight black pants and a low-cut, white silk blouse emphasized every curve. She was gorgeous. And scary as hell. Power radiated from her like heat from an active volcano.

"What do you want, Mara?" Johnny asked.

"Nothing. I simply wanted to meet your friend. The family was curious."

"The family? And how does *the family* know about us?"

"Well, when I told them to stop looking for a suitable mate, they naturally wondered why."

Giovanni shook his head. "Go tell *the family* that my friend and I are *ever* so grateful for their concern but to mind their own damn business and let me take care of mine."

Mara grinned broadly. She had rarely heard him swear and she found it infinitely amusing. "*Buona notte*, Giovanni. Cassie, dear, I do hope to see you again."

Though that was the last thing she wanted, Cassie nodded politely. She felt another ripple in the air and the woman was gone as if she'd never been there. "Who *is* she?"

"Like I said, an old friend. I've known her for centuries. She is the oldest of our kind and a law unto herself."

Mara. Of course, Cassie thought. The vampire who lived during the time of Cleopatra. "She scared the crap out of me."

He chuckled. "She's good at that."

"Wait a minute. Did you say you'd known her for *centuries?* As in, hundreds of years?" Cassie asked, certain she had misunderstood. And then wondered why it was such a shock. Impossible as it seemed, Mara had lived even longer.

"Yes."

Cassie shook her head. It was beyond comprehension that anyone, even a scary creature of the night, should live so long. Maybe someday she would ask Johnny how long he'd been a vampire, but right now, she didn't want to know.

"Come on," Giovanni said, "we'd better get you home so you can get ready for work."

"What? Oh, right." Suddenly, she couldn't wait to get there; she needed something to remind her that she wasn't living in some kind of alternate universe. Schlepping drinks at the Winchester would ground her back in the real world, where she belonged.

Giovanni sat at the bar in Rick's, nursing a glass of red wine. The last few weeks had been filled with surprises. He had met Cassie. He'd taken human life. He had discovered that centuries of abstinence hadn't left him impotent.

Not only had he learned his sire's name, but that Alric was very much alive. And Mara had insinuated herself in his life in ways he found both irritating and amusing.

He could only wonder what the future held.

The thought had barely crossed his mind when Angelica perched on the stool beside him. "How are you, Father?"

"Fine. And you?"

"Doing well, thank you."

Giovanni frowned. "Did Mara send you?"

"No, why do you ask?"

He made a vague gesture. "She's been snooping in my life quite a bit lately, sticking her nose in where it doesn't belong. I thought . . . Never mind. Do you come here often?"

"Now and then. Why? Am I trespassing in your territory?"

"Not at all." At a loss for words, he sipped his wine.

"Actually, I was looking for you."

"Oh?"

"I was wondering if you'd like to go out tomorrow night."

"I thought you said we had no future together."

She ran her hand up and down his thigh. "I'm not infallible," she murmured, her voice low and sultry. "I think I may have made an error in judgment. So, what do you say?"

"I'm afraid it's out of the question. I'm seeing someone."

"Really? Is it serious?"

"It is on my part."

"One night," she coaxed. "The girl need never know."

Giovanni shook his head. "There are no secrets between us."

Angelica stared at him in disbelief. "None?"

"None."

"Then she knows that you're . . . ?"

"Yes. I told her everything."

"And she doesn't care?" Angelica shook her head, surprised by an unexpected wave of jealousy for a mortal female.

"I'm sorry, Angelica, but I have to go."

"Late date?"

"You could say that." He took a last sip of wine and centered the glass on the cocktail napkin. "It was nice seeing you again."

Grabbing his arm, she said, "Are you sure you won't change your mind?"

Frowning at the note of desperation in her voice, he removed her hand. "I'm sorry," he said again. "Good night."

He felt her angry gaze on his back as he left the nightclub.

Cassie was waiting for him outside the lounge when he pulled up to the curb. Smiling, she opened the door and slid into the seat. Her smile faded when she saw his expression. "What's wrong?"

Giovanni shook his head as he put the car in gear and pulled into the right-hand lane. "Nothing."

"Hey, weren't you the guy who said no secrets?"

"Yes," he said with a sheepish grin. "I just don't know how to explain it. Before I met you, Mara tried to set me up with someone."

"Oh?"

He nodded. "She was a vampire-witch. We met at a bar one night. After we talked awhile, she said we weren't right

for each other, but that I was going to meet someone else."
Johnny reached over and squeezed her hand. "I can only
think she meant you."

Cassie grinned at him. "I sure hope so."

"Anyway, she showed up out of the blue tonight and
asked me out."

"What? I hope you said no!"

"Of course, I did." Cassie was jealous, he thought,
pleased. "I'm just wondering what changed her mind."

"He turned me down," Angelica said, not meeting Alric's
eyes. "He's dating someone."

"You must not have tried very hard."

"I could hardly seduce him right there with the bartender watching," she retorted.

He swore a vile oath. "Stop making excuses! You're a
vampire and a witch! Are you telling me you're helpless
against a priest?"

"What do you want from him, anyway?"

"I want Mara. I tried to get him to give me her whereabouts, but he refused, and when I tried to force him, she
blocked me."

"Going after Mara is suicide, Alric. You must know
that. Everybody in the supernatural community knows that.
She's practically indestructible."

Alric stared at her, black eyes narrowed ominously. "Do
you know where she is?"

"She could be anywhere."

His hand closed over her arm, bearing down until she
grimaced. "You'd tell me if you knew, wouldn't you?"

She gasped, "Of course I would," as pain splintered
through her.

His hell-black eyes burned into hers. "If you're lying to me . . ."

It took all her self-control to still her trembling and meet his gaze. "I'm not!"

Alric released her arm even though he wasn't convinced. If she hadn't been a witch, he might have tried to read her mind to see if she was telling the truth. But that was risky, as he well knew. Though her vampire powers weren't as strong as his, she was a master of her craft. It was a potent combination. Even ancient vampires such as himself knew it was dangerous to run afoul of a practicing witch, especially one with three hundred years of experience behind her.

Dammit!

Chapter 16

Mara paced the floor in front of the living room fireplace, muttering under her breath all the while.

"You're going to wear out the rug," Logan remarked from in front of the TV as he tracked her progress back and forth. "Ordinarily, I wouldn't care, but it's brand-new."

"Alric is getting to be a pest. Now he's hounding Angelica. What if he goes after Abbey? She's still a young vampire."

"She's married to Desanto. If Nick can't protect her, no one can."

"That's not the point."

"Then end it. Call Angelica and have her tell Alric where we are."

"I hate to kill a man without a good reason."

He stared at her, one brow lifted. "It wouldn't be the first time."

"That was ages ago," she said, with an airy wave of her hand. "I'm much more civilized now."

"Yeah, right."

"Keep it up, Hektor, and you'll be next."

Laughing, he grabbed her arm and dragged her onto his

lap. "No way. You'd miss me too much," he said, nuzzling her breast.

"You think so?"

"I know so."

She closed her eyes as his lips trailed along the side of her neck, sending shivers of delight down her spine.

"Let me," he murmured against her throat as his hands slid restlessly up and down her back.

She turned her head to the side in silent invitation, gasped with pleasure as he bit her, ever so lightly. The wonder of it drove every other thought from her mind save her need for this man and this man alone.

Chapter 17

Giovanni awoke from the Dark Sleep smiling, as he had every night for the last five weeks, because he knew Cassie would be waiting for him at his house. They had quickly fallen into a routine. Their lives had merged together almost seamlessly, he thought. He met her when she got off work at 2:00 A.M. and drove her home, where they spent an hour or two together, mainly locked in each other's arms. He stayed in the house until dawn, then sought his lair. Since they stayed up so late, she slept a good part of the day. On the nights she worked, he rose a couple of hours before sunset so he could spend time with her before she had to leave for the Winchester. Her days off were the best. He had taken her night fishing at Huntington Beach. They'd gone to the Griffith Observatory in Los Angeles to look at the stars, spent an evening at the Hollywood Bowl. So many things to do and see, things he had done before, yet they were all so much more enjoyable when Cassie was with him. He wanted to show her the world, wanted to see it anew through her eyes.

He found her in the kitchen, loading dishes into the dishwasher, when he arrived that evening.

Moving up behind her, he slipped his arms around her waist and nuzzled her neck. "You smell so good," he murmured.

"I bought a new shampoo."

"I wasn't talking about your hair."

She stilled in his arms.

"I'm sorry," he said quickly. "Sometimes I just can't help myself."

She turned in his embrace. "How can you smell my blood?"

"I don't know, but it's driving me crazy. Why aren't you wearing your crucifix?"

"I left it in the bathroom after I took a shower. Do I need it?"

"No." He shoved his hands in his pockets and backed away from her. "Shall we watch some TV before you go to work?"

"Okay."

They settled on the sofa in the den, his arm around her shoulders. He loved sharing his house with Cassie. Loved spending so much time with her. She was good company, easy to get along with, a tidy housekeeper. For the first time since he'd been a young boy, he had a home. A real home. True, there were nights when the scent of frying meat turned his stomach, nights when his need to taste her tested every bit of his self-control, but it was a small price to pay for the happiness she brought him.

There was only one drawback. The more time he spent with her, the more he wanted her. He had kept his desire in check for so long that just holding Cassie in his arms was sometimes painful. As his need to make love to her grew ever stronger, so did his desire for her blood. Holding her close, kissing her, touching her skin, her hair, listening to the strong, steady beat of her heart. . . . He blew out a shaky breath in an effort to cool his ardor.

"Johnny?"

"What?" he asked, his voice thick with barely suppressed need.

"You're hurting me."

It took him a moment to realize his fingers were digging into her shoulder. Lowering his arm, he muttered, "Sorry."

"Are you okay?"

"No." Pushing off of the sofa, he put some distance between them.

"What's wrong?" she asked. Then, seeing the taut lines of his face, the faint red glow in his eyes, she said, "Oh."

Hands tightly clenched, he let his gaze lower to the pulse throbbing in the hollow of her throat.

"Johnny?"

"I need to go out."

Cassie bit down on her lower lip, unable to believe what she was about to say. "Would it help if you . . . you drank from me?"

"Maybe." He raked his fingers through his hair. "I don't know." It might help to ease his hunger and satisfy his curiosity, he thought. Then again, it might make it worse. "Go get the crucifix."

She hurried to do as bidden. In the bathroom, she took several deep breaths as she picked up the chain and slipped it over her head. The silver, thick and strong and reassuring, felt cold against her skin.

In the living room, she perched on the edge of the sofa. "What should I do?"

"Just stay still." He sat beside her. Slipped his arm around her waist. Pushed her hair out of the way. "If you get scared, just hit me in the face with the cross."

Nodding, she clenched her fingers around the crucifix. "Will it hurt? When you . . . you bite me?"

"No," he said, his voice tight. "Are you ready?"

"Wait! It won't turn me into a vampire, will it?"

"Definitely not."

"Okay, then." Her whole body tensed as his arm tightened around her.

"Relax," he said, though he had to admit his own nerves were wound tighter than a spring. He kissed her cheek. And then, as gently as he could, he bit her just below her ear, careful to avoid the chain around her neck.

Cassie let out a gasp of surprise that quickly turned to a sigh of pleasure. Who would have thought something so gross would feel so amazing? For a moment, caught up in the thrill of it, she closed her eyes. Only to open them seconds later. What if he was taking too much? How was she to know? She lifted her hand, wondering if she should press the cross to his cheek. She heard his voice telling her that silver against preternatural flesh burned like hell and left a nasty scar. She didn't want to hurt him. But she didn't want to die, either. Before she could decide, he lifted his head.

Her gaze searched his. "Did it help?"

He nodded. Then, cupping her cheek in his palm, he kissed her. "Thank you."

"You're welcome. You never told me it would feel so wonderful. Why didn't it hurt? I mean, I've seen your fangs. They look very sharp."

"I can make it hurt the next time, if you like."

"What makes you so sure there will be a next time?"

He grinned a knowing grin. "Because you liked it the first time."

"How do vampires make other vampires? I saw a movie where the vampire had to bite the girl three times to change her. But in *Dracula,* he drank her blood and then she had to drink his."

"Are you thinking of joining the ranks of the Undead?"

"Heavens, no! Just curious."

"The film, *Dracula,* had the right idea. To turn you, I'd have to drain you to the point of death and then give you some of my blood."

"Eww. That sounds worse than gross. And dangerous. What if you took too much by mistake? Would I die?"

"Probably."

"Have you ever turned anyone?"

"No. That's one thing I don't have on my conscience."

"So, vampires don't go around making lots of other ones?"

He shook his head. "No. Too many vampires would only draw unwanted attention to our kind. It's safer for the public, and for us, if we keep our numbers small."

"What happens when you make a new one?"

"What do you mean?"

"Do they stay with you?"

"Your sire—that's what you call whoever made you— is supposed to stay with you for a year or so while you're a new vampire—a fledgling. They're supposed to teach you how to hunt, hopefully how to feed without killing your prey. Teach you what you can and can't do."

"Kind of like vampire kindergarten?"

He grinned at her. "I guess you could call it that."

"Was your sire a good teacher?"

"I wouldn't know. He turned me and left me." Funny, that still rankled, even after all these years.

"But you survived."

"Barely."

"Were you scared?"

"Terrified. I woke up in a cave not knowing what had happened to me. Or what I had become. I had a voracious hunger, but I didn't know what I was craving." He paused. "Are you sure you want to hear this? It's not a very pretty story."

She nodded, fascinated by what she was learning.

"I came across a man who was bleeding. As soon as I smelled the blood, I went kind of crazy. I attacked him and drained him dry." The guilt he felt for that man's death and the others that followed plagued him to this day. "It took me a while to learn that I didn't have to kill," he said, his voice thick with regret. "That I could satisfy my hellish thirst without doing any harm."

"It wasn't your fault. You didn't know. Your sire is accountable for those lives, not you."

"There's no excuse for what I did. I was a priest." He groaned low in his throat. "I was supposed to provide comfort and ease suffering, not take human life."

Hearing the anguish in his voice, Cassie put her arms around him. "I'm sorry, Johnny. But I'm so glad you survived."

He buried his face in her shoulder, finding a measure of peace in her touch, in the nonsense words she crooned as she stroked his hair. He had done nothing to deserve her, he thought, even as he murmured a silent prayer of thanks that Cassie Douglas had come into his life.

I've been bitten by a vampire. It was Cassie's last thought as she tumbled into sleep that night, her first when she woke the next morning.

Sitting up, she lifted a hand to her neck. Had it left a permanent mark, like in the movies? If she looked in a mirror, would she find two little puncture wounds in the side of her neck? Would she have to wear scarves the rest of her life?

Curious, she threw back the covers and padded into the bathroom. Opening a drawer, she pulled out her hand mirror and turned her head this way and that, but found no telltale marks.

"You're in love with a vampire, Cassie," she told the image in the mirror. "So, what are you going to do now?"

What did people do when they fell in love with a creature of the night? She supposed there were only two options—stay or go. The third option popped, unwanted, into her mind. Or she could become a vampire, too.

She grimaced at her image. "Do you think there are people who actually want to be turned?"

She couldn't imagine it. And yet . . . he had told her that some of the women he considered family had asked to become vampires. What if Johnny asked her to marry him? It was a long shot, sure, but the man had been a priest. He was still a virgin. Did that mean he didn't believe in sex outside of marriage, even though he was no longer a practicing clergyman? Did she love him enough to give up her humanity to be with him? How did anyone make a life-changing decision like that?

With a shake of her head, she put the mirror back in the drawer, then turned on the shower. She absently massaged the side of her neck while she waited for the water to heat, then stepped under the spray. Johnny was still a virgin.

Would he still care for her when he learned she wasn't?

Chapter 18

Alric grinned with satisfaction. It had taken several nights, but he had finally found a link to Mara's whereabouts. It wasn't a member of her family, as he'd hoped, but a part of her inner circle nonetheless. And he'd found it quite by accident when he ran into an old acquaintance of his in a tavern. Alric's ears had perked up when Reynolds mentioned a vampire bar in Dune, New Mexico, run by a couple of vampires named Edna Mae and Pearl.

"Edna and Pearl," Alric murmured as he headed for his lair. They were well-known in the vampire community. A couple of old broads, they had once been vampire hunters until they ran afoul of one of Vince Cordova's twin sons. The women had been in their seventies when Rafe turned them both. Alric chuckled. He still found it amusing.

Tomorrow might, he would head for New Mexico and pay them a visit.

Edna Mae smiled at Pearl as Monroe and James hung the new sign over the entrance to the combination bar and café. Bright red letters proclaimed the grand opening of the Bloody Mary Café and Motel.

"It's about time, don't you think?" Edna Mae asked. "I never liked the old name."

"I didn't either, dear," Pearl agreed.

"Coming here was the best decision we ever made," Edna Mae said, watching her husband.

Pearl nodded. "Yes, indeed. And not just because we're getting rich," she said with a grin.

Edna Mae laughed. "But money helps."

"What are you two gabbing about?" James asked as he slipped his arm around Edna's waist.

"We were just saying how happy we are to be here."

"That makes two of us," James said.

"Four of us," Monroe added, coming up beside Pearl. "Let's go inside and drink a toast to our good fortune."

Alric stood outside the Bloody Mary Café. Through the open window, he could see perhaps a dozen people inside. His nostrils told him most of them were vampires imbibing wine heavily laced with blood. It was easy to pick out the old broads. One, dressed in jeans and a flowered blouse, was short and plump with curly hair that looked too red to be real. The other, tall and angular, with shoulder-length white hair, wore pants and a bright green shirt. They sat at a round table with two men, who were also vampires.

Gathering his power, Alric strolled through the door.

Edna Mae looked up as a strange man strode toward their table. Without asking if he could join them, he pulled a chair from an adjoining table and sat down.

"Can we help you?" Monroe asked.

"Butt out!" Alric said brusquely. "I'm here to see the ladies."

Edna Mae and Pearl exchanged glances.

"What do you want?" James asked.

"This doesn't concern you, either," Alric snapped. "I'm looking for Mara."

"Mara!" Pearl exclaimed "Whatever for?"

"That's my business, you old bat. Where is she?"

Pearl and Edna Mae exchanged glances again.

"I'm sure we don't know," Edna Mae said, shrugging. "We haven't seen her in quite a while."

"I don't believe you," Alric snarled as he grabbed Monroe by the neck. "I'd advise you to tell me what I want to know."

A hint of preternatural power flooded the room.

"Wait!" Pearl glanced around the bar, dismayed to see all eyes were turned in their direction.

Three of the human patrons rose quietly and practically tripped over each other in their haste to leave the café. The vampires simply vanished from sight.

"Stop! Don't hurt him anymore!" Pearl begged as Alric loosed the full force of his power on Monroe. "The last we heard, Mara was spending the summer in her castle in Transylvania."

Alric snorted. "A castle in Transylvania? I don't believe you."

"It's the truth! Tell him, Edna."

"She has a castle there," Edna Mae said. "She's had it for centuries. I thought everybody knew that."

Alric's gaze bored into hers for a moment. Then, digging his fingers into Monroe's neck, he looked back at Pearl.

Unflinching, she stared at him.

Alric grunted. So, Mara had a castle. He shook his head. And then he grinned. It had been three hundred years or so since he'd been to the home country. He could revisit the place of his birth and destroy his enemy.

Monroe slumped over the table when Alric released him.

Alric stood, his narrow-eyed gaze fixed on Pearl. "If you're lying about this, I'll come back and finish the job."

Pearl nodded. She didn't doubt it for a minute.

A wave of his hand and the vampire was gone.

"Are you all right?" Pearl asked, reaching across the table to grasp Monroe's arm. "I don't think I've ever been so scared in all my life!"

"I'm okay," Monroe said. "I just hope to hell I never see him again."

"Me, too." Pearl smiled at Edna Mae. "Thanks for backing me up."

"I'm so proud of you!" Edna Mae said. "How did you ever think of telling him that?"

"I don't know, dear. But what are we going to do when he finds out we lied to him?"

"I don't know. Maybe we should call Mara and warn her that some vampire is looking for her," Edna Mae suggested.

"I think that's a good idea," James said. "I don't know who that guy was, but I don't mind telling you, he scared the crap out of me."

"The four of us together don't have that much power," Monroe muttered, rubbing his neck. "I say call Mara."

Mara glanced at her ringing phone and then at Logan. "You won't believe who's calling," she said as she answered. "Edna, this *is* a surprise."

"I hate to bother you, but we're in trouble and you might be, too. Some rude vampire that I've never met before is looking for you. We told him you'd gone to Transylvania and he seemed to believe us. But we're worried about what he's going to do when he finds out you're not there." Edna Mae paused to take a breath. "We need help."

"What did this vampire look like?"

"He was tall, with black hair and a tattoo on his neck."

"Alric," Mara muttered. "I knew he was looking for me, but thanks for your concern. As for your problem, why don't you close up the café for a while? You can go stay at my home in Northern California, if you like. You should be safe there."

"That would be wonderful! We'll leave as soon as we get packed. Thank you so much!"

"I'll send Logan to let you in and reset the wards."

"I don't know how we can ever repay you."

"I'm sure I can think of something. Logan will be waiting for you at the house when you get there," she said, and ended the call.

"Nice of you to volunteer me," Logan said. "What do I get in return?"

A lazy grin spread over her face. "What would you like? As if I didn't know." She slapped his hands away when he reached for her. "Don't you ever think of anything else?"

"Not when you're in the room."

She laughed softly. "Maybe later."

"What's wrong with right now?"

"Have you forgotten? You're going to Northern California."

Chapter 19

Cassie found herself thinking about becoming a vampire at random times during the next few days. She considered the pros and cons while taking a walk around the block in the morning, while changing the sheets on the bed, or while eating a cheeseburger and drinking a soda. Of course, hamburgers and fries and the like hadn't existed when Johnny was turned, but there must have been foods he missed, at least at first. Still, being a vampire didn't seem as awful as she had once imagined. Johnny wasn't a blood-thirsty maniac who went around terrorizing the countryside. She never would have guessed what he was if he hadn't told her. He had just seemed like a nice, ordinary guy who had once been a priest. Even now, she sometimes forgot what he was . . . except for times like this evening, when she knew he had gone hunting.

How did he do it? Did he sneak up on people and take them unawares? Knock them unconscious? Use some kind of vampire magic to hypnotize them?

She put the question to him as soon as he came home.

"You ask the darnedest things," he muttered, following her out of the kitchen and into the living room.

"Well, can you blame me?"

"I guess not."

"After all, I am living with a creature of the night," she said, kissing the tip of his nose. "Who better to help me sort fact from fantasy?"

She sat on the sofa and he dropped down beside her. "Sometimes I find my prey in bars, sometimes it's just someone walking down the street. I speak to their minds, assuring them that I'm not going to hurt them. After I take what I need, I wipe away the memory of what happened and send them on their way, none the wiser."

"What does it taste like?"

He frowned at her. "Like blood, what else?"

"Well, I've tasted my own when I get a paper cut or something like that, but I've never actually *drunk* any. Isn't it kind of gross?"

He shook his head, amused by the train of her thoughts. "I thought it would be disgusting the first time I preyed on someone, but it wasn't. It's warm and coppery and a little salty. And I can't live without it." He thought a moment before adding, "I can exist on animal blood if there's nothing else."

"Yuck," she said, grimacing, "That's really disgusting!"

"Blood is blood," he said matter-of-factly. "But yours is sweetest of all."

"I'm not sure that's a compliment."

"Trust me, it is." He thought for a moment, then said, "Now that I think about it, not all blood tastes exactly the same. But none of it satisfies me the way yours does." Although he had no idea why that should be. Perhaps it was because of the emotional connection he felt between them.

Cassie nodded, and then she grinned. This had to be the

strangest conversation she'd ever had. "In the movies, when a vampire bites someone, there's always a mark."

"You can't believe everything you see in the movies," he said with a wink.

"I guess not." She pursed her lips, her brow furrowed. "So, what about garlic?"

"What about it?"

"Does it bother you?"

"Only on your breath," he said with a lopsided grin.

Cassie stuck her tongue out at him. "What about holy water?"

"It burns." Another reason why he was no longer a practicing priest.

"What about mirrors?" she asked, only then realizing the only one in the house was the hand mirror she had brought with her when she moved in.

"That myth is true. Vampires cast no reflection. And no shadow, either."

"Why?"

He shrugged. "Some say it's because we have no soul."

"Do you believe that?"

"I don't want to."

"Wait a minute. Don't people notice your lack of a reflection? Doesn't it freak them out?"

"You haven't."

Cassie frowned. Surely when they passed by store windows or were in restaurants with mirrors on the walls, she would have noticed that it looked as if she was alone. But she hadn't. "Why didn't I?"

"You saw me, but it was an illusion."

"I don't believe you." Pulling her phone from her pocket, she tapped the camera and held it out in front of them for a selfie. "You're in the picture," she said as she clicked the photo button. A gasp escaped her lips when she clicked on the photo. She showed up just fine. But it looked as if she was alone on the couch. "That is so weird. Doesn't it make you feel kind of . . . I don't know what."

"I think *invisible* is the word you're looking for. I have to admit, it was a little disconcerting at first, but you get used to it."

"I'm sorry to be such a pest. You're probably tired of answering all my questions."

"You have every right to know what you're dealing with. Who you're living with."

Cassie smiled at him. But she couldn't help wondering how lady vampires applied their makeup or arranged their hair.

After Cassie left for work, Giovanni willed himself to a neighboring city. Walking down the dark streets, he thought about her questions as he searched for prey. Was she merely curious? Or was she wondering what it would be like if she became a vampire? He shook his head. He wouldn't wish this life on her—or on anybody. And yet . . . he gazed up at the vast midnight-blue vault of the sky. It wasn't all bad. He had watched the world change, seen inventions that were not even thought of in his day. He had traveled the globe and seen wondrous things. He had visited Machu Picchu, located high in the Andes Mountains in Peru, walked along the Great Wall of China, stared in awe at the giant statues created by the ancient Rapa Nui people on Easter Island, visited the monuments at Stonehenge, and toured many other places located in distant parts of the world. Would he want to give all that up for one mortal lifetime? In a New York minute, he thought, smiling, if he could spend it with Cassie.

He was waiting for her at the Winchester when she got off work. "How was your night?" he asked as he opened the car door for her.

"Busy, thank goodness. Makes the time go by faster." She grinned at him as she got into the car. "I guess time doesn't matter much to you, does it? I mean, you've pretty much got forever."

He shrugged. "Lately, the only time that matters are the hours I spend with you."

Cassie pressed a hand to her heart as he walked around the car and slid behind the wheel, thinking that was the sweetest thing anyone had ever said to her. Leaning toward him, she kissed his cheek. "Johnny, I think I'm falling in love with you."

Taking her hand in his, he gave it a squeeze. "Good. Because I'm already in love with you."

She smiled all the way home. As soon as they were inside, she threw her arms around him and kissed him.

"What was that for?"

"Because you're so sweet and caring and way too good for me."

"Hardly."

"It's true. You're the nicest, most considerate man I've ever known."

His arms went around her waist, pulling her closer. "You're the only woman I've ever really known," he said quietly. "And I want to know everything about you." He kissed her brow, the tip of her nose. "Everything." His lips slid across her mouth, followed by a long, lingering kiss

as his tongue dueled with hers. And then they were stag-
gering toward the sofa, falling onto the cushions, their
mouths fused together. Desire spiked within him, hotter
than sunlight on preternatural flesh. He moaned low in his
throat, certain he would perish from the exquisite agony
of holding her but not possessing her.

"Johnny. Johnny . . ." Her hands moved restlessly over
his back, then slid under his shirt to caress his bare skin.

It was very nearly his undoing. Twisting out of her arms,
he bolted to his feet.

She stared up at him through heavy-lidded eyes. "What's
wrong?"

"I want you."

She held out her arms. "I'm here."

He raked trembling fingers through his hair. She was
so tempting and he wanted her so desperately, yet fear held
him back. What if he disappointed her? What if she
laughed at his clumsy attempt? And it was morally wrong,
he thought glumly. Vow or no vow, it was a sin to make
love to her outside the bonds of matrimony. "Heaven help
me, I want you more than you can imagine," he said, his
voice little more than a growl. "But I need more time."

She stared up at him, her eyes bright with tears of disappointment. "I understand," she murmured. He'd been a
priest. No doubt it was hard for him to commit what he
surely thought was a sin. Shoulders sagging, he slumped
down beside her, hands dangling between his knees.

"It's all right," she said, wrapping her arm around his
shoulders. "I can wait."

He smiled grimly, afraid that, sooner or later, his longing for her would prove stronger than his self-control. He'd
once heard an old Jesuit say, *Once a priest, always a priest.*

Apparently, it was true, even after all these years.

Chapter 20

Filled with rage and betrayal, Alric returned to New Mexico. He had gone to Transylvania. He had located Mara's castle. She wasn't there. Had he been able to get inside, he would have trashed the place.

The Bloody Mary Café was shuttered tight when he arrived. He stormed into the motel office. A middle-aged man wearing a golf shirt sat behind a desk reading a travel magazine.

"Where are they?" Alric demanded brusquely.

"Are you looking for a guest?"

"No, you fool! I'm looking for the owners."

"They've gone on vacation. I'm not sure when they'll be back."

"Where did they go?"

The man shrugged. "I don't know. They didn't tell me."

Furious at being thwarted yet again, Alric sprang over the desk and buried his fangs in the man's throat. He drank his fill, then tossed the empty husk aside.

Steeped in anger, high on fresh blood, he prowled through the motel rooms, killing everyone he found.

After exiting the last room, his hands and clothing

covered in blood, he set fire to the café and the motel. He watched them burn for several minutes before he willed himself to his lair to get cleaned up. Edna and Pearl had lied to him, and for that, they would pay dearly when he found them again.

And find them, he would.

Chapter 21

Cassie sighed as she washed her breakfast dishes. Things had been a little tense between her and Johnny since last night and she didn't know what to do about it. Had he not been a priest, she would have seduced him. Not that she had much practice at seduction. But how hard could it be? He wanted her. She wanted him. All they had to do was let nature take its course.

She tried to understand how he felt. As a priest, he'd been celibate. No doubt he had preached against sex before marriage, heard numerous confessions from men and women who were tormented by guilt for having broken the law of chastity, or being unfaithful to their spouses. It couldn't be easy for him to turn his back on the tenets of his religion. But he hadn't been a practicing priest for a long time. Surely whatever vows he had once made were null and void by now. Weren't they?

Wiping her hands on a dish towel, she told herself to be patient. After all, they had only known each other a short time. It was probably better for both of them to wait awhile. Maybe he was just nervous, she thought with a wry grin. After all, he'd never done it before, but she loved him enough, wanted him enough, to give him all the time he needed.

Tossing the dish towel aside, she went into the den and turned on the TV. She flipped through the channels and picked an old miniseries set in Australia. To her astonishment, the story involved a priest who had an affair with a young woman.

Cassie shook her head. What were the odds that she'd chance upon this movie now? Was it an omen? A warning? Or just a coincidence? Watching the movie, she gained a bit of insight into Johnny's conflicting feelings. Like the priest in the movie, Johnny was fighting years of guilt ingrained in him by his religion.

Hopefully, she and Johnny would live happily ever after, unlike the priest and his love interest in the movie.

Cassie glanced at the clock. Almost sundown, she thought, and then froze. She knew Johnny was near even before he materialized in the room. How was that possible? Was it because he had tasted her blood?

Her heart skipped a beat when he appeared in the living room.

"What's wrong?" he asked. "You look surprised to see me."

"I knew you were almost here," she said, her voice laced with wonder. "How is that possible?"

"Because I drank from you. It forms a bond between us. I probably should have warned you about that."

"What does it mean, exactly? This bond?"

He sat in the chair across from the sofa. "It means I'll be able to find you whenever and wherever you are."

She stared at him. "So, it's like vampire GPS?"

"You could say that."

"Why didn't you tell me?"

"I guess I was too caught up in the moment. I'd wanted to taste you for so long, I couldn't think of anything else. It works both ways, if that's any consolation."

"You mean I'll be able to find you?"

"No. But we'll be able to communicate without words." He smiled faintly. "Sort of like a vampire walkie-talkie."

She mulled that over, then frowned. "So, you can read my mind now?"

"I always could."

That was disconcerting. "Can I read yours?"

"No. You'd have to take my blood for that."

She grimaced at the thought, then decided to see if he could really read her mind. *I'm off tonight. What do you want to do?*

"Whatever you'd like to do," he said with a grin. "Did I pass the test?"

"That's amazing."

He nodded. There were *some* good things about being a vampire.

"Is there a cure for what you are?"

"Sadly, no," he said, and then frowned. "You remember I told you about Mara? The oldest of our kind?"

"Oh, yeah." Having met the woman, she didn't think she would ever forget her. "Did she find a cure?"

"No, but she reverted to being human. No one knows how or why. Some think it was because she had lived so long it was some sort of natural regression, but no one really knows. While she was human, she had a child, and when that child's life was threatened, she asked Logan, the man who had loved her his whole life, to give her the Dark Gift."

"Why?" It was inconceivable that anyone would *want* to be a vampire.

"Because it was the only way she could find her son."

"So, she willingly gave up her humanity?"

Johnny nodded.

Cassie stared at him, wide-eyed. "Was she sorry afterward?"

"No. I think Mara was born to be a vampire. The most amazing thing is, even when she was a fledgling again, she was just as powerful as she'd ever been."

"Would you be human again, if you could?"

"Maybe I will be," he said, with a wink. "If I survive long enough."

"I'm serious. Would you?"

Leaning forward, he clasped her hands in his. "If it meant spending my mortal life with you, then yes, definitely."

Feeling that she was melting inside, Cassie gazed into his eyes. When he reached for her, she gladly fell into his embrace.

With a low groan, he lifted her onto his lap and wrapped his arms around her, holding her so tightly she could scarcely breathe.

"What is it?" she asked, her fingers delving into the hair at his nape. "What's wrong?"

Not meeting her eyes, he said, "I'm afraid of losing you."

"You won't."

"I know we've only been together a short time, but . . ."

"But what?"

"Do you think there's any chance you'd ever consider being my wife?"

Astonished, she could only stare at him. "You want to get married?"

"Is the idea so repellant?"

"Well, no, but we've only known each other a few weeks. And you really don't know anything about me."

"I know I love you and I don't want to live without you. As for your past, whatever happened before we met doesn't matter."

"How can you be sure you love me? I mean, you've never had a girlfriend. Maybe you're just, I don't know, infatuated, and once you get to know me better, you'll be disappointed or . . . or realize that what you're feeling is just lust and not love," she ended breathlessly.

Cupping her face in his hands, he kissed her tenderly. "I know what I feel, Cassie. I know what I want. You don't have to give me an answer now. But will you think about it?"

What *would* it be like to be married to him? she wondered. She had dated a few guys in high school, had a couple of serious relationships since then. Made the mistake of sleeping with her last boyfriend, only to find out Tom was married with two kids and one on the way. She'd thought herself in love with him, but she knew now she'd been blinded by his easygoing charm and Hollywood good looks. Once she'd taken him to her bed, he quickly moved on. Just one more reason not to trust anyone. But Johnny wasn't like that. He was warm and caring and sincere, easily the most honest man she had ever known. He had probably never told a lie or had an unkind thought in his whole life.

Nodding, she said, "I'll think about it."

He kissed her again, more deeply this time. And she was lost. Still, she intended to think it over for a week or two at least, even though, right or wrong, smart or foolish, she was sure her answer would be yes.

Later that night, after Cassie had gone to bed, Giovanni went in search of prey. It felt as if he were walking on air as he strolled down the street. He had asked Cassie to marry him, and although she'd said she wanted to think about it, he'd stolen into her thoughts and knew she had already made up her mind.

He was stalking a young couple when Mara appeared in front of him.

"I thought I had you blocked," he muttered as she fell into step beside him.

"You were broadcasting so loudly, I wouldn't be surprised if the satellites circling Earth were picking up your thoughts," she said with a grin, then gestured at the young couple. "Do you want the man or the woman?"

"What do you think?"

At a word from Mara, the couple stopped in the shadows cast by a large tree.

"No killing," Giovanni warned.

She made a face at him as she gathered the man in her embrace and ran her tongue along the side of his neck.

With a shake of his head, Giovanni spoke to the woman's mind, telling her there was nothing to fear as he bit her ever so gently, wishing, all the while, that it was Cassie in his arms. But she was not prey and the good Lord willing, she never would be.

When he finished, he licked the wounds to seal them, erased what had happened from the woman's memory, and sent her to join her companion.

Mara licked a bit of blood from her lower lip. "A tasty morsel."

Giovanni grunted softly. "You didn't come here to hunt with me. What do you want?"

"As if you didn't know. You've proposed to your little mortal and she's likely to say yes."

He nodded.

"Did you mesmerize her?"

"Of course not! You think that's the only way I could get a woman?"

She laughed, a deep-throated sound of pure amusement. "No, my old friend. I'm just amazed that you waited so long. You will let us know when you set a date, won't you? The whole family will want to be there." She lifted one brow when he didn't answer. "Giovanni, you *will* tell us, won't you?"

He nodded. What other choice did he have? Mara would likely know anyway, whether he told her or not.

Cassie woke smiling. Johnny had asked her to marry him! To wed or not to wed, that was the question. She mulled it over while she fixed breakfast. She was perfectly happy with things the way they were. But it would be wonderful to be his wife, to know that he was hers, and only hers. Of course, with his track record, she wasn't really worried that he'd cheat on her, she mused with a wry grin. Marriage wouldn't really change anything between them, she thought, and then shook her head. It would change everything. He wouldn't have to worry about breaking his vow of chastity, or feel guilty when they made love, because she was sure that, marriage or not, he couldn't hold out much longer.

If she married Johnny, she would never have kids. Cassie considered that during breakfast. She had never really given any thought to being a mother, had never been around babies, or even held one. She had no idea what it would be like to raise a family. Her own childhood had been miserable, her own mother and father poor examples of parenting.

Cassie remembered thinking once that she never wanted to be a mother. She supposed, if she had a sudden maternal urge, they could adopt a baby. Johnny had mentioned that one of the couples he considered family had done that. But, at the moment, it was the last thing she wanted.

She was doing the dishes when the phone rang. It was Harris, her boss at the Winchester, telling her he needed her to come in at four that afternoon instead of eight that night.

"Can you make it?"

He wasn't really asking, she thought, not in that tone of voice. "I'll be there."

"Good," he said curtly, and ended the call.

Sliding her phone into the pocket of her robe, Cassie quickly wiped down the counter and the stove, then tossed a load of her work clothes into the washer. She grinned inwardly as she imagined Johnny doing laundry.

She dressed quickly, made a run to the grocery store to pick up a few things, then stopped at a Chinese place for takeout.

At home, she threw her clothes into the dryer, ate a late

lunch, then wrote a note for Johnny telling him she'd been called into work four hours early, but would be home at the same time as usual.

After getting ready, she picked up the keys to the Mustang. She had never taken it before, even though he had told it would be hers to use if she moved in with him.

Cassie bit down on her lower lip. It was either take the car or call a cab. She added a PS to her note, advising him she'd taken his pride and joy, then went out to the garage, praying that she wouldn't get into an accident.

Cassie was waiting on an elderly couple who couldn't decide whether they wanted beer or wine when her friend Darla entered the lounge. Cassie hadn't seen Darla since her disastrous date with Lynx.

After turning in the couple's order, Cassie approached her friend's table. "What are you doing here?"

"Have you seen Lynx?"

Cassie went cold all over. "No, why?"

"He's missing. So are Brad and Fin. No one's seen them for weeks."

Cassie shook her head.

"His father's worried about him."

"I don't know what to tell you. Can I get you a drink?"

"No, thanks. Did you move? I stopped by your place a few days ago and someone else was living in your apartment."

"I had to get out of that place. I couldn't stand it any longer. Listen, I've got to get back to work. Let me know if you hear anything about Lynx."

With a nod, Darla stood and made her way to the door.

Cassie stared after her. What had Johnny done with the bodies of Lynx and his buddies that their remains hadn't been found?

Darla met Lynx's brother, Rico, in the parking lot behind the Winchester. "She says she hasn't seen him."

"Do you believe her?"

"No. I'm sure she was lying."

"What do you think happened to him?"

She shrugged. "Whatever happened to him, I don't believe she had anything to do with it. But I think she knows who did."

With a nod, Rico slipped her a fifty. "I'll keep in touch."

Johnny arrived at the Winchester right on time.

"I'm sorry I had to take your car," Cassie said as they walked through the alley to the parking lot.

"Why? I said you could use it."

"I know, but I also know how much you love it."

"I love you more." Taking her hand, he kissed her palm. "I can buy another car," he murmured. "But no one can replace you."

And she fell a little more in love with him.

It wasn't until they got home that she thought about Lynx again. "Darla came by the lounge tonight."

"Darla?"

"My friend."

"Ah."

"She asked if I'd seen Lynx and I told her no." Cassie hesitated before asking, "What did you do with them?"

"I buried them where no one will find them."

"Oh."

"Does it bother you, what I did that night?"

"No," she admitted slowly. "And it bothers me that it doesn't. Do I need to repent?"

"Why? You didn't do anything wrong."

"I know, but shouldn't I feel remorse for their deaths?"

"They were going to rape you, Cassie. I read his thoughts and those of his companions. You wouldn't have been the first woman they attacked and killed. Nor would you have been the last. Put your mind at rest. Believe me, the world is better off without their kind."

Cassie tried to take comfort in what Johnny said, but it still left her with a sick feeling in the pit of her stomach.

Chapter 22

Edna Mae glanced around as she stood in front of the sandstone fireplace in Mara's Northern California retreat. Never in her life had she been in such a luxurious place. The house was like something out of California's Ten Most Beautiful Homes magazine. The living room was large, with plush white carpeting and dark red velvet drapery. A pair of black sofas faced each other across a rosewood coffee table. In one corner, a round ebony table polished to a high shine sat between a pair of overstuffed red velvet chairs. Several expensive-looking paintings of landscapes decorated the walls. A sword in a silver sheath hung above the mantel.

"I can't get over this place," James said, slipping his arm around her waist. "She must be one wealthy woman."

"Undoubtedly," Monroe agreed.

"How long do you think we should stay?" Pearl wondered aloud. "I don't feel very safe here. It's all so . . . so open."

"Mara said it was warded against intruders, so I'm sure we're safe enough," Edna Mae murmured, though she had doubts of her own. There were windows everywhere, not to mention the balcony with its double glass doors. Still, if Mara couldn't protect them, no one could. "What do you think, James?"

"I think. . . ." His voice trailed off when Pearl let out a gasp.

"What is it?" Edna Mae asked, alarmed by Pearl's stricken expression.

Holding out her cell phone, Pearl said, "Edna, look at this!"

Edna Mae peered over her friend's shoulder and let out a gasp of her own. "Oh, no!"

"What is it?" James asked, concerned by the stunned expression on her face.

"It's a news story. Our café burned down. The motel, too. A number of guests were found in the ashes."

"All those poor people," Pearl murmured. "What are we going to do?"

"Nothing," James said adamantly. "Unless you want to go back and face the police and their endless questions. None of us can afford to have them snooping into our pasts."

"True," Edna Mae agreed. "Good thing we bought the place under assumed names."

Monroe nodded. "What the hell do you think happened?"

"My guess is that vampire Alric happened," Edna Mae said, a tremor in her voice. "He obviously went to Transylvania and knows that we lied to him."

Chapter 23

Sitting at the breakfast table late the next morning, Cassie thought about Johnny's proposal. She weighed the pros and cons for over an hour, wondering if she should listen to her head or follow her heart.

Pouring another cup of coffee, she picked up her phone and read her horoscope. *The decision you make today will change your life forever.* She laughed softly. If only it had told her whether that decision should be yes or no. And then she sobered. She was twenty-six years old, barely making enough money to provide for herself. Unmarried. She had several failed relationships and one disastrous one behind her.

And then there was Johnny. He treated her with love and respect, made no demands on her. He was kind. Generous. And sweet.

And a vampire.

She hadn't had any luck with mortal men, Cassie mused. Maybe it was time to try something different.

Johnny frowned as he materialized in the living room. Dozens of candles cast a warm glow on the walls. Soft music filled the air. A bottle of red wine and a pair of crystal goblets waited on the coffee table. "Cassie?"

"Welcome home."

He turned at the sound of her voice, let out a wolf whistle when he saw her standing in the doorway, her hair framing her face like a golden halo.

"What's the occasion?" he asked.

She wore a V-neck white sweater and a pair of slinky red pants. A matching flower adorned her hair. Perching on the edge of the sofa, Cassie patted the cushion beside her. "Come here. I have something to tell you."

"Okay."

"You asked me to marry you and I've decided to give you my answer."

He nodded, wondering if the wine was to soothe a *no* or celebrate a *yes*.

"If you haven't changed your mind, I'd love to be your wife."

"Cassie!" Not knowing whether to laugh or cry, he drew her into his arms. "I swear I'll make you happy all the days of your life," he murmured. "I'll do everything in my power to make your every wish come true."

"I love you, Johnny."

"I love you," he murmured. "And I've never said that to any other woman."

"I'm glad I got to be the first."

"Cassie, how did I survive so long without you?"

"I don't know," she said, her voice little more than a whisper. "But you'll never be alone again."

He hugged her close, wishing that was true. In time, she would go the way of all the earth and he would be left behind, heart-broken and empty. Shaking off his morbid thoughts, he kissed her. She was young and healthy. The good Lord willing, she had many years ahead of her.

He kissed her again, amazed that he could hold her and caress her, that she didn't find him lacking, that she responded enthusiastically to his kisses. She seemed as eager as was he to hold and be held. A miracle, indeed.

He had waited centuries for this woman, but it had been worth the wait.

"I'm sorry I have to go to work tonight," Cassie said as he pulled up in front of the Winchester.

"Yeah, me, too."

"I would have called in sick, but we're already short-handed."

"It's okay."

Leaning over, she kissed his cheek. "See you later." After opening the door, she stepped out of the car and waved at him. He winked at her as he pulled away from the curb.

Cassie stood there a moment, staring after him, wondering how she'd gotten so lucky. She was about to enter the lounge when someone called her name. Turning, she came face-to-face with two men wearing well-worn jeans and black leather jackets. One held a gun. Before she could scream, the second man was on her, one hand covering her mouth while he dragged her into the alley beside the Winchester and into the parking lot behind the building.

A third man waited by a black Chevy. When they emerged from the alley, he opened the rear door and the guy holding Cassie pushed her inside, before climbing in after her.

Cassie scrambled across the back seat, her hand reaching for the door handle, but he grabbed a fistful of her hair and yanked her backward.

She screamed as the car lurched forward.

Shaking uncontrollably, Cassie huddled in the corner. The next ten minutes passed by too slowly and at the same time, all too fast.

Her mouth went dry when the car pulled up in front of an abandoned warehouse on the outskirts of the city. There were no other houses or buildings in sight. The streetlight on the corner was broken.

Her heart pounded like a runaway freight train as the men dragged her out of the car and hustled her into the warehouse.

She flinched when the door closed behind her. There was a flash of light as someone lit a lantern. She stared at the three men. One of them looked vaguely familiar. "What . . . what do you want?" she stammered, so scared she could hardly speak.

The man who looked familiar said, "I want to know what happened to Lynx."

Fear congealed in the pit of Cassie's stomach at the sound of his name. "Who . . . who are you?"

"His brother, Rico. Where is he? You know, don't you?" he growled, his voice thick with menace.

She shook her head vigorously.

Taking a step forward, he slapped her across the face.

Cassie reeled back from the force of the blow, one hand pressed to her cheek.

"Don't lie to me, you slut. Where is he?"

"I don't know," she sobbed. "I swear I don't know."

"I tried to do this the easy way," he warned. "Now we'll do it the hard way."

She let out a wordless cry when he pulled a small dagger from inside his boot. "I don't know!" she wailed. "Please, believe me!"

"Tony, Max, hold her!"

Cassie kicked and flailed as the men grabbed her arms, but she was no match for them. They easily caught her and held her between them. She tried to scream for help, but her throat was dust-dry. *This can't be happening,* she thought. But it was. Unable to look away, she watched as Rico's blade opened a long, narrow gash from her right elbow to her wrist. She stared at the bright red blood welling from the shallow wound. The pain was worse than anything she had ever known.

She went cold all over when Rico took hold of her other arm. Knowing what was coming, she began to struggle anew, sobbed, "No, don't," when he laid the knife against her skin and dragged it down her left arm.

The sound of her heartbeat thundered in her ears as the world began to spin, dragging her down into oblivion.

Her last conscious thought was that it was too bad Johnny wasn't there to lap up the blood.

Giovanni frowned when he sensed Cassie was in danger, bolted upright in the chair when her screams reverberated in his mind. Springing to his feet, he opened the link between them. Fear lanced through him when he felt her pain, her terror, heard her cry out again.

Summoning his preternatural power, he stormed out of the house, his senses focused on the blood link that bound them together.

* * *

It took him only seconds to hone in on her whereabouts—an abandoned building on the outskirts of town. A thin sliver of light emanated from inside. Moving silent as a shadow, Giovanni dissolved into mist and drifted through the crack beneath the door. There were three men huddled together inside, speaking in hushed tones. Cassie lay on the floor, curled into a fetal position, bleeding from long, shallow cuts on both arms. Her left cheek bore the unmistakable imprint of a man's hand. *A dead man,* he thought.

Rage engulfed him, blinding him to everything but the need to kill the men who had caused his woman pain. And shed her blood.

Quiet as a wraith, he resumed his own form. A breath blew out the lantern, plunging the building into total darkness.

"Who's there?" one of the men demanded.

"What the hell?" another exclaimed.

He moved through them like a scythe, cutting then down one by one, relishing their cries of fear, their screams of terror as he broke the neck of one, crushed the spine of another, sank his fangs into the third and drank his fill before ending his life.

Tossing the empty husk across the room, he ran to Cassie's side.

Cassie cowered on the floor, the pain of her wounds forgotten as she listened to the cries, pleas, and screams that echoed off the walls. She couldn't see anything, but every cry seemed worse than the last. The coppery scent of blood filled the air and she knew it wasn't all hers.

She let out a harsh cry of fear and denial when hands touched her.

"Cassie, don't be afraid. It's me. Johnny."

"Johnny!" She sobbed with relief when he stood, lifting her into his arms, cradling her to his chest.

"Hang on, *cara mia*. I'm taking you home."

She clung to him as the world began to spin. Before she could fathom what was happening, they were in his kitchen.

Johnny set her on the counter, then let the faucet run until the sink filled with warm water. Soaking a rag, he washed the blood from her arms and then, to her shock, he licked the wounds. The bleeding stopped immediately and the pain was gone.

She looked at him, her gaze searching his. "Why didn't you lick up the blood?"

He shook his head. "You're not prey, Cassie. I never want to feed off you."

"But you drank from me before."

"That's not the same thing." Slipping one arm around her waist, he said, "Thank the Lord that I did, or I wouldn't have been able to find you so fast."

She rested her head on his shoulder. Then, needing to know, she said, very quietly, "You killed them, didn't you? All of them."

"Yes."

"One of them was Lynx's brother. He wanted to know where Lynx was."

"Why didn't you just tell them that I killed him?"

She lifted her head. "I would never do that. They would have come after you, and . . ."

Johnny arched one brow in amusement. "You could have saved yourself a lot of fear and pain if you'd just told them the truth," he remarked with a wry smile. "The results would have been the same."

Knowing that Cassie was upset with what had happened that night, Giovanni stayed by her side, hoping his company would ease her fears. She put on a brave front, but he knew being kidnapped and wounded had been traumatic for her, even though she tried to pretend she was fine.

"Do you want to talk about it?" he asked.

"No." She wrapped her arms around her middle. "I just want to forget it happened." As if she could ever forget her terror, the memory of being cut, the agonized screams of Rico and his friends.

He held her close, lightly stroking her hair, until she fell asleep.

Taking her in his arms, he carried her to bed, removed her shoes, undressed her down to her bra and panties, and tucked her under the blankets. He sat there for an hour, tortured with the thought that, had he not taken her blood, he might not have found her in time. No doubt she would be better off without him, he thought. But what would he do without her?

He was about to leave the room when she let out a cry and began thrashing about under the covers.

"Cassie." He shook her gently, but she was trapped in a nightmare. "Cassie! Wake up."

She lashed out at him. "No! No!"

"Cassie, shh, it's me." He shook her again, more roughly this time.

"Johnny? Oh, Johnny." Trembling from head to foot, she threw her arms around him.

"I'm here, love," he murmured. "No one will hurt you while I'm here."

"Don't leave me."

"No, never."

Lifting her onto his lap, he whispered to her mind, his voice lulling her to sleep, telling her there would be no more bad dreams that night.

Propping his back against the headboard, he held her in his arms until the sun chased the moon from the sky.

Cassie slept late the next morning. Reluctant to face the memory of what had happened the night before, she pulled the blankets over her head. But, try as she might, she couldn't get back to sleep. Johnny had killed six men that she knew of. All because of her. If she stayed with him, would he have to defend her again and again, adding more deaths to his conscience?

Did vampires even have a conscience?

There was so much about Johnny that she didn't know. Things she might never know. Things she might be better off not knowing. Had she made a mistake in telling him she would be his wife?

Sitting up, she glanced around the room. For the first time, she wondered if this had been his room before she moved in. He was such a nice guy. She could easily imagine him giving her the biggest bedroom. Johnny. She loved being with him, loved the sound of his voice, the pleasure of his kisses. She hadn't known him long and yet, already, she couldn't imagine her life without him. He made her feel wonderful, as if she was someone special and not just some girl who was so unlovable even her parents hadn't wanted her.

Flinging the covers aside, she glanced at her arms. There were no scars, no sign that she had been hurt at all. Amazing.

Picking up her phone, she looked at the time. It was too early to call the Winchester, she thought. But that was a good thing. It would give her more time to come up with a plausible excuse for missing work last night.

Rising, she pulled on her robe and padded barefooted into the kitchen. She had finally learned how to set the coffeemaker so that coffee would be hot and ready when she woke in the morning. She popped two slices of bread into the toaster, then sat at the table. She wondered about the vampire he called Mara, the one who had lived during the time of Cleopatra. What were the others like? And how many were there? Did he see them often? If they married, would he expect her to entertain them? How did one entertain vampires? Offer them a bite?

Grinning, she shrugged her worries about the future aside. She loved Johnny. For now, that was all that mattered.

Chapter 24

Alric stormed through the night, his rage at being lied to still fresh in his mind. With his emotions running hot, he preyed on every mortal he found, killing some, leaving others alive, doling out life and death with no rhyme or reason.

He had contacted old friends, but no one knew where to find Mara. How was that possible? She was a powerful vampire, true. But she wasn't invisible. She had to be somewhere. He had searched the Internet. He had mesmerized a cop and compelled him to search every database available to law enforcement, but to no avail.

Maybe she *was* invisible. Or, more likely, living under an assumed name. Or perhaps out of the country altogether. Dammit! Where the hell was she?

"You can't hide forever," he raged. "I'll find you sooner or later, if it takes a year or a century!"

No sooner had he spoken the words than his ire cooled as he remembered the force of her power moving through his mind. The gut-wrenching fear. The sheer agony she had inflicted upon him.

A hunter, he thought. What he needed was a hunter. Let someone else run the risk of her wrath.

And once he'd settled his debt with Mara, he would teach his fledgling to have a little respect for the man who had sired him.

Chapter 25

Late that night, after Cassie had gone to bed, Giovanni went for a stroll through the town. The scent of fresh blood assaulted his nostrils, leading him from one body to another. Men and women alike, some dead, some barely breathing. Each victim carried the lingering scent of his sire.

Giovanni shook his head. Unlike Alric, he had never enjoyed killing for sport. He hadn't taken a life in centuries save for Lynx and the other five men he had killed recently. But he felt no guilt or regret for those six deaths. The victims had laid hands on his woman and the penalty would always be death.

He was turning away from a corpse when he heard the wail of a siren coming from the direction of the last body he'd found. In minutes, the screech of a dozen sirens filled the air.

Dissolving into mist, Giovanni willed himself to the next city.

Damn Alric. Why hadn't he done his killing somewhere else instead of the town where Giovanni and Cassie lived? By tomorrow morning, the front page of every newspaper would carry a lurid story about bodies drained of blood. In no time at all, the media would make the jump to vampire and before long the talk shows would pick up the story. It was only a matter of time before the town would be crawling with reporters from the major networks.

And most likely a hunter or two.

Cassie's eyes widened as she read the morning headlines on her phone. There had been a rash of killings from one end of town to the other. The dead had been drained of blood. The survivors, too, had been drained of blood, though not to the point of death. When asked if they had seen their attacker, men and women alike remembered nothing but hideous red eyes. Some of the reports put the blame on a maniacal killer. Others mentioned puncture wounds and hinted at vampires.

Surely Johnny hadn't committed these atrocities. She knew he was capable of it. He had killed half a dozen men that she knew of, but only to save her. Who knew how many other lives he might have taken in his long existence? She shook her head. He'd been a priest. She couldn't imagine him killing anyone in cold blood, refused to believe it. There were other vampires. Mara. Johnny's sire, Alric, and who knew how many others?

Deeply worried, and more than a little apprehensive at the thought of another vampire in town, she went through the house, making sure all the doors and windows were locked.

It didn't help. She felt vulnerable, uneasy at being alone in the house even in broad daylight. For the first time, she wondered if there were other creatures out there.

If there were vampires, why not werewolves, demons, and zombies?

As always, when she was upset, she cleaned house. Not that there was much to clean, with just the two of them living there. But she dusted and vacuumed with a vengeance, refusing to think about bodies drained of blood.

She prepared an elaborate dinner for herself, something she rarely did, not because she was hungry, but because it kept her hands and mind occupied.

She had just sat down at the table when Johnny materialized in the room. Sometimes being a vampire seemed as if it might be fun, she thought. He could zap himself wherever he wanted to go. What would that be like? What else could he do?

She put the question to him when he sat down across from her. "So, how many other supernatural powers do you have?"

"I don't know. I've never taken the time to count them. I have the strength of thirty men. I can levitate off the ground. I can dissolve into mist, though I must tell you, that takes a lot of concentration and is more than a little frightening the first time or two. I can shape-shift, which is also a little disconcerting."

"Wow. You should do a magic act. I'll bet you'd make a fortune. No one would ever figure out how you disappeared or did any of those other things."

"I don't think that's such a good idea," he said with a wry grin. "I've spent centuries learning not to draw attention to myself. Although Rane Cordova, one of the vampires in the family, spent some time doing just that. He went from town to town for years, doing magic shows under various names."

"I guess it's like they say, there's nothing new under the

sun." And then, without meaning to, she blurted, "You didn't have anything to do with all those dead bodies that are on the news, did you?"

The look of disappointment on his face made her instantly regret asking the question.

"I'm sorry," she said quickly. "I know it wasn't you."

"But you still felt the need to ask." Why wouldn't she? He was more than capable of it and she knew it all too well.

Cassie looked away, cheeks flushing with shame.

"It's all right," he said quietly. "I can't blame you for wondering. Alric killed them."

"Why?"

Johnny shrugged. "He likes it."

She shuddered with revulsion. How could anyone enjoy such wanton killing? Hoping to take her mind off her morbid thoughts, she said, "I'm off tonight. Do you want to go do anything?"

He shrugged. "Nothing in particular."

"Maybe we'll just stay in then."

She was afraid to go out, he thought. Well, what normal human woman wouldn't be apprehensive after reading about last night's bloodbath? "Cassie?"

"Hmm?"

"You haven't changed your mind about marrying me, have you?"

"Not exactly, but . . ."

"But you're having second thoughts."

Rising, she put her dishes in the dishwasher, then gestured for him to follow her into the living room. She sat on the couch and he sat beside her, afraid of what her answer would be.

"Cassie?"

"There's a lot to consider, you know? Don't be mad, but

I think I need to give it a little more thought. My feelings for you haven't changed," she said quickly. "But . . ." She lifted a hand and let it fall, not knowing how to explain.

"It's all right, Cassie. I understand."

"Do you?" she asked tremulously.

He nodded. "Marrying a vampire is a big decision. You shouldn't rush into it." He wouldn't blame her if she changed her mind. But it hurt like hell, just the same.

Sensing that she was cold, he concentrated on the hearth. A moment later, a fire sparked to life.

Wide-eyed, Cassie looked at him. "Did you do that?"

"Yeah," he said with a grin. "I guess I forgot to mention that particular talent."

He really was a remarkable man, she thought. What was it like to summon fire at one's command, or turn into mist? "Do all vampires have the same powers?"

"As far as I know, although it wouldn't surprise me if Mara has a few that no one else has or even knows about."

"Tell me about the vampires you call family."

Settling back on the sofa, he hesitated a moment, then slipped his arm around her, pleased when she didn't pull away. Maybe there was hope for them, after all. "Well, there's Roshan. He fell in love with the photograph of a woman who was burned at the stake as a witch back in the sixteen-hundreds. I'm not sure how he did it, but he time-traveled back to the past and brought her to the present. Turns out Brenna Flanagan really was a witch.

"They adopted Cara, who eventually married Vince Cordova. I told you about them, remember? He married Cara and she gave birth to the twins, Rane and Rafe. The boys were human until they reached puberty and then they morphed into vampires."

"No way!"

"Way. Rafe married Kathy McKenna. Rane married Savannah Gentry. Rane and Savannah had Abbey Marie by artificial insemination. Abbey married Nick Desanto, one of the ancient ones.

"By a strange twist of fate, Mara's son, Derek, turned out to be vampire on his mother's side and a werewolf on his father's. Derek married Sheree Westerbrook."

Cassie shook her head. "That's some unusual family, to say the least."

Johnny nodded.

"And now all the women are vampires."

He nodded again.

"And none of them are sorry they gave up their humanity?"

"As far as I know, they have no regrets."

She made a soft, contemplative sound.

"I promised I wouldn't turn you, Cassie. And I meant it."

"But I'll get old. And you won't."

"Let's not worry about that now."

Easy for him to say, she thought, somewhat glumly. *He* wasn't going to get all wrinkled and gray. . . . She smiled faintly. He was already gray at the temples. But on him, it looked good. Maybe someday she would ask him to make her what he was.

Maybe.

Someday.

Reaching up, she cupped his face in her palms and kissed him. "I love you, Johnny."

"You don't have to marry me, Cassie," he said quietly. "I'm happy just having you in my life for as long as you can stand me."

"Stop talking and kiss me," she murmured.

He crushed her close as he rained kisses on her cheeks,

the tip of her nose, her eyelids, before teasing her lips. And she forgot all about vampires and everything else except the magic of his kisses, the way his touch made her melt like butter left too long in the sun. Wanting to be closer, she slipped her hands under his shirt, reveling in the way his muscles flexed at her touch. His power surrounded her, heightening every sensation, making every touch, every kiss, more intense, more pleasurable.

Feeling bold, she ran her tongue along his lower lip before delving inside.

He gasped in surprise as her tongue dueled with his.

The next thing she knew, they were lying on the sofa, their bodies pressed together as their hands went exploring.

Cassie was panting when he suddenly bolted upright, then stood.

"What . . . what's wrong?" she asked. And then, seeing the faint red glow in his eyes, she knew. He had warned her that his hunger and his desire were closely woven together, the one spiking the other.

Heaving a sigh, she sat up and straightened her clothing. Smiling seductively, she murmured, "Maybe we should get married real soon."

"Cassie!" His gaze searched hers as hope sprang to life inside him. "*Cara mia!* Do you mean it?"

Batting her eyelashes at him, she murmured, "I think it's the only way I'll ever get you into my bed."

Lifting her into his arms, he swung her around and around.

"Johnny! Stop," she said as laughter bubbled up inside her. "You're making me dizzy."

Setting her on her feet, he said, "You make *me* dizzy with happiness. You mean more to me than you'll ever know." Tilting her face up, he kissed her ever so gently, both prayer and promise. He grinned inwardly, eager to tell Mara he was getting married. But just in case Cassie changed her mind again, he decided it might be best to keep the news a secret until his future bride actually set a date.

Chapter 26

Alric strolled through the town. He loved everything about this new century! He had quickly adapted to the wonders of computers and cell phones. He loved the soft, supple clothing, the way the language had changed, the pictures that moved. Cars and airplanes fascinated him.

He loved the big cities like Seattle and San Francisco and Los Angeles. Thousands of homeless people lined the streets, a veritable smorgasbord for a hungry vampire. Easy pickings for his kind. When one of them disappeared, there was no family to raise the alarm.

He loved that you could find anything you wanted on the Internet. He had hired a private detective to locate Mara, and a vampire hunter to destroy her. It wouldn't give him the same satisfaction as killing her himself, but it would be the next best thing. And a hell of a lot safer!

And once Mara was out of the way, he intended to go after Pearl and Edna.

And the priest.

Chapter 27

In the morning after breakfast, Cassie drove to the next town. She had told Johnny she would marry him and for that she needed a dress.

She parked in front of Barbara's Bridal Shop, took a deep breath, and hurried inside. There were racks and racks of gowns—long and short, white and pink and blue and even black. She grinned, thinking ebony might be the perfect color for a vampire wedding. What would Johnny think?

She looked through the dresses and found three that she especially liked——one mermaid style, one princess style, and an A-line. They were all so beautiful, she thought with a shake of her head. But black just didn't seem right for a bride.

She walked across the aisle and looked at the white ones. In the end, she chose a lace and tulle mermaid confection with sheer, three-quarter-length sleeves and a short train. The matching veil was so delicate she was almost afraid to try it on.

It would take her months to pay for the dress, she thought, but it was worth every penny. It didn't need much in the way of alterations, which, thankfully, were included in the price.

She smiled all the way home.

"You're looking very pleased with yourself this evening," Johnny remarked when he arrived at home that night.

Cassie looked up from the book she'd been reading. "Do I?"

"Indeed." He smiled as he sat beside her and kissed her cheek. "Might I ask why?"

"You may."

"I'm asking."

Laying her book aside, she said, "I went shopping today."

He arched one brow.

"And I bought a wedding dress," she said in a rush. "It's going to take me months to pay for it, but wait until you see it!"

"And where did you find this remarkable gown?"

"At Barbara's Bridal Shop. It's so beautiful!"

"And I'm sure you look beautiful in it."

Her smile stretched from ear to ear. "I hope so."

"I know so."

Holding her close, he pressed his lips to hers in a long, lingering kiss that stole her breath away and made her heart beat faster. Somehow, they were lying on the floor in front of the hearth, their bodies pressed intimately close together. Without conscious thought, he tucked her beneath him as desire rose hot and swift within him. Her hands slipped under his shirt to move restlessly up and down his back.

He groaned when she moved beneath him. "Cassie," he gasped. "Please set a date now! I don't think I can wait much longer."

Cupping his face in her hands, she begged, "Don't wait, Johnny."

Rearing back a little, he gazed down at her flushed cheeks, her lips swollen from his kisses, her eyes smoky with need.

"Please, Johnny."

How could he refuse her sweet entreaty?

How could he deny what he, himself, wanted so desperately?

He was on the verge of surrendering to his desire when the bells of a distant church chimed the hour.

Cassie swore softly as they tolled seven and the moment was gone. "Looks like you're saved by the bell," she said with a wry grin. "Just as well, I guess. I've got to get ready for work."

Rolling swiftly to his feet, he pulled her up beside him, wishing he knew what to say.

"It's all right." Cassie kissed him lightly. "I guess I'm glad nothing happened. I don't want you feeling guilty when it does."

"And you? You'd be all right with that?"

Cassie bit down on her lower lip. "I guess, before we get married, I should tell you that . . . that I'm not a virgin."

He nodded, his expression troubled.

"Does it make a difference in how you feel about me?"

"No," he said, slowly. "I told you before, whatever you did in the past is of no consequence."

"But you're disappointed."

He smiled a crooked smile. "Maybe a little."

"I love you, Johnny. When I get home tonight, we'll set a date, if you still want me."

"Of course I do, *cara*."

"It was only one time," she said. "And he finished so quickly, the only thing I remember is how glad I was when it was over."

Taking her hand, he gave it a squeeze. "We'll find our way together."

After Cassie left for work, Giovanni picked up the book she had been reading and settled on the sofa. But he couldn't concentrate on the words. His vampire senses had told him she wasn't a virgin. It made no difference in the long run, but he was glad she had told him before the wedding. He liked her the more for her honesty.

Laying the book aside, he left the house. Then, on a whim, he transported himself to Mara's house in the Hollywood Hills.

The look of surprise on her face when she opened the door was worth the trip.

"Giovanni! What's wrong?"

"Nothing. Can't an old friend stop by to say hello?"

"Well, sure," she said, taking a step back so he could enter. "It's just that, in all the years we've known each other, you've never dropped in for a visit."

"Well, there's a first time for everything."

"Like the kisses you've shared with your young woman." Leading the way into the living room, she said, "Logan, we have company."

"Hey, *Padre!*" Logan rose to shake his hand. "It's good to see you. Is something wrong?"

Giovanni laughed softly as he took the seat Mara offered. "No. I guess a visit from me really is unexpected. So, what's new with you two?"

"Mara killed a hunter last night," Logan said.

"Really?" Hardly surprising, Giovanni thought, with Alric leaving bodies all over town.

She shrugged. "Your sire is getting to be a problem."

"A hunter came *here*?" Giovanni exclaimed. If they could find Mara, they could find anyone. Including him, he thought, feeling a stab of concern for Cassie's safety.

"No. I ran into him on Sunset Boulevard while *I* was hunting. Alric's stink was all over him. Before he died, he told me Alric had sent him after me."

Giovanni nodded. "There might be others."

"I'm sure there will be. But I'm not worried. Sooner or later, I'm going to have to destroy Alric."

"I'm surprised you haven't already," Giovanni remarked.

Logan laughed softly. "That's what I said."

Mara glared at her husband and then at Giovanni. "I'm trying to be more . . . more . . ." Her voice trailed off.

"Kind?" Logan suggested.

"Compassionate?" Giovanni added.

"Patient!" she snapped.

Logan and Giovanni exchanged amused glances, then burst out laughing. They stopped abruptly as her power wrapped itself around them, stealing their laughter and their breath.

She withdrew it abruptly. "Still feel like laughing at me?"

Logan smiled at her. "Woman, you know we weren't laughing *at* you."

"Do I?" she asked, her voice as frosty as a winter morning.

Giovanni watched as Logan crooked his finger at her,

amazed when Mara went into her husband's arms and kissed him.

He looked away, not wanting to intrude on such a private moment, all the while hoping that he and Cassie would one day enjoy that kind of intimacy and affection, and that their love would last as long.

"We're ignoring our guest," Logan said after a moment.

Mara smiled at Giovanni. "I'm sorry, Father."

He dismissed her apology with a wave of his hand. "I do have some news." He looked at Mara, one brow raised. "Unless you already know what it is."

She shook her head. "Tell us."

"I asked Cassie to marry me. And last night she said yes."

"I'm so happy for you, Giovanni!" Mara exclaimed.

"Congratulations, *Padre*." Then, looking at his wife, Logan said, "I told you he didn't need any help."

Giovanni thought about Mara's incredible power when he returned home. She could have killed him and Logan both with little more than a thought. He knew other powerful vampires. Nick Desanto was one of them. He was almost as old as Mara, and he had been turned by her, which made him even more deadly. Logan, too, had been sired by the Queen of the Vampires.

Giovanni frowned into the fireplace. He hadn't been turned by Mara, but he carried her blood in his veins. He had never considered himself to be above average in the strength department, but maybe he had underestimated the effect of her ancient blood. He had rarely used his preternatural abilities for anything other than calling his prey, transporting himself from one location to another, and occasionally defending himself, though those occasions had been rare.

Feeling restless, he decided to walk to the Winchester Lounge and ride home with Cassie.

He was three blocks from the lounge when he caught the scent of a hunter approaching from behind. Giovanni slowed, all his senses alert. He had lived here for fifteen years and in all that time, he had never encountered a hunter. Was this one somehow in league with the one Mara had killed? Or had the killings mentioned in the paper drawn him to town?

Or had the hunter come here searching for him?

Dissolving into mist, he floated upward, drifted past the man, then materialized behind him. "Looking for me?"

The hunter reached into his jacket pocket, gasped with pain when Giovanni grabbed his wrist and twisted his arm behind his back.

"Who are you?" Giovanni hissed.

"Go to hell."

"Not yet." Giovanni yanked the man's arm upward. "What's your name?"

"Rocco."

"Why are you following me?"

"I wasn't!" He let out a howl when Giovanni gave his arm another twist.

"Next time I'll break it." Giovanni reached into the hunter's pocket and withdrew a nasty-looking wooden stake and a bottle of holy water. He tossed both aside, then reached into the man's other pocket, only to let out a hiss when his fingers closed over a pair of handcuffs. But they weren't ordinary cuffs. They were coated with a thin layer of silver. He threw them away, hand clenching in pain as his skin burned and blistered. "Were you planning to use those on me?"

The hunter's silence was damning.

"How did you know I was here?" Giovanni asked, his voice silky soft with menace.

"I was hired to find you," Rocco muttered.

"By who?"

Rocco shook his head. "I can't tell you that. He'll kill me."

"What makes you think I won't?"

The hunter cringed, his gaze darting left and right in search of help that wasn't there as Giovanni's power slammed into him.

"Alric. His name was Alric. But he didn't want you dead. I was supposed to bring you to him."

"I guess he wants to take my head himself."

Rocco stared at him, eyes wide with fear.

"Next time I see you, you won't get off so easy." Giovanni gave the hunter's arm one last twist, then released him.

The man sprinted down the street without a backward glance.

Giovanni grimaced as he stared at his burning palm, then at the fleeing hunter. Damn. He should have held on to the man a few more minutes, he thought glumly. A little fresh blood would have quickly eased the pain.

Hand throbbing, he transported himself to the Winchester parking lot.

Cassie let out a gasp when she saw someone sitting in the front passenger seat of the car, heaved a sigh of relief when she realized it was Johnny. "Hi," she said, smiling as she opened the driver's side door. "This is a nice surprise. What . . . ?" She gasped when she saw his expression. "Are you all right?"

"No. But I will be."

She frowned at the stress in his voice. "What's wrong?" she asked, sliding behind the wheel. "What happened?"

He quickly related his encounter with the hunter, then showed her his hand.

"Oh, Johnny, that looks awful. Just touching silver did that?" She shook her head. "Let's get you home. I've some burn ointment that will ease the pain and help it heal faster."

"I'm afraid it will take more than that."

Brow furrowed, Cassie looked at him, wondering what he meant, until he glanced at her throat. And then she understood. Swallowing hard, she asked, "Can you wait until we get home?"

Mouth set in a hard line, he nodded.

She drove as fast as she dared. A sideways glance in his direction made her flinch. She could only imagine the pain he was in. Regular burns hurt like hell, but his skin was charred almost black. The pain must be beyond bearing.

At home, she parked in the driveway, then hurried around to open his door. He followed her into the house, then dropped onto the sofa, his injured hand resting, palm up, on his knee.

He glanced at her high-necked sweater. "Are you wearing your crucifix?"

Her eyes widened. "Am I going to need it?"

"I hope not," he said, though he couldn't guarantee it. The pain of the silver searing his flesh was excruciating.

She sat beside him, her expression wary, her heart pounding.

"Don't move," he warned, his voice tight. "And don't let me drink for more than a minute or two."

Cassie went still all over. It hadn't hurt when he'd taken her blood before. Quite the opposite. But he hadn't been injured then. What if he lost control? He was in terrible pain. After seeing what silver did to him, how could she even think of causing him more injury? Still, if causing him a little added pain would stop him from taking too much . . . She took a deep breath. "Okay." She wrapped her fingers around the cross. "I'm ready."

He didn't take her in his arms this time. Brushing her hair out of the way with the back of his good hand, he feathered kisses along the length of her neck and then, when she was more relaxed, he bit her gently.

Giovanni closed his eyes as a slow river of warmth ran over his tongue. No matter how often he fed, he was always surprised at how it affected him. Her blood warmed him inside and out, strengthening him, easing the agony in his hand to the point that it was bearable.

And still he drank.

And drank.

"Johnny. Johnny, stop!"

Just a little more, he thought. She tasted so good. Surely she could spare just a little more.

"Johnny! Don't make me hurt you!"

The panic in Cassie's voice penetrated the haze of pleasure that engulfed him. With a low groan, he lifted his head and looked away, not wanting her to see the hellish red glow in his eyes, his fangs stained with her blood. "Are you all right?" he asked gruffly.

"I'm okay. How are you?"

"Much better." He closed his eyes, willing himself to relax as he ran his tongue over his teeth. When he felt he was in control again, he turned toward her and kissed her cheek. "Thank you, *cara mia*."

The love in his voice, the gratitude in his eyes, almost made her sorry she'd had to ask him to stop.

When he was in control again, he took her in his arms. "I'm sorry," he murmured. "I didn't mean to scare you."

"I'm glad I could help, although I admit, I was worried for a moment there at the end."

"I know." He brushed his knuckles along her cheek. "You can't imagine how good you taste. You're so sweet. Drinking from you fills the emptiness inside me—drives the darkness from my soul and gives me hope."

"Darkness?"

"*Guilt* would be a better word, I guess. Remorse for the lives I took when I was first turned. For drinking from you when you mean so much more to me."

Laying her head on his shoulder, she murmured, "I love you, too."

Cassie's words filled his heart and banished the pain in his hand as nothing else could. He claimed her lips with his, thinking he had never been happier or more content in his life.

But he couldn't help wondering how long it would last, with Alric still out there looking for vengeance.

Chapter 28

Cassie was in the midst of rearranging the contents in one of the kitchen cupboards when she heard a knock at the front door. Wondering who it could be, she went into the entry way and looked out the door's peephole. A woman with long, black hair stood on the porch. Mara.

Oh, Lord, Cassie thought. What was the so-called Queen of the Vampires doing here? And in the daytime? Why wasn't she resting in her coffin? But then, she was older than dirt. If Johnny could be awake during the day, surely the vampire queen could, too.

Stalling for time, she called, "Who's there?"

"Mara."

What to do, what to do? Johnny had told her not to invite anyone in during the day. Did that include his friend?

"Are you going to invite me in, Cassandra?" the vampire called, a note of impatience in her voice. "Or should I come down the chimney? Like the Big Bad Wolf?"

Before Cassie could decide what to say, the front door swung open and the Queen of the Vampires stood framed in the doorway. As always, she looked too perfect to be real. Today, she wore a deep green dress and a pair of matching stiletto heels.

Cassie retreated into the living room until she came up against the back of the sofa. Grasping her crucifix in her hand, she stammered, "What . . . what do you want?"

"We didn't have a chance to chat last time we met," Mara said, her voice smooth as black silk. "Giovanni speaks so highly of you, I decided to pay you a visit. Do you mind if I come in?"

"Would it matter if I said no?"

"That's not very friendly, but I can see why Giovanni loves you." Mara's gaze moved over Cassie from head to toe. "You've got spunk, and you're really quite lovely."

"So are you." The woman was even more stunning than Cassie remembered, with her long, dark hair and flawless skin. Her eyes were a bright, mesmerizing green.

"Why, thank you."

Questioning her better judgment, Cassie's fingers tightened around her crucifix. "Please, come in."

Mara seemed to flow into the house, almost as if her feet weren't touching the floor. "I hear you're going to marry our priest."

"Yes." Remembering her manners, she said, "Would you like to sit down?"

"I'm not staying. I just wanted to let you know how grateful I am to you. Giovanni has been alone far too long."

"I love him."

"And he loves you. Once you wed, you will become a part of my family. As such, we will be here for you if you ever need us."

"Did you really know Cleopatra?"

"Told you that, did he?"

Cassie nodded.

"It's true. I knew her quite well. I was there when Antony died in her arms. I offered to give her the Dark Gift, but she refused. With Antony dead and the prospect of being made a public spectacle in Rome, she had no desire to live."

"That's so . . . tragic," Cassie murmured. She had seen the movie *Cleopatra,* of course, but hearing the queen's fate from someone who had actually been there made it all the more real.

"Our Giovanni is a kind and gentle man," Mara remarked. "Be good to him."

Though the words were softly spoken, Cassie didn't miss the warning underlying them. "Can I ask you something?"

"Of course, though I don't promise to answer."

"I thought vampires had to sleep during the day."

"Most do," Mara said. "Direct sunlight will destroy fledglings. Ancient ones, such as myself and Giovanni, can be active during the day, although bright sunlight quickly weakens most of us. I've given my blood to some of the family, which also allows them to be awake when the sun is up. But it is natural for our kind to rest until nightfall, although most vampires are able to rouse themselves from the Dark Sleep if they sense danger nearby. Is there anything else?"

"No. I was just curious."

"Very well," Mara said. "I hope to see you again soon, Cassie Douglas. Perhaps at the wedding."

Cassie nodded again.

And Mara vanished from her sight.

Cassie stared at the place where the vampire had been. How on earth did they disappear like that?

Feeling as if she had been a bug under a microscope, she dropped down on the sofa. Mara had done nothing more than enter the house, and yet her power, invisible as the wind, had permeated the room. Cassie couldn't help thinking that if the vampire had chosen to do so, she could have leveled the house and everything in it with no more than a casual thought.

Giovanni hesitated when he reached his house that night and caught Mara's lingering scent. *What the devil had she been doing here?*

When he materialized in the living room, he found Cassie huddled on the sofa, the remains of her dinner on the coffee table. "Are you all right?"

"I had an unexpected guest today."

"Yes, I know."

"You know? Did you send her?"

"Of course not." Seating himself beside Cassie, he took her hand in both of his. "What did she want?"

"She said she'd just come by to say hello and that she hoped to see me again soon. Perhaps at the wedding. I know you like her, but she's scary."

Giovanni laughed softly. "She can be. She's mellowed a lot since I first met her."

"She didn't seem very mellow to me."

He grunted softly. Mara's residual power still lingered in the air.

"She didn't say it in so many words, but I got the distinct impression that I'd regret it for the rest of my life—however long or short it might be—if I did anything to make you unhappy."

He arched one brow in wry amusement. "She's worse

than a mother hen," he said, kissing the tip of her nose. "But you've got nothing to worry about, my love. Once we're married, you'll be family and she'll defend you to the death."

To Cassie's surprise, she found that oddly comforting.

"Have you decided on a day yet?"

"What? Oh. For the wedding. How about Halloween?"

He stared at her. "Are you serious?"

"What better day to marry a vampire than on All Hallows' Eve?"

"If that's what you want."

"I'm kidding, silly! But how about October first?"

"Sounds good." Two weeks, he thought. Fourteen days until she would be his. The thought was exhilarating. And terrifying.

He called Mara with the good news that night, after Cassie had gone to bed.

"So, he's getting married," Logan said when Mara ended the call. He shook his head. "Hard to believe, after all this time. Do you suppose his equipment works?"

Mara stared at him from across the bedroom, then burst out laughing. "I hope so! For both their sakes. How's yours?"

"I haven't heard any complaints from you in the last nine hundred years," he said with a wink. "But feel free to check it out for yourself anytime."

Eyes twinkling, Edna Mae said, "That was Mara on the phone."

"What did she want, dear?" Pearl asked.

"You'll never guess!" Edna Mae exclaimed. "Father Lanzoni is getting married!"

"Really? When's the big day?"

"October the first! You know we have to be there."

"Of course, dear, but . . . do you think it's safe for us to leave here?"

"Oh. I hadn't thought of that. But it seems a shame to miss the wedding." Edna Mae drummed her fingers on the arm of the sofa. "You know, I was thinking, maybe we should go back home."

"We have no home to go back to," Pearl said. "Alric burned it down, remember?"

"I meant Texas. We've been gone for ages. No one will remember us there. We could buy a little place, come back here for the wedding, then scurry home to Texas."

"It could be risky, dear," Pearl warned.

"Maybe it's time we took a little risk."

"I don't know. Maybe. Maybe we should talk it over with Monroe and James when they get back."

"If you like," Edna Mae agreed. But she had already made up her mind. She was going back to Texas—and to the wedding—whether Pearl went or not.

"Hey, Sheree," Derek called. "The priest is tying the knot in two weeks."

"I don't believe you!" she said, looking up from the book she'd been reading.

"It's true. I just got a text from my mother. She's not one for practical jokes, you know."

"Or any other kind," Sheree muttered. And then she smiled. "I'll need a new dress!"

Roshan DeLongpre shook his head. "I don't believe it."

"Believe what?" Brenna asked. "Who was that on the phone?"

"Mara. You remember Father Lanzoni?"

"Of course."

"He's getting married."

"Really?"

Roshan nodded. "I never thought it would happen."

"Well, good for him. He's been alone far too long. I wonder what she's like, the woman who finally won his heart?"

"We'll find out in two weeks," he said, grinning. "I'll bet the whole clan turns out!"

Rafe stuffed his cell phone into his pants pocket. "Did you hear any of that?"

Rane grinned at his brother over his prey's head. "Wait until we tell Savannah and Kathy. They won't believe it."

"I know. But it's great news. I can't wait to see the looks on their faces when we tell them."

"Mom's and Dad's, too," Rane added. "They're coming over tonight, remember?"

"Right. We'd better get a move on then. You ready?"

"Yeah." Rane released his prey from his thrall, waited for his brother to do the same. "Been a while since we hunted together."

"We should do it more often," Rafe said. "Race you home!"

Abbey Marie was smiling when she tossed her cell phone on the footstool and settled back in Nick's arms. "What do you think?"

"I think miracles never cease," he said. "What do you think?"

"I'm happy for him. Aren't you?"

"I guess so."

"You guess so?" she asked, frowning.

"Yeah, poor man. It's like I told you before. He waited centuries to find the right woman, but I've already found her."

Chapter 29

Alric moved through the dark streets like a scythe, mowing down everything and everyone that had the misfortune to cross his path. Damn Mara! She had killed the first hunter he'd hired and when the second hunter heard the news, then met Lanzoni, he'd quit.

Maybe he should just forget about her and concentrate on his ungrateful fledgling. You'd think the stupid priest would have a little gratitude for the gift he'd been given. If he hadn't sired Lanzoni, the man would have died centuries ago. Alric swore a vile oath. His fledgling had lived long enough, as far as he was concerned. Though how he'd find him now that Mara had severed the link between himself and the priest remained a mystery. Damn the woman's interference!

Well, to hell with incompetent hunters. And to hell with detectives. Yanking his cell phone from his pocket, he called the detective he'd hired and fired him.

He'd been going about this all wrong, he thought as he made his way to a bar with public Wi-Fi. He did a quick search online for Goth magazines and booked ads in each one, promising a hefty reward to anyone having knowledge of Mara or Father Giovanni Lanzoni or their whereabouts. Then he contacted an advertising firm and arranged for them to print posters offering the same reward for the same information and have the posters sent out to all the Goth clubs in the Western United States. If Lanzoni was in the area, there was a good chance Mara was, too, he decided. He was betting that even the Queen of the Vampires had to be somewhere in the vicinity when she tampered with his mind.

He would find her or the priest, one way or another.

No matter what it cost.

Chapter 30

She was getting married in two weeks, Cassie thought as she lounged on the sofa, scrolling through Google looking for ideas on planning a hasty wedding. Two weeks! And suddenly she didn't think she'd left herself enough time to prepare. She was stunned by all the details she hadn't considered—such as flowers and pictures and someone to walk her down the aisle and a bridesmaid. Not to mention where to have the reception and what to serve.

And where to go on their honeymoon . . . ?

Maybe they should just elope, she mused. Laying her phone aside, she leaned back against the sofa. She didn't have any family, so she didn't have anyone to walk her down the aisle. Her only friend was Darla, who really wasn't much of a friend. And Cassie didn't want her at the wedding anyway. So, no bridesmaids. No guests other than the vampires Johnny considered family. And since they were all vampires, there was no need for food or champagne—or even a cake. She grinned as she imagined a fancy three-tiered affair with a bride and a vampire groom on top.

Maybe she'd ask Mara to be her maid of honor, Cassie

thought, and burst out laughing. She sobered just as quickly as she realized that everyone attending the ceremony would be a vampire.

Except the bride.

What was she doing? Thinking? She would be as helpless as a lamb in a den of wolves.

"Cassie."

Startled, she bolted upright. "Johnny! What are you doing here?" She glanced at the window. "Is something wrong? The sun is still up."

"I know. It's an added benefit for some ancient vampires." Her chaotic thoughts had disturbed his rest and brought him home hours before dark.

Brow furrowed, she cocked her head to the side. "How ancient *are* you?"

It was a question he had dreaded.

"Johnny? No secrets between us, remember?"

"I've been a vampire for thirteen hundred years, give or take a decade or two." To his knowledge, only a handful of vampires were older—Mara was thought to be over three thousand years old, even though she'd had a brief period as a human before being turned again. But her stint as a mortal hadn't diminished her powers in the least. She remained the most powerful vampire in the world. Nick Desanto was around two thousand, Alric, fourteen hundred.

Cassie stared at him. *Thirteen hundred years, give or take a decade or two.* He had already lived over a dozen lifetimes before she'd even been born.

"Does it matter?" he asked.

"I don't know." She tried to imagine what it would be like to live so long. To see everything she knew change or disappear, to watch everyone she knew grow old and die.

She thought of the myriad changes he must have seen in all that time. Inventions that she took for granted would have been unthinkable a thousand years ago. Thirteen hundred years. He should have been dust long ago, she thought morbidly, and then she frowned. Was she seeing the real Johnny? Or was there some sort of monster hidden beneath his handsome exterior?

Giovanni watched the play of emotions flit across her face. He didn't have to read her mind to fathom her thoughts, or to know she was wondering if he was some kind of freak. Hell, maybe he was. Maybe he'd been a fool to think he could have a lasting relationship with Cassie, or with any mortal woman.

Not knowing what to say and not willing to wait around to hear her say it was over, he simply vanished from the house.

"Johnny?" Frowning, Cassie stared at the place where he'd been standing a moment ago. Where had he gone in such a hurry?

And why?

Giovanni materialized on the front porch. He had intended to leave, but what if he had misjudged her reactions? What if he was projecting his own thoughts and insecurities onto Cassie? What if she wasn't thinking he was some kind of monster? What if she'd just been astonished at how old he was? If he wasn't a vampire and someone told him they had lived thirteen hundred years, he would probably be speechless, too. And who could blame her for having second thoughts about marrying a vampire? Maybe he had been attributing his own fears to her. Maybe he should go back inside.

Johnny? Her voice, in his mind.

I'm here.

Why did you leave?

I thought . . . I thought you'd feel different about me now.

Because you're so old?

He frowned. Was she laughing at him?

I was just surprised, that's all. I mean, even without the added thirteen hundred years, you're an old man. I mean, you are on the downside of thirty.

Cassie . . .

Johnny, come home.

The words were scarcely out of her mouth when he materialized in front of her. It didn't startle her nearly so much this time.

"I was afraid you were having second thoughts," he said. "That you were thinking I'm some kind of . . . of . . ."

"Freak?"

He frowned at her. Had *she* been reading *his* mind?

Taking his hand, she tugged him down beside her. "I *was* having some doubts," she admitted. "And I let my imagination run away with me for a few minutes. But mostly, I was fretting over the wedding. I don't know anything about planning one, and while I was looking up suggestions online, I realized I'm not your average bride. I don't have any family. Or any close friends to be my bridesmaids, or anyone to give me away. And then it occurred to me that I would be the only human at the ceremony, like a . . . a lamb among lions and it . . . it scared me."

Giovanni put his arms around her, thinking they were two of the most insecure people he knew.

"My family would never hurt you, Cassie. None of them is a killer . . . well, unless it's necessary to preserve their own life or that of their mate. If you didn't know they were vampires, you'd think they were just ordinary people. Well . . . except for Mara. There's nothing the least bit ordinary about her."

"That's for sure," Cassie muttered.

"So, are we still getting married?"

"Yes. I think I just had a case of bridal jitters." The minute she'd thought she had lost him, Cassie had known she didn't want to live without him.

"I'm sure Mara's son, Derek, would love to walk you down the aisle," Johnny said. "I'll ask him, and then I'll talk to Logan about being my best man. And we'll get Mara to be your maid of honor."

Cassie smiled inwardly, remembering how she'd considered that earlier and how the mere idea had made her laugh.

"You don't like that plan?"

"No, it's fine." She frowned as a new thought occurred to her. "I'd like to be married in a church. Is that going to be a problem?"

"Why would it be?"

"Well, it's holy ground. I'd hate for the groom and all the guests to go up in flames."

"There's nothing to worry about, love," he said, grinning. "I promise you that won't happen. We can text invitations as soon as you pick a time and a place."

"Who will we get to perform the ceremony?"

He frowned. In days past, he had officiated at the family weddings. "I'm sure we can find someone."

She snuggled against him, content to be in his arms. Vampire or not, she loved him more every day.

And in two weeks, he would be hers and she would be his for as long as she lived. She closed her eyes as a little voice in the back of her mind whispered, *It could be forever, if you were a vampire, too.*

The next day, Cassie went online looking for a nearby church. She found a small, nondenominational one close by. The pictures showed a lovely white brick building set amid a swath of green grass surrounded by trees. Noting the phone number, she called and learned the day she wanted was available. A minister could perform the ceremony for a small donation to the church.

Smiling, she booked a reservation, then looked at her checklist. Dress, yes. Church, yes. Maid of honor and best man, yes. Someone to walk her down the aisle, yes. Flowers . . . ?

Another quick phone call and she crossed that off her list. She debated about a photographer, but then, remembering Johnny didn't show up on her cell phone and he'd told her vampires didn't cast a reflection or a shadow, it seemed unlikely that their image could be captured on film. She crossed photographer off her list. If she wanted pictures of herself as a bride, she could always use her cell phone. It took better pictures than her old camera ever had.

When she saw Johnny tonight, she'd ask where he wanted to spend their honeymoon. She didn't really care, as long as they were together.

Johnny arrived with the setting of the sun. "How are you, my lovely bride-to-be?" he asked, taking her in his arms.

"Wonderful. I missed you."

"I missed you, too. Have you had dinner?"

"Yes. Have you?"

His gaze moved to her throat. "Is that an invitation?"

"If you want it to be."

"Very much so."

She pulled her hair back, baring her neck to his gaze.

"Ah, Cassie." He rained kisses along the length of her throat before biting her. The scent of her blood, the taste of it, was like nothing else. Hot and sweet and filled with vibrant life. It went through him like sunshine, warming him from the inside out. He took only a little, but it was enough. A flick of his tongue sealed the tiny wounds.

"Finished so soon?" she asked.

He kissed her lightly. "You're my dessert," he said. "I'll have dinner later."

She smiled at him as he sat in the big easy chair and pulled her down on his lap. "I have to get ready for work soon."

"I know."

"I was thinking about our honeymoon today."

"Oh?" A thrill of excitement swept through him at the thought of holding her, making love to her for the first time.

"Where do you want to go?" she asked.

"I don't care, as long as you're with me. Where would *you* like to go?"

Cassie shrugged one shoulder. "I don't know. I've never been anywhere. But you must have been everywhere."

He made a vague gesture with his hand. "I've seen a place or two in my time."

"What was your favorite one?"

"Italy."

"Isn't that where you were born?"

He nodded. "It's home."

"I'd love to go there. I've always wanted to see Rome

and the Colosseum and Venice and the Leaning Tower of Pisa and Vesuvius. But . . . can we afford it?"

"Money is no object, *cara mia*. We can visit Italy and anywhere else you'd like to go."

She beamed at him, then sighed. "I've got to get ready for work."

"You can leave that job any time you want, Cassie. I know you don't like working there."

"I'd love to quit, but I like having my own money. I know I'm not contributing anything to the household, but at least I can pay for my own clothes and things."

"Maybe after we're married, you could look for another job," he suggested. "One where you'd work days. Isn't there something you've always wanted to do?"

"I always wanted to be a hairdresser, but I could never save enough money to go to school."

"I'll pay your way." He held up his hand when she started to protest. "Once you're my wife, half of everything I have will be yours. Consider it an investment in our future."

Cassie smiled, then kissed him. "You're so good to me." She kissed him again. "But now I really have to get ready for work."

He stared after her as she hurried into the bedroom to change. He could get used to this, he thought. Holding Cassie on his lap, having her kiss him spontaneously, knowing he could kiss her in return . . .

He shook his head. Life couldn't get any better than this.

Chapter 31

Cassie frowned as she stared at the return address on the envelope in her hand. Try as she might, she couldn't imagine why Mara would be writing to her. Muttering, "Only one way to find out," she slit open the envelope and withdrew a single sheet of paper.

It was an embossed invitation to a bridal shower in her honor to be held at Mara's home in Hollywood the following night. Cassie frowned. Talk about short notice!

She blinked at the invite and blinked again. A bridal shower, given by the Queen of the Vampires. Unable to help herself, she burst out laughing, wondering if her life could get any more bizarre.

Johnny shook his head when she showed him the invitation that night. "You just never know what that woman's going to do next. Well, you have to go."

"You'll go with me, won't you?"

"I'll take you and pick you up when it's over."

"But . . . you can't mean to leave me there, alone, with her."

"I'm sure she's invited the other women in the family."

"But I don't know any of them! And they're all . . ."

"Vampires?"

"Yes."

"If you marry me, you're marrying into the whole bunch of us. You know that, don't you?"

Cassie bit down on her lower lip. "I knew it, but . . . I guess it never really hit home until now."

His whole being went still as he waited for her to say she'd changed her mind.

"You won't be far away, will you?"

"No. If the other men come, we'll go downstairs and find something to do. Either way, I'll be nearby."

"All right. Do I need to write a reply? Or can you just call her?"

Giovanni called Mara later that night, after Cassie was asleep. "Is this shower thing on the up-and-up?"

"Of course, it is," she said, sounding deeply hurt that he would ask. "Why would you think otherwise?"

"It doesn't seem like the kind of thing you would do."

"Well," she huffed, "that just proves how little you know me."

Giovanni shook his head when he heard Logan laughing in the background. "Apparently I'm not the only one who finds it hard to believe." He grinned when he heard Mara tell Logan to shut up.

"She is coming, isn't she?" Mara asked. "I've gone to a great deal of trouble to arrange it."

"No tricks?"

"No tricks. I just thought it would be nice for the women of the family to meet the bride before the wedding."

"The men aren't coming?"

"No, but Logan will be here to keep you company."

"All right, we'll be there."

Cassie was a nervous wreck when Johnny knocked on the door of Mara's home. Knowing the vampires would be able to sense her uneasiness made her even more nervous.

She grabbed Johnny's hand when the door opened and Mara stood there looking like a New York supermodel in a pair of black silk hostess pants and a white, off-the-shoulder sweater.

Cassie swallowed hard. She was always surprised by the vampire's sheer beauty, the perfection of her features, the power that radiated from her.

"Welcome, Cassie," she purred.

"Thank you for doing this," Cassie replied, surprised that her voice came out sounding almost normal.

Taking a step back, Mara said, "Come in, won't you? Giovanni, Logan is downstairs watching a movie."

Giovanni squeezed Cassie's hand. "Have a good time, *cara mia.*"

She forced a smile, then followed Mara into a living room that threatened to take her breath away. Pale blue walls, pristine white carpet, tables made of polished ebony. On the walls hung pictures that Cassie was certain had been painted by Old Masters. A pair of long sofas faced each other in front of a large white brick fireplace. Two overstuffed chairs covered in a burgundy print took up the space between the ends of the sofas farthest from the hearth.

"I recently had the place redecorated," Mara said.

"It's lovely."

"Thank you." The vampire gestured at the women seated on the sofas. "Ladies, this is Giovanni's fiancée, Cassie. Cassie, these are your guests. Abbey Marie is married to Nick, Brenna is married to Roshan, Savannah and Kathy are married to Cara's twin sons, Rafe and Rane. And this is Sheree, who is married to my son, Derek."

Cassie nodded to each one in turn as Mara introduced them, thinking it was nice to put faces to the names as she took the chair Mara indicated. Johnny had been right about them, Cassie mused. If she had met these women on the street, she never would have suspected they weren't human. And yet . . . there were subtle differences. They were all lovely, but it was more than that. Their hair had an added luster, their skin was flawless, almost translucent, and they moved with a kind of innate grace, as if they were lighter than air. But none of them radiated the same degree of power that Mara possessed.

Mara took the chair next to Cassie's. For a moment, there was only silence.

Then Abbey Marie said, "Cassie, we're all so pleased to meet you. We didn't think Father Lanzoni would ever marry. How did the two of you meet?"

Cassie felt herself relax as she related how Johnny had saved her from Lynx and his friends.

"Were you surprised when he told you he's a vampire?" Savannah asked.

"You could say that."

The ladies smiled as they exchanged knowing glances.

"We've all been where you are," Kathy said. "You must have questions."

"Dozens, but mostly I wonder how one makes a decision to become a vampire."

Savanah smiled wistfully. "It's an easy choice if you really love him and want to be with him forever."

"It's a good life," Abbey Marie remarked. "I never got to make the choice and, yes, it takes some getting used to, especially if it's thrust upon you. There are adjustments to be made, but in the end, if you love him, it's worth it."

As Johnny had said, none of the women seemed to have regrets, at least none they were willing to share. "He's not at all what I thought a vampire would be like," Cassie remarked. "Not that I ever imagined I'd meet one. Or even believed they existed."

"What *did* you expect?" Brenna asked.

The question brought a flush to Cassie's cheeks. "Well . . . you know . . . I've seen the movies. . . ."

"Were you disappointed when he didn't sparkle?" Sheree asked, stifling a grin.

"Ladies, we're embarrassing her," Mara said. "Maybe it's time we opened the presents."

Abbey Marie and Cara hurried into the other room. They returned moments later carrying armloads of colorful bags and gaily wrapped boxes.

Mara handed Brenna a small notebook and a pen. "Why don't you write down each gift and the giver?"

Brenna nodded.

"This first one is from Savannah," Abbey Marie said, handing Cassie a large rectangular box.

With every eye watching her, Cassie lifted the lid. "Oh!

It's lovely," she murmured as she pulled a long, black silk nightgown and matching peignoir from the box.

"I'm sure Giovanni will love it!" Kathy exclaimed.

There followed a wide assortment of negligees—long and short, silk and satin, and one, from Mara, that was little more than a whisper of white lace. There were numerous sets of sexy underwear, as well, mostly black or red.

By the time the last gift was unwrapped, and the last bottle of wine had been consumed, Cassie had forgotten the guests were vampires. They oohed and aahed like women everywhere, winking at her from time to time as they teased her good-naturedly about wedding a vampire priest who had been celibate for hundreds of years.

It was late when Johnny came upstairs. He held up his hands in self-defense as the women all clustered around to give him hugs and congratulate him on his upcoming marriage.

"So," he asked Cassie on the long drive home, "did the good ladies talk you out of marrying me?"

"No," she said. "Just the opposite. They all love you."

"They're the only family I've known since I was turned."

"Will they expect you to turn me?"

"Probably. But that choice will be yours. I would never force a life-altering decision like that on you or anyone else."

Good to know, Cassie thought. She couldn't imagine ever wanting to be a vampire. And yet. . . . She looked at Johnny. He appeared to be a young man in his late thirties and he would always look that way. How would she feel when he still looked thirtyish and she was fifty? Or sixty? Or eighty, if she lived that long? Would he be sorry he'd married her when she was as wrinkled as a prune?

Would she still love him when she grew old and he didn't? Or would she hate him because he remained a virile, sexy, younger-looking man and she was an old woman?

It was a thought that lingered in her mind when they reached home, and followed her to sleep.

Chapter 32

Alric stared at the text on his phone. The sender's name was unknown, but the message was short and sweet. I don't know where she lives, but I know her daughter-in-law's whereabouts.

He read the words again, then called the number listed. The phone rang twice before a man picked up. "Hello?"

"Are you sure she's related to Mara?" Alric asked.

"I'm sure."

"Where is she staying?"

"There's the little matter of a reward first."

"You'll get it. Where are you?"

"In New York. Meet me at Pike's in New Jersey tomorrow night at ten. And bring the money."

"How will I know you?"

"I'll be the only one not wearing black," the man said, and disconnected the call.

A slow smile spread across Alric's face as he slid his phone into his back pocket. All that time and money wasted on hunters and detectives, he mused. But, no matter.

Tomorrow night at ten, if luck was with him, he might have something to bargain with.

Alric arrived at the appointed place at nine-thirty. Pike's was a high-class Goth club that catered to the rich and famous who wanted to mingle with the strange and bizarre. Two walls were black, two were gray. The bar was ebony-colored marble veined with gold, the tables covered with alternating black and gray cloths, each one adorned with a white vase of blood-red roses.

He took a place at the end of the bar, his gaze sweeping the room. He counted four vampires in the crowd—three male and one female. As his informant had said, everyone wore black.

At exactly ten o'clock, a vampire dressed in navy blue slacks and a light blue jacket sauntered into the club. He glanced around the room, then headed toward Alric. "You got the money?" he asked briskly.

"You got the information?"

The vampire nodded. "Let's see the cash."

Alric pulled a fat envelope out of his coat and lifted the flap, exposing a sheaf of one hundred-dollar bills.

"She's staying at the Windsor Hotel with another female. For the last two nights, they've attended one play or another and then come here for drinks afterward, usually around ten-thirty, eleven."

"What does she look like?"

"She's young, real pretty, with dark blond hair. Her name's Sheree. You'll know her when you see her. I'm not sure who the other woman is, but she's a looker, too." The vampire held out his hand.

"Good work." Alric slapped the envelope into his palm. "You won't say anything about this to anyone, will you?"

The man shook his head. "Nice doing business with you."

"Uh-huh." Alric waited until the vampire left the bar, then followed him outside. As far as he was concerned, the only people you could trust to keep a secret were dead ones.

Alric leaned against the bar, a glass of red wine in his hand. A glance at his phone showed it was ten-fifty. He was beginning to think his informant had sold him a pack of lies when two women glided into the club.

He whistled under his breath. They were both lookers, all right. And both vampires, though not particularly powerful. They looked around, then headed for a small table in a far corner. Perfect.

Leaving his glass on the bar, he strolled in their direction.

Sheree sipped her wine, then put the glass aside. "So, what did you think of Cassie the other night?"

"I liked her," Abbey Marie said. "And I'm guessing Mara does, too. I mean, seriously, did you ever think the Queen of the Vampires would throw a bridal shower?"

"Not in a million years," Sheree admitted. "But she's always been full of surprises. I'm just glad Father Lanzoni has finally found someone. So, what shall we see tomorrow night?"

Abbey Marie thought a moment, then said, "There's a revival of *Les Miz* that looks good."

"I hate sad endings."

Abbey Marie grinned at her friend. Sheree had the kindest heart of anyone she had ever known. "Well, Cinderella is playing off-Broadway. How about that?"

"Better. This trip is the best birthday present I've ever received. I'm still surprised that Derek . . ." Sheree's voice trailed off as she sensed a vampire standing behind her. A moment later, he was beside her, a small dagger pressed against the side of her throat.

"What are you doing?" Abbey Marie gasped. "Do you know who she is?"

"Not really."

"Abbey, don't tell him anything." Sheree glared at the stranger, her heart pounding with trepidation. He was one of the ancient ones. She could feel his power coalescing around them, preventing those nearby from noticing what was going on at their table, preventing her and Abbey from transporting themselves to safety. She thought of contacting Nick through their blood bond but decided against it. At least for now.

"Since you're a vampire, you must have heard of Mara," Abbey Marie said. "Well, this is her daughter-in-law. I suggest you go away and we'll forget this happened."

The vampire snorted. "I forget nothing. I have a score to settle with the much-vaunted Queen of the Vampires. All I want is her whereabouts."

"Abbey, don't tell him anything," Sheree said again.

The vampire increased his pressure on the knife at Sheree's throat, hard enough to draw blood. "Shut up," he hissed. Glaring at Abbey, he said, "You'd better tell me what I want to know right now, or I'll cut her damn head off."

"All right!" Abbey Marie cried. "I'll tell you whatever you want to know. Just leave her alone."

"That's better." He eased the pressure against Sheree's neck but didn't remove the dagger. "Where is Mara?"

"The last I knew, she was at her home in the Hollywood Hills."

"What's the address?"

"I don't remember. It's the only house on Crow Haven Lane."

"And the priest? Where does he live?"

"I don't know," Abbey Marie said, fighting tears. "He moves around a lot."

The vampire stared at her, eyes blazing with hatred.

And then he was gone.

Abbey Marie grabbed a napkin and pressed it against the wound in Sheree's throat. "Are you all right? I should have called Nick, but I was so scared of what that monster might do."

"You made the right decision." Sheree smiled grimly. Nick was very protective of her friend. She'd been pretty sure the vampire wouldn't kill her. Whoever he was, he was a dead man, because if Mara didn't kill him, Derek and Nick certainly would.

Alric strolled down the street, oblivious to the lights and the crowds. He chuckled softly. The Queen of the Night had been right under his nose the whole damn time. Filled with exhilaration, he crossed the street, heedless of the traffic as he plotted his next move.

He glanced up at the sound of screeching tires in time

to see a long-bed truck bearing down on him. Before he could vanish, the vehicle slammed into him.

Pain engulfed him as he felt bones shattering, breaking, before he pinwheeled through the air, then skidded across the road, leaving pieces of skin and bone behind.

Barely able to move, he dragged himself into the darkness.

Chapter 33

Mara muttered something very unladylike under her breath when the doorbell rang.

"Don't answer it," Logan said, his soapy hands resting on her shoulders. "I haven't washed the best part yet."

"Very funny." Climbing out of the tub, she grabbed her robe and wrapped it around herself. "It's Abbey Marie and Sheree."

"What the hell are they doing here? I thought they were in New York."

"Only one way to find out," Mara said. "Something's wrong. I think you'd better get dressed."

"Might as well," he said sourly.

The man had a one-track mind, she thought as she answered the door. Abbey Marie and Sheree stood on the porch, both dressed for a night on the town.

"Well, this is a surprise," Mara said, gesturing for them to come inside. She glanced from one to the other, thinking something was definitely wrong.

"Sheree was attacked," Abbey Marie explained.

"When?" Mara's gaze ran over her daughter-in-law,

but there was no visible sign of injury. Still, there *was* something—Alric's distinctive scent. "Sit down, you two." She glanced over her shoulder when Logan strolled into the room wearing a pair of sweatpants and a tee shirt, his hair still damp.

"What's going on?" he asked.

"I'm trying to find out," Mara said impatiently. "Abbey, what happened?"

"We were having a drink in Manhattan when a vampire came up behind us and put a knife to Sheree's throat. He wanted to know where to find you," Abbey Marie said, her words tripping over themselves. "He threatened to take Sheree's head if I didn't tell him. I'm so sorry, but . . ."

"Don't worry about it," Mara said. "I'll take care of the matter. Sheree, you tell Derek to stay out of this if he knows what's good for him. We don't need an angry werewolf running wild in the streets. Alric is mine."

"I had the same thought," Sheree said, smiling faintly. "So, you know this vampire, then?"

"Yes. We have some history between us. Do you two want to spend the night?"

Abbey Marie shook her head. "Nick's coming to get me."

"And I just want to go home," Sheree said with a weary sigh. She had contacted Derek through their bond on the way to Mara's house.

No sooner had she spoken the words than Derek appeared in the room. He went immediately to Sheree's side. "Are you all right? I'll kill the bastard who dared lay a hand on you."

"No, you won't," Mara said.

"Like hell!"

Mara stared at her son as her power swept through the room. "I said I'd take care of it."

"Dammit, she's my wife!" Derek swayed as pain knifed through him, but he stayed on his feet, his eyes red and glowing with rage.

"Yes, I know. And I'm warning you to stay out of it. All of you. This is between Alric and me." Her gaze bored into him, and then softened. "Do you understand?"

Hands clenched at his sides, he nodded once, curtly.

Withdrawing her power, Mara said, "Why don't you take Sheree home? She's had a bad night."

"If you don't destroy him, I will." Derek's whole body vibrated with barely subdued rage as he wrapped his arm around his wife's shoulders and left the house.

Rising, Abbey Marie said, "Mara, I'm so sorry."

"What's done is done. Tell Nick . . ."

"Tell Nick what?" Desanto said, materializing in the room. His gaze moved over Abbey before he took her in his arms. "What the hell's going on?"

He listened intently as Abbey related the events of the night.

"I told Derek to stay out of it," Mara said. "And now I'm telling you. This is my fight and I'll handle it in my own way. Is that clear?"

"Dammit. . . ."

"Are we clear?"

Nick scowled at her. "Fine. You can have first crack at him—then he's mine." Taking Abbey's hand in his, they vanished from the room.

"Well, that was fun," Logan muttered. "Nothing I like better than being interrupted when taking a bath with my woman."

Mara took a deep breath as the last of her power faded away. "We can always go back and refill the tub," she said, absently.

"What are you going to do about Alric?"

"He hasn't given me any choice, has he? The fool seems determined to confront me." She reached for Logan, then stilled. Lifting her head, she closed her eyes.

"What's going on?"

"I have no sense of him."

"What do you mean?"

"He's either dead or gone to ground again."

Logan grunted softly. "Forget about him for now. He's taken up enough of our night." Swinging Mara into his arms, he carried her into their bedroom, raining kisses on her cheeks, her brow, her lips before he lowered her to the bed.

She lay back on the pillows, her eyes smoky with desire as he removed her robe, then shed his own clothing. Stretching out beside her, he drew her into his embrace.

"I hope I never get on your bad side," he murmured, nuzzling her neck. "Not that I've ever seen one. You look good all over."

"Sheree, why didn't you come to me instead of going to Mara's? Hell, why didn't you contact me from the restaurant?" Derek asked when they reached home.

"Alric threatened to kill me if Abbey didn't tell him where Mara lived. I felt Mara should know what happened right away but Abbey was afraid to face her by herself. We weren't hurt," she said, with a reassuring smile. "As for why I didn't contact you . . ." She caressed his cheek. "I was afraid you wouldn't be able to control your temper.

As your mother said, we didn't need an angry werewolf prowling the streets. Besides, I was pretty sure Alric wouldn't kill me."

He snorted. "Pretty sure?"

"I knew you'd come if we needed you."

"You're damn right. And if Mara doesn't kill him, I sure as hell will."

Chapter 34

Giovanni strolled aimlessly down the dark streets. Cassie had gone to bed an hour ago. He had tried reading. He had tried watching TV, but nothing held his interest. In ten days, she would be his wife. And he was plagued by doubts. What if she grew tired of him? What if he disappointed her in bed? What if she laughed at him?

He rarely cursed, but he swore now. He was a vampire, a powerful being, yet he felt as vulnerable as the weakest mortal. He had spent centuries keeping mostly to himself. Marrying Cassie would put an end to that. At the moment, they spent most of their time together, just the two of them, and she seemed content with that. But what if, once the newness wore off, she wanted to go out, make friends, mingle with humanity? He wasn't sure he was ready for that. He generally avoided crowds of people. The lights, the noise, the ever-constant temptation of all those beating hearts. . . . He shook his head, determined to put his doubts behind him. Fate had put a wonderful, beautiful woman in his path. Was he going to let his fears of something that might never happen ruin what he had now?

He was about to turn toward home when Mara appeared beside him.

"Good evening, Giovanni."

"Mara." He slid a sideways glance at her. Something was wrong. "What's up?"

"Alric attacked Sheree earlier tonight."

"What the hell? Is she all right?"

"She's fine. She was with Abbey Marie at the time. Alric threatened to take Sheree's head if Abbey refused to reveal my whereabouts."

Giovanni grunted softly. Anyone who messed with Mara was a fool.

"I thought you should know I've been unable to locate any trace of him. I think he's gone to ground."

"Why would he do that again so soon?"

"I'm not sure. The only reason I can think of is that he's been badly hurt."

"Hurt?" He looked at her sharply. "Did you . . . ?"

She made a sound of disgust low in her throat. "If he'd crossed my path, he wouldn't be hurt. He'd be dead."

Giovanni chuckled. "Thanks for letting me know."

"Keep your guard up," she warned. "Wounded animals are the most dangerous kind."

Troubled by Mara's words, Giovanni decided to return home and check on Cassie before he went back to his lair. He felt a jolt of fear when he saw there were lights on in the house. Materializing in the living room, he was surprised to find Cassie awake and curled up on the sofa.

"What's wrong?" he asked. "What are you doing up so late? It's almost morning."

"I had a nightmare."

Nodding, he sat beside her and put his arms around her. "Do you want to talk about it?"

She shook her head vigorously.

"That bad, huh?" He barely remembered what it was like to dream. As a vampire, he was awake one minute and unless he fought it, the next he was lost in the Dark Sleep of oblivion until the setting of the sun. "Can I get you something?"

"No." She looked up at him. "Would you stay here with me tonight?"

"If you like." Rising, he gathered her into his arms and carried her down the hall to her room, waited until she'd settled into bed.

When he turned to leave, she caught his hand. "Don't go."

"That must have been some hellacious nightmare."

She nodded. "I don't want to be alone."

"All right." Sitting on the end of the bed, he took off his boots and socks, then stretched out on top of the covers beside her.

She nestled against him, her head resting on his shoulder, one arm lying across his waist.

Giovanni took a deep breath. It was the wrong thing to do. The fragrance of her hair and skin tickled his nostrils, the warm, rich scent of her life's blood teased his hunger. He clenched his hands as he fought for control.

And then she rose up on one elbow and kissed him.

With a low groan, he pulled her into his arms. Her lips were warm and soft and pliable. Heat shot through him when her tongue slid over his lower lip and dipped inside to duel with his. They had kissed and cuddled before, but never like this. Every breath carried her scent, every touch stoked his desire, weakening his resistance. Murmuring his name, she slid her hand under his shirt, her fingers stroking his chest, sliding back and forth over his belly.

Lost in a fog of sensual pleasure, he caressed her in turn, each touch growing bolder when she didn't protest.

She unbuttoned his shirt, then bent her head and ran her tongue over his bare chest, his neck. "Johnny," she whispered, her voice thick with need. "Don't make me wait any longer."

"Cassie . . ."

She pressed her fingers to his lips to silence him and then kissed him again, longer, deeper, until he was on fire for her, the wall of his resistance shattered by a need that would no longer be denied.

Murmuring, "Heaven, forgive me," he threw the covers aside. A thought removed his clothing and her nightgown. His gaze caressed her for a long, lingering moment, and then, capturing her lips with his, he sheathed himself deep in the warmth of her love.

Reality returned slowly. He felt listless, drained, and yet invigorated. For a moment, Giovanni thought he had dreamed the whole thing. But that was impossible. He didn't dream. And then he realized there was something warm and soft pressed against his back. A musky scent hung heavy in the air.

He rolled over slowly, surprised by the wave of tenderness that swept through him when he saw Cassie sleeping beside him.

He had never shared a bed with a woman. His gaze moved over her, lingering on the pulse throbbing in her throat, sliding down to one bare shoulder peeking from beneath the rumpled blankets, and then to a length of silky thigh.

Giovanni let out a deep, shuddering breath as his desire stirred to life again. He grinned faintly, surprised that he could want her again so soon. That instead of feeling guilty, he was filled with a sense of peace, of acceptance and belonging.

He knew a moment of embarrassment when her eyelids fluttered open and he realized he was naked beneath the covers.

A slow smile spread over Cassie's lips and then, seeing his expression, she frowned. Was he angry because she had begged him to make love to her? Was he wracked with guilt because she'd seduced him into breaking his vow of chastity? "Say something."

"I love you."

"You're not angry?"

His brows shot up. "Angry? Why would I be angry?"

"Because we . . . because I know you wanted to wait until we were married."

"Ah, Cassie," he murmured, drawing her into his arms. "No matter what the future holds, I'll never be sorry for tonight. You've given me a rare gift, one I'll never forget or regret."

She sighed with relief at his words.

He cleared his throat. "The sun won't be up for another hour. Do you want to . . . I mean, could we . . . ?"

She laughed softly. "If you're asking what I think you are, the answer is yes. Most definitely yes."

Cassie woke hours later with a smile on her face. Yawning, she reached for Johnny's pillow and buried her nose in it, inhaling his scent. For a man who claimed to have no experience, he hadn't had any trouble finding his way. The first time had been fire and fury. The second time had been filled with tenderness and a sense of wonder.

Slipping out of bed, she walked barefoot into the bathroom to shower and brush her teeth. She hoped he would wake up in his lair feeling as happy as she had, but she couldn't help worrying that, even though he'd denied it earlier, he might feel some sense of regret. He had been so determined that they not make love until they were married.

Well, she thought as she dressed, what was done was done.

In the kitchen, she fried several strips of bacon, scrambled three eggs, popped two slices of bread into the toaster, filled a glass with orange juice, poured a cup of coffee. She grinned when she sat at the table, thinking that a night of great lovemaking had certainly increased her appetite.

Soon, they would be man and wife and she would be able to seduce him wherever and whenever she wanted. And then she laughed. If she was this famished every time they made love, she would soon be as fat as the proverbial pig.

After breakfast, Cassie headed back to her room and made the bed. She glanced at the bridal shower gifts, still in their boxes on the chair in the corner. Perched on the edge of the mattress, she opened them one by one, felt her cheeks grow warm as she ran her fingers over the white lacy gown Mara had given her. Of them all, it was her favorite. She could hardly wait to wear it, she thought as she folded her gowns and placed them in one of the dresser drawers.

In little more than a week, she would be Johnny's wife. She would quit her job at the lounge and find a good beauty school. For the first time in her life, she had someone in her corner, someone to encourage her in her endeavors. Someone to share her laughter and her tears, to lift her when she was down. It was a good feeling. And she would be there for him, too, if and when he needed her.

She hadn't prayed much in her life but now, standing in the middle of her bedroom, she bowed her head and silently thanked Heaven for sending such a wonderful man her way.

And then she had a terrible thought. They were supposed to be wed in nine days. What if he didn't want to marry her, now that they'd made love? What was that old saying? Why buy the cow when the milk is free? Did he think less of her now? Sure, he'd said he wasn't sorry they'd made love, but what if he was? He was an honorable man. What if was only marrying her because he'd promised to do so?

Eager to see Cassie, Giovanni woke while the sun was still low in the sky. He dressed quickly, hoping that she didn't have to work tonight. He was anxious to hold her in his arms again, even if they didn't make love. He laughed softly as he ran a comb through his hair, surprised that the guilt he had expected to be waiting for him when he woke up never materialized.

He said a silent prayer, thanking the good Lord for sending her his way. She was the best thing in his life. He admired her spunk, her sense of humor. It hadn't been easy for her, growing up alone with no one to care for her, making a decent life for herself, but she'd done it. He had never heard her complain or rail at fate because her parents had abandoned her. She had managed to survive on her own, and he respected her for that. She could have been bitter or filled with anger. Instead, she'd kept moving forward. She had filled his life with hope and love and sunshine, and for that, he would be forever grateful.

And soon, soon, she would be his wife, and he would love her and cherish her as long as she lived.

Whistling softly, he transported himself to their home, eager to hold her in his arms again.

Cassie smiled uncertainly when Johnny materialized in the living room. "Hi."

"Hi." He wanted to hold her, yet was oddly reluctant, which was strange, after what they had shared the night before. He wondered if she felt the same, excited and yet sort of shy. Deciding one of them had to make the first move, he sat beside her and put his arm around her shoulders. "Are we okay?"

"Are we?"

"What do you mean?"

"Do you . . . ?"

"Do I what?"

"Do you still want to marry me?"

"Of course. Why would you think otherwise?" He frowned when she didn't answer. "Cassie?"

"I was afraid that you might change your mind after last night."

"I was afraid you'd be sorry."

"Sorry?" She smiled. "Are you kidding? I've been trying to get you into my bed for weeks."

He grinned at her. "Did I do all right? Were you disappointed?"

She couldn't help laughing, even though she knew she shouldn't.

"That bad, huh?"

"No, you fool! It was wonderful. *You* were wonderful."

"You're not just saying that to soothe my masculine ego, are you?"

"No, Johnny. Are you sure you've never done it before?"

"I think that's something I'd remember," he said dryly. "But I'd sure like to do it again."

Rising, she tugged on his hand. "Well, come on, then," she said, her grin spreading from ear to ear. "I don't want you to forget how."

Later, lying amid tangled sheets, the air thick with the scent of their lovemaking, Giovanni was overcome with a sense of wonder. Rolling onto his side, he lifted a lock of Cassie's hair and twined it around his finger. "Is it this way for everyone?"

"How could it be? All those other poor women only have regular guys in their beds. I've got the Italian stallion in mine."

At her reference to Rocky Balboa, he groaned out loud.

"Sorry," she said contritely, even though she wasn't sorry at all. The man had amazing stamina.

"Cassie?"

"Again?" she asked, eyes twinkling. "Are you trying to make up for lost time?"

He nodded as he rose over her, eyes dark with desire. "Thirteen hundred years' worth, give or take a decade or two."

"I'll never survive," she exclaimed in mock horror, even as she lifted her hips to receive him.

Chapter 35

The following night, Cassie was in the kitchen stuffing dishes into the dishwasher when Johnny appeared in the doorway. Glancing over her shoulder, she smiled at him.

"You about done there?" he asked.

"Yeah, why?"

"We're going out."

"We are? Where?"

"It's a surprise."

"Really? I love surprises!" she exclaimed, although she'd had few good ones in her life. And then she smiled, thinking Johnny was the biggest and best surprise she had ever received. She looked down at her jeans and T-shirt. "Just let me change my clothes."

Cassie felt a rush of excitement when Johnny pulled up in front of a jewelry store.

He grinned when he saw the look on her face. "That's right," he said when he came around to open her door. "It's time you had a ring."

She was too excited to speak as he took her hand and helped her from the Mustang.

"Pick out whatever you want," he said as they entered the store. "Price is no object."

Cassie stared at the display of wedding and engagement rings, wondering how she would ever make up her mind. In spite of what Johnny had said, she perused the cheapest ones.

He noticed, of course. "Look at all of them," he chided. "You're going to be wearing it for a long time and I want you to get the one you love the most."

"But . . . these are so expensive."

"Don't think about it."

She worried her lower lip between her teeth as she moved slowly along the display cases. Silver, of course, was out of the question. She walked up and down twice, but kept coming back to an emerald-cut diamond engagement ring set in platinum. The matching wedding ring had smaller diamonds all around the band.

"I really love this one," she said. "But, Johnny, it's almost four thousand dollars."

"No problem. I can sell the Mustang to pay for it."

"What?" She looked at him in alarm. "No way. You love that car."

"I love you more," he said. "Besides, I was kidding. We can buy the ring and keep the car. We'll take these," he told the salesman who had been patiently waiting to help them.

The man took Cassie's ring size and smiled. "We have your size in stock, if you'd like to take it with you."

"Wrap it up," Johnny said as he reached for his wallet and withdrew a credit card.

Cassie frowned when she caught a glimpse of his driver's license. "Who's Paul Langley?"

He tapped his chest with his forefinger. "Me, of course."

"So, will I be Mrs. Johnny Lanzoni or Mrs. Paul Langley?"

"Both. On paper, you'll be Cassie Langley. I alternate names every fifty years or so. As far as the world is concerned, Johnny Lanzoni died half a century ago. Fifty years from now, I'll be Johnny Lanzoni again."

"What will it say on our marriage license?"

"With a little vampire magic, we'll get two, one for each name. If you don't like that idea, you can use your maiden name. It's up to you."

"Oh." While he paid for the rings, Cassie stared out the window. In fifty years, he'd be Lanzoni again. A half a century from now she would be old and gray and wrinkled, if she lived that long. It was a sobering thought.

"You're very quiet," Johnny said as they left the store hand in hand. "Did you change your mind about the ring?"

"No. I was just thinking of what you said, about coming up with a new name every so often. Fifty years is a long time."

He grunted softly. He didn't have to read her mind to know what she was thinking. He drove to a secluded area near a stand of timber and parked the car. "Come on," he said, "let's go for a walk."

They followed a narrow dirt path to a stone bench located between a bubbling fountain and the statue of a stag. When she sat down, he knelt in front of her. Taking her hand in his, he unwrapped the engagement ring and slid it on her finger. "I love you, Cassie."

"I know. I love you, too."

"But you'll grow old and I won't," he said. "Is that what's bothering you?"

She blew out a sigh. She had known that would happen, had thought she was prepared for it. Until today. Seeing his driver's license had made it all very real. "Is that the reason the women in Mara's family chose to be vampires?"

"Pretty much. Some sooner than others. But, as I said before, some were turned against their will." His fingers tightened around hers. "But they're all happy now, *cara*. I've never heard any of them say they were sorry, even the ones that had no say in the matter. I know being a vampire might seem like a terrible life, but it isn't. Sure, it's a trade-off—you lose the sun and food, but you gain unlimited health and strength and the ability to heal yourself. If you should decide to become one of us, you'll stay the age you are whenever you're turned. But whether you're old or young, vampire or not, I'll always love you and be with you."

"Will you?"

"I swear it." Turning her hand over, he kissed her palm. "You have years to decide."

Cassie nodded. She was only twenty-six, after all. She had plenty of time to make up her mind. Still, she'd have to decide in the next ten or twelve years or so, because she certainly didn't want to look older than her future husband!

Rising, he sat beside her. "Are we good?"

"Yes." There were no guarantees in life. She could be hit by a car tomorrow. Though he wasn't likely to succumb to accidents or illness, even Johnny wasn't indestructible. Vampire or mortal, no one was guaranteed tomorrow. "Yes," she said again. "Let's go home."

* * *

The next few days flew by. She picked up her wedding dress and veil, went shopping for a pair of white heels, then bought a couple of suitcases to take on their honeymoon. She also bought a new handbag and a pair of slippers.

Wandering through the men's department, she searched for something to buy for Johnny. She couldn't think of anything he needed and then, on impulse, she bought a pair of black silk bikini briefs.

And immediately had second thoughts. Would he think them too sexy? Even though they'd been intimate, she hadn't noticed what kind of shorts he wore. She started to return the briefs, then changed her mind as she pictured him wearing them on their wedding night. And nothing else.

Two days before the wedding, Mara stopped by the house.

"So, are you ready for the big day?" she asked with an airy wave of her hand. "Or night, as the case may be?"

"I think so."

"You never mentioned a reception."

"I didn't think there was any need for one. I mean, well, there's no need for food or . . ."

"You still need a reception. I've arranged for one at the Park Hyatt Hotel. I hope you don't mind."

"No, of course not."

"Good. I've arranged a wedding supper for you and lots of wine for the rest of us. And a band, of course. I've also rented the bridal suite," Mara added. She frowned, and then grinned. "Something tells me you've already had the honeymoon."

Cassie felt her cheeks grow hot as she stared at the vampire. How could she possibly know that?

Mara shook her head. And then she laughed. "So, the walls of Jericho finally came down."

Giovanni frowned when he went home that night and found Cassie sitting on the sofa, arms crossed over her breasts and not looking very happy. "Does that expression have anything to do with the fact that Mara's been here?"

"In a way. She came by to let me know she's arranged for a reception at the Park Hyatt Hotel, complete with a wedding supper for me, wine for the guests, and a band."

"Are you all right with that?"

"I guess so, if you are."

"What else did she say?"

"She knew we'd made love. Did you tell her?"

"Of course not!"

"Then how did she know?"

"It's complicated."

Cassie tilted her head to the side, her fingers drumming impatiently on the arm of the sofa.

"I don't know how to explain it. Vampires can sense that kind of thing." Taking the seat beside her, Giovanni reached for her hand. "Are you okay?"

"Better than okay. Just think, day after tomorrow we'll be married."

"I'll try to make you happy."

"You already make me happy. I found an ad for a beauty

school today. When I called, they said a new course starts in six weeks, so I signed up for it."

"Good for you. I know you'll do great."

"I hope so." She looked at him, a smile playing over her lips. "Haven't you forgotten something?"

"Have I?"

"You haven't kissed me tonight."

"I'm a cad."

"I know how you can remedy that."

"So do I."

Cassie closed her eyes as he pressed his lips to hers in a long, slow kiss that made her toes curl.

"Don't go to work tonight," he said, his hand stroking her thigh. "Stay here and keep me company."

"I'd love to, Johnny. You know I would. But it's my last night and it's too late to find someone to take my place."

"Right." He kissed her again. "I guess you'd better go get ready."

"You don't have to drive me tonight. If I can, I'll come home early. If I have to stay late, I'll let you know."

"I don't know. . . ." Alric's whereabouts were still unknown. As far as anyone knew, he had gone to ground. Surely, if he'd surfaced again, Mara would have said something.

"I'm a big girl," Cassie said. "I'll be fine. You can't keep me wrapped up in cotton wool my whole life."

He grunted softly, thinking it was a hell of a good idea.

Cassie hummed softly as she showered, then dressed for work. This time tomorrow, she would be Johnny's wife. Feeling giddy, she twirled around the room. She was getting married to the most wonderful man in the world. And she didn't care if she was Mrs. Langley or Mrs. Lanzoni, as long as she was his.

She could hardly wait.

Tomorrow night, all her dreams would come true.

Chapter 36

Rising through layers of dirt, grass, and leaves, Alric emerged from the depths of the earth, uncertain of how long he'd been lost in the Dark Sleep. He stretched his arms and back. The worst of his injuries had healed, but his ribs were still sore. He had been injured numerous times in the course of his long existence, but never like this. He possessed incredible strength, but his body wasn't immune to pain or physical trauma. It would be another day or two before he was fully recovered. In the meantime, he needed blood.

Lots of blood.

He grinned inwardly. Every cloud had a silver lining. Filled with renewed purpose, he prowled up and down the streets of New York City, feeding from multiple victims so as not to call attention to himself.

In a few days, he would be strong enough to go after Mara, he thought. And then he paused. Being so badly wounded had reminded him that he was vulnerable. And that Mara could do a hell of a lot more damage than a five-ton truck.

She could destroy him with little more than a thought.

Perhaps he could hurt her in other, less dangerous ways. The priest was a particular favorite with the Queen of the Vampires. Taking him out could serve as revenge, not only for Calidora's death, but for the vampire's complete lack of respect for his sire. Alric dragged a hand over his jaw. Destroying the priest seemed like a far wiser—and safer—course of action.

With a thought, he transported himself to the last place he'd seen the priest. He found himself in front of a third-rate bar. The Winchester Lounge. The place was packed, he noted, as he swaggered through the door. The music of a hundred beating hearts assaulted his ears. He pushed his way through the crowd to the bar, where he ordered a glass of red wine.

Turning toward the room, he opened his senses. So many interesting scents, such a variety of men and women and blood types. A veritable feast to satisfy a hungry vampire's thirst. He had chosen his prey when a waitress sauntered by. He inhaled sharply, his eyes narrowing as he watched her. She had recently been with Lanzoni. The other vampire's scent was all over her. Who was she? And what was she to the priest? A customer? An acquaintance? Or something far more intimate?

Keeping her always in sight, he faded into the background.

Just before closing time, Cassie reminded the manager that it was her last night. He wasn't happy about it, cheap help was hard to find, after all, but he thanked her gruffly and promised to give her a good recommendation should she ever need one.

Feeling lighthearted, Cassie left the lounge and headed

for the parking lot. She had just unlocked the Mustang when a man stepped out of the shadows.

Alarm bells went off in her mind but before she could get in the car or scream for help, he was on her, his hands like iron where they gripped her arms.

Fear turned to terror when his eyes—eyes tinged an unholy red—locked on hers. *Vampire.* She tried to look away, tried to connect with Johnny, but she couldn't tear her gaze away from that hypnotic stare, couldn't focus enough to send out a silent, desperate plea for help.

And then it was too late.

She felt the vampire's power crawl over her, stealing her mind, her will.

And then everything went black.

Chapter 37

It was later than usual when Giovanni headed for home. Bored with prowling the same familiar streets in the next town, he had gone farther afield in search of a new hunting ground. The city he had chosen was twice the size of his usual haunt and he had spent some time just wandering through the business district before heading for the residential area. He had found a two-story house for sale. It sat on a large lot with an abundance of shrubs and flowers. The backyard looked like a park. A number of trees grew along the fence line. There was a covered patio and a kidney-shaped pool with a diving board, a slide, and a spa.

The house was vacant so he willed himself inside and went exploring. A living room with a red rock fireplace and built-in TV, dining room, bathroom, kitchen with all the modern appliances, and a good-sized laundry room were situated on the first floor. He found a master bedroom and two smaller ones upstairs, each with a walk-in closet and its own bath. There was also a linen closet and game room. Everything looked new.

It would, he thought, make a wonderful wedding present for his bride, who would be waiting for him and perhaps wondering where he was.

Whistling softly, he transported himself home. He caught the smell of smoke seconds before he materialized inside the house.

Veering to the right, he took on his own form across the street, eyes narrowed as he watched the fire department attempt to put out the blaze.

Cassie!

Racing across the street, he grabbed a fireman by the arm. "Was there anyone inside?"

"We don't know. Please, sir, stay back."

Giovanni retreated, his gaze fixed on the flames. He tried to sense her presence in the house, but the smoke and the fire made it impossible.

Feeling sick, he turned away. He refused to believe she had been inside. He had taken her blood. He would have sensed it if she was gone. Yet, when he tried to find the bond between them, there was only emptiness.

Unwilling to believe she was dead, he transported himself to the Winchester Lounge, but it was closed, the doors locked and bolted. Only a faint night-light burned inside.

Filled with despair, Giovanni hurried around the building to the parking lot. If her car was still here, then there was hope she had been detained. He felt a wave of relief when he saw the Mustang across the lot. She hadn't gone home.

But where was she?

And why couldn't he sense her whereabouts?

Pulling his keys from his pocket, he walked swiftly toward the car. As he drew closer, he found the answer to his question in Alric's foul scent.

Giovanni groaned low in his throat. He had failed her. She would have been better off in the flames.

Dropping to his knees, he buried his face in his hands.

Moments later, he felt Mara's presence at his side. "He's got her," he said, his voice thick with despair.

"I should have killed him centuries ago when I had the chance," Mara said.

"You once told me you can find anyone. Where is he?"

Lifting her head, she closed her eyes. Power rose all around her, then evaporated.

"Well?"

"I can't sense him."

"What? Why the hell not?"

"I'm not sure. Either he's left town, or he's found a way to block others of our kind, which usually involves a witch."

"Angelica?"

"Perhaps. But I don't think so. If he'd left on foot, we could follow his scent, but transporting doesn't leave any trace to follow. Have you tried tracking Cassie's presence?"

He nodded. "There's nothing there. You don't think she's . . . ?" He couldn't say the word.

"No. You'd feel it if she were dead. Most likely she's unconscious. I think he's sealed his lair in such a way that it blocks all outside supernatural powers. Sort of like a vampire threshold to keep our kind out. Or . . ."

"Or he's turned her and the link between us is gone," he said flatly.

Mara's silence told him the thought had also occurred to her.

"So, there are some things even the Queen of the Vampires can't do," he muttered. "Where the hell does that leave us?"

"It will be morning in a few hours," Mara said. "Why

don't you come home with me and take your rest at my place?"

"Thanks, but no."

"Don't be discouraged, Giovanni. I'm sure she's still alive. Perhaps you'll be able to track her tomorrow."

"Perhaps," he said. But there was no conviction behind his words.

"I'll do what I can to find him," she promised, laying her hand on his arm. "If I learn anything, I'll let you know."

He nodded again, touched by the concern in her eyes.

She gave his arm a squeeze and then she was gone.

Driving to the abandoned church where he made his lair, Giovanni parked his car behind the building. Inside, he prostrated himself in front of the altar and sent a heart-felt cry for help toward Heaven.

Cassie woke in the dark with a splitting headache and no memory of where she was or how she had gotten there. She lay very still, eyes straining to pierce the blackness that surrounded her. There was no light, no sound, yet she sensed she wasn't alone.

She let out a yelp when she felt a hand at her throat.

"Be still."

The voice rumbled through her like thunder and she obeyed instantly.

"How do you know the priest?"

She didn't want to answer but his voice compelled her to do so. "We're engaged to be married."

"Interesting."

A light came on, momentarily blinding her. When her vision cleared, she saw a man standing beside the bed. He was tall and dark and muscular, with an ugly snake tattoo on the side of his neck. She felt an odd sensation and when it passed, she was no longer unable to move. Sitting up, she scrambled to the far side of the room, her hand reaching for her crucifix. Only it wasn't there.

"There's no place for you to go," he said. "I want you to call Giovanni."

"Who?"

"The priest, you stupid girl. Don't play the fool with me."

Cassie shook her head. "I don't have a phone."

"You don't need a phone and we both know it. Just think his name. He'll hear you."

Cassie shook her head again. She didn't know who this guy was, but some instinct told her to refuse.

"Call him," the stranger hissed. "And tell him to come alone if he wants to see you alive."

Giovanni's head jerked up as the blood link that bound him to Cassie sparked to life. He knew a moment of soul-shattering relief—thank the good Lord, she was alive—followed by mounting despair as he sensed her fear. He swore again when he heard her voice in his mind, warning him to come alone or her life would be forfeit.

Stay strong, cara. I'm on my way.

Leaving the church, he honed in on his link to Cassie and followed it to a small, dark, windowless building. Alric's stench was strong here.

Giovanni swore under his breath. Every instinct he possessed warned him that it was a trap and Cassie, the bait. It was suicide to go in there, he thought, but he couldn't leave her in Alric's hands.

A harsh cry of pain torn from Cassie's throat had him bursting through the door. The interior was pitch-black but he didn't need light to see that she was tied hand and foot to a narrow wooden cot. The blank look on her face told him she was under a spell of some kind.

He had barely come to a stop when hands reached for him, wrestling him to the ground, binding his wrists with silver shackles before he could break free of their grasp. Transporting himself out of there and leaving Cassie behind never occurred to him.

He swore under his breath as a rush of preternatural power filled the room. He could feel it surrounding him like an invisible shield, expanding to engulf the entire building—the same kind of shield that had kept him from sensing Cassie's presence the night before. He should have called Mara before he came here, he thought bleakly. Now it was too late.

And then Alric was standing over him, flanked by two men who were under the vampire's thrall.

Alric grinned, baring bloodstained fangs.

Giovanni rolled to his side and lurched to his feet. "What do you want, Alric?"

"A little respect," the vampire hissed. "Perhaps a thank-you for sparing your life all those centuries ago."

"Go to hell."

He had no sooner spoken the words than Cassie let out a hoarse cry as one of the revenants struck her across the face. Hard. Twice.

"Damn you!" Giovanni growled. "Leave her alone. She has nothing to do with what's between you and me."

"If you want her to live to see tomorrow, you will get down on your knees and beg for my forgiveness."

"Forgiveness?" Giovanni sneered. "For what?"

Another cry from Cassie sent him to his knees. Forcing the words past his lips, he said, "I'm sorry for whatever wrong I've done you."

"Master."

"Master."

Gloating, Alric walked around his prisoner. Stopping in front of him, he glanced over his shoulder at Cassie. "What does she taste like, I wonder."

Before Giovanni could respond, Alric was bending over Cassie's neck, his fangs tearing into the soft, tender skin of her throat.

"No!" Giovanni lunged forward and slammed his shoulder into Alric, driving him away from the bed.

Alric let out a roar of outrage as he spun on his heel. A wave of his hand sent Giovanni crashing into the far wall. He gestured at his two revenants. Moving like wooden soldiers, they each grabbed one of Giovanni's arms and dragged him across the floor. One of them took hold of a rope that dangled from the ceiling and dropped it around his neck while the second man fastened his shackles to a thick iron ring in the wall. The rope had been fashioned into a noose and dipped in silver.

Alric padded toward him, Cassie's blood smeared on his lips. "You shouldn't have done that," he said, sneering. A word removed Giovanni's shirt. Then, hands curled into claws, Alric raked his nails down Giovanni's chest and arms, opening long gashes several inches deep.

Giovanni sucked in a breath as pain splintered through him, adding to the agony of the silver binding his wrists and blistering the skin on his neck. The silver, the loss of blood, left him feeling lightheaded and weak.

And from far away, he heard Alric's voice.

"So, pretty lady, what shall I do with you? If I drink you dry, you will please me, but only for a few moments. If I bring you across, you'll entertain me for decades, perhaps centuries."

Giovanni sobbed a strangled, "No!"

But Alric only laughed before sinking his fangs into the side of Cassie's neck again.

Mara came to an abrupt halt as she lost track of Giovanni. One minute she'd had his scent and the next it was gone.

"Damn Alric," she hissed.

"What happened?" Logan asked, skidding to a stop beside her.

"I lost him. Alric has mastered some kind of shield that blocks us from finding him."

"How the hell did he manage that?"

"How should I know?" She frowned. "Giovanni thought he might have sought Angelica's help."

"Would she do that?"

"I don't know. She told me Alric had been in touch with her a couple of times when he was trying to find out where I live. Maybe she concocted a talisman of some kind for him."

Logan shook his head. "Why would she help him? Hell, she'd be a fool to make an enemy out of you."

Mara grunted softly. "There are other witches."

"If it's you he wants, why take Cassie? Or Lanzoni, for that matter? Sheree told him where to find you."

"Maybe he's not after me anymore. Or maybe he just lost his nerve."

"He's always been the impetuous type, acting before he thinks. Why would he be so cautious now?"

She gave him a quelling look. "Maybe he finally realized I can put an end to his miserable existence like that," she said with a snap of her fingers. "Any day of the week."

"Is that so? How about tonight?"

She glared at him. "I think I'm right on several counts. One, Alric has always been a coward. Two, he has a grudge against Giovanni. Three, he knows that hurting our priest would hurt me, too. Four, I'm sure he's employed a witch."

Logan snorted. "If what you say is true, he's dumber than I thought. He has to know if he kills Lanzoni, he'll have you to answer to. Not to mention the rest of the family."

Cassie groaned as she struggled to sit up. She'd had the world's worst nightmare. Rubbing the sleep from her eyes, she wondered why it was still dark. And then she realized it hadn't been a nightmare. She was in the same dark room she'd awoken in before. The air felt thick and heavy, like an invisible blanket weighing her down. It made her feel sluggish.

Alarmed, she glanced around, but she couldn't see a blessed thing. Where were Alric and his goons? And Johnny? Where was he? Was he still here? Still alive? Or had Alric killed him while she was unconscious?

It took her a moment to realize she was no longer tied to the bed. Sitting up, she cocked her head to the side. Was it day or night? Was she alone?

Swinging her feet over the edge of the cot, she stood on shaky legs. Then, blindly reaching out in front of her, she moved slowly forward until she touched a wall. If she remembered correctly, the room was totally empty save for the cot.

Step by slow step she made her way around the room, searching for the door, even though she was sure it would be locked. And it was. She kept going, then let out a startled cry when she tripped over something. She gasped when her hand hit a leg. It didn't move at her touch. Was it Johnny? Had Alric killed him and left his body behind? Or was he just trapped in the Dark Sleep of his kind? Not dead, only at rest.

She shuddered at the thought as she ran her fingers tentatively up his thigh to his shoulder, then to his neck. She gasped as she touched his skin, which felt raw and blistered, cursed when she felt the noose. As carefully as she could, she lifted it over his head, then tied a loop in the rope to keep it out of the way.

They needed to get out of here, but how? There were no windows. The only door was locked. Giovanni was bound with silver and helpless. She felt weak from the blood the vampire had taken from her. She lifted a shaky hand to her throat. Was she a vampire now? But no. If she was, she, too, would be trapped in the deathlike sleep.

Tired and discouraged, she rested her head on Johnny's shoulder and surrendered to the misery that engulfed her. She was hungry and afraid—afraid that Alric would kill Johnny, afraid of what he might do to her. She tried to think positively, to cling to some shred of hope, but there was none in sight.

The sound of Cassie's tears roused Giovanni from the Dark Sleep. "*Cara?*"

Sniffling, she sat up. "Is it night already?"

"No. Are you all right?"

"I'm fine," she lied. He had enough to worry about. It grieved her to know he was in pain and that it was her fault. If not for her, he wouldn't be here now. She bit down on her lower lip. She could help him, if she had the courage. "Johnny?"

"What?"

"I want you to drink from me."

"Are you out of your mind?" The chain binding him to the wall rattled as he struggled to a sitting position.

"I know you're hurting. I want to help." She forced a smile into her voice. "No sense both of us being hungry. Besides, it will make you stronger, won't it?"

"Yes." He forced the word through clenched teeth.

"Then do it." She held out her arm, knowing he could see it, even though the room was dark.

Giovanni closed his eyes. Took a deep breath. "Don't let me drink for more than a few seconds," he warned. And bent his head toward her wrist.

With his hands shackled, he couldn't get a good grip on her arm, which was a good thing, Cassie thought as she felt his bite. She counted to ten, then jerked her arm away.

He growled in protest, then murmured, "Thank you." Knowing how she must feel, trapped in the dark, he summoned what little power he had and turned on the bare light bulb that dangled from the ceiling.

Murmuring, "Oh, Johnny," she burst into tears. Besides the awful blisters on his neck, she could see dried blood down the length of his chest and both arms. What had Alric done to him?

"It's not as bad as it looks," he said.

"Liar." She glanced around the room. "How are we going to get out of here?"

"I wish I knew." His gaze moved over her face. Her fear was a palpable thing. Not that he could blame her. She was trapped in a room with a hungry vampire and at the mercy of another one.

Sighing, he closed his eyes.

Today was to have been their wedding day.

Chapter 38

Mara paced the floor in the living room, oblivious to the fact that the sun was high in the sky. What sort of voodoo was Alric practicing that kept her from discovering his whereabouts? She cursed softly, wishing she'd had occasion to take his blood. Perhaps then she would have been able to find him—regardless of whatever magic was blocking her.

She should have killed the cur centuries ago.

She glared at Logan when he started to speak. Smart man that he was, he closed his mouth.

Earlier, she had contacted the rest of the family to let them know what was going on and that the wedding was off.

She had also called Angelica to see what she knew, but the witch denied having given Alric any kind of talisman or spell and offered to use her magic to see if she could locate Giovanni.

"Damn," Mara muttered as she sank down on the sofa beside Logan. "Damn, damn, damn. If I get my hands on Alric, I swear I'll tear him to shreds."

"And I'll help you," he said. "But first we have to find him."

Chapter 39

Cassie paced the floor, too worried to sit still. From time to time, she tried the door, even though she knew it was locked. Once, out of sheer frustration, she pounded her fists against it, then kicked it, but it remained stubbornly closed, and all she had to show for her efforts were a couple of bloody knuckles.

She prowled the room, hoping to find a weapon, but there was nothing to find. Just a lumpy cot with no pillow and no blanket.

Discouraged, she sank down on the floor beside Johnny. "We're never going to get out of here, are we?"

"Don't give up, *cara mia,*" he murmured. "There's always hope."

"Is there?" She stared at him through haunted eyes. "He's going to kill you and drink me dry, isn't he?"

"I imagine that's his plan, although I can't blame him for wanting to 'drink you dry,' as you put it. Heaven knows I've thought about it myself from time to time."

"Well, if someone's going to do it, I'd rather it was you."

He laughed then, though there was little humor in the

sound. "I love you, Cassie. I'm sorry I got you into this mess."

She rested her head on his shoulder, her fingers absently toying with a lock of his hair. "I'm sorry *I* got *you* into this mess."

"This isn't your doing, *cara*. And who knows, we might see the other side of this yet."

"I don't see how."

"I don't, either," he admitted and then frowned as a new thought took shape in the back of his mind. The building was warded against supernatural creatures. It had blocked his thoughts and prevented Mara from connecting with him.

But Cassie was mortal.

Sitting up straighter, he said, "I have an idea."

"What is it? Tell me."

"I want you to drink my blood."

"What! How is that going to help?"

"It might not, but it's worth a try. Alric has cast some kind of preternatural ward around this place to keep supernatural creatures from contacting each other. I can't contact Mara and she can't locate me. But you're not a vampire or a witch. If you drink my blood, there's a chance, however slim, that if you reach out to her with your mind, she might hear you. Are you willing to give it a shot?"

"At this point, I'm willing to try anything. But if Alric has somehow blocked you from contacting Mara, won't whatever it is block her from contacting me?"

"There's always that chance. If it was anyone but Mara, I wouldn't even try. What do you say?"

"Where should I"—she grimaced at the thought— "bite you?"

"You don't have to." Lifting his arms, he bit into his left wrist, just above the cuff of the shackle.

Cassie stared at the dark red blood that oozed from the two tiny wounds. Then, unable to believe what she was about to do, she leaned forward and lapped it up. It sizzled through her like liquid lightning.

"That's enough."

She was surprisingly reluctant to stop.

"Are you all right?" he asked, his gaze moving over her face.

"I think so. I feel sort of . . ." She shook her head. "I don't know how to describe it. So, what do I do now?"

"Focus on Mara. Try to call her."

Cassie bowed her head as though in prayer. Closing her eyes, she pictured the vampire in her mind. *Mara. We need you. Please come and find us. Please.*

A minute passed.

Two.

Shoulders slumped, Cassie said. "Nothing. It didn't work."

He swore softly as the seconds ticked by. Dammit, Mara was their only hope.

Cassie? Are you with Giovanni?

Yes! "She heard me!" Cassie exclaimed.

Keep your mind focused on me. I'm on my way.

"She's coming!" Cassie threw her arms around Johnny. "She's coming!"

She had barely spoken the words when the door flew off its hinges and crashed into the wall. A shimmer of power exploded through the room like a blast of hot air, and then Mara and Logan appeared in the doorway, bathed in sunlight.

"I've never been so glad to see anyone in my life," Giovanni said. "Get us the hell out of here."

"The threshold, combined with whatever spell he's using, is keeping us out. But I don't think it's warded to keep *you* in, so you'll have to come to us." Mara gestured for Cassie to join her.

"No, I'm not leaving Johnny."

"We won't. Now come here."

Reluctantly, Cassie crossed the threshold and stood beside Logan.

She shivered as Mara's power coalesced around them.

Eyes narrowed, Mara focused on the shackles connected to the chain in the wall. Power thrummed through the air, sending shivers down Cassie's spine. There was an audible *crack* as the shackles broke in half.

Giovanni struggled to his feet, then staggered toward the door. Pain ripped through him like shards of glass when he stepped across the threshold.

"Let's get out of here," Mara said. "Logan, bring Cassie."

With a nod, Logan wrapped his arms around her.

Mara glanced at Giovanni. "You look like hell. Are you ready?"

"More than ready."

She winked at him as she slipped her arm around his waist.

In moments, the four of them materialized in Mara's living room.

Giovanni sank down on the sofa, leaned back, and closed his eyes.

Cassie stared at Johnny. The skin around his neck was red and blistered, as was the skin on his wrists. She couldn't imagine the pain he was in.

With a low groan, he opened his eyes and glanced at Mara and Logan. "I owe you one," he said. "Both of you."

"You're welcome." Mara sat beside him and offered him her arm. "Drink. You'll feel better."

Nodding, he bent his head to her wrist. Her blood was ancient. In an instant, it flooded him with strength and preternatural power, and he lost himself in the warmth of it. He felt Mara's power move through him, healing the blistered skin on his neck, easing the pain of the silver burns on his wrists, healing the gashes in his arms and chest.

Cassie watched in amazement as his wounds healed. She could see the strength flowing into him as he drank. And drank. The blisters on his skin disappeared, the red fading from pink to nothing. The scars on his wrists also disappeared. How was that possible? He had told her silver left nasty scars.

"Enough," Mara said.

Giovanni clutched her arm tighter, wanting more. Wanting it all.

"Enough!"

Reluctantly, he released her. "Sorry," he muttered, embarrassed by his need, his lack of control.

She smiled at him. "No need to be sorry." She well knew the power of her blood on those of her kind. "Cassie, why don't you go run some water in the tub? I'm sure Giovanni would like to get cleaned up. Logan, see if you can find him something to wear."

Nodding, Cassie left the room.

Logan followed her.

"I can't believe you found us," Giovanni said, a note of wonder in his voice. "Even when I told Cassie to try to contact you, I didn't think it would work. I felt the wards around the place. They were incredibly strong, and not all his." He shook his head. "How *did* you get through them?"

Mara tilted her head to the side, her expression a trifle smug. And then she grinned. "To tell you the truth, I have no idea."

"What?"

"You heard me. I think my powers have grown stronger because I've tasted Logan's blood, and yours, and that of other vampires. And that of witches, too, now and then, though their blood is vile. Over time, I think drinking from others of our kind has somehow magnified my own power, making it even stronger. As for how I was able to respond to Cassie, I have no idea. It shouldn't have been possible." She shrugged. "Perhaps it's because she's mortal. She drank from you and you've tasted both of us."

Giovanni grunted softly. It was as good an explanation as any. He smiled when he heard Cassie's footsteps in the hallway.

She smiled tentatively. "The tub's almost full."

Giovanni stood, stretching his back and shoulders. Crossing the room, he took Cassie in his arms and kissed her. "I told you," he said, jerking his chin toward Mara. "There's always hope."

Mara's bathroom was the size of a master bedroom. It held a stall shower big enough for three, as well as an oval tub. Both had gold faucets.

Giovanni took a quick shower, rinsing the dried blood from his chest and arms before he sank into the bathtub. He lingered there until the water grew cool, then, wearing his briefs and a pair of Logan's gray sweatpants that he found on the bed, he strolled into the living room. Mara and Logan sat on the sofa with their heads together. "Where's Cassie?"

"She fell asleep on the sofa while you were getting cleaned up," Mara said. "Logan put her to bed in the guest room."

Giovanni didn't like the sound of that.

Mara grinned as a muscle throbbed in Giovanni's jaw. "Relax. He *put* her to bed. He didn't *take* her to bed."

"A subtle difference." Giovanni dropped into an overstuffed chair and stretched his legs out in front of him.

"How are you feeling?" Logan asked.

"I'm all right. There's nothing like a little ancient blood to cure what ails you, as well you know."

Logan nodded. "It's like the Fountain of Youth."

Mara grinned at her husband.

"I want him, Mara," Giovanni said. "I want to tear him apart."

"You'll have to get in line," Logan muttered.

"That line forms behind me," Giovanni said. "If I can't take him down, then you two can have a try at him. Dammit! He drank from Cassie. For that alone, I'm going to rip out his heart and shove it down his throat."

"You'll have to find him first," Logan remarked.

"Yeah. I never should have let Mara break the link between him and me."

Mara looked thoughtful. "So, Alric drank from Cassie."

"Didn't I just say that?" Giovanni snapped. And then he frowned. "I wonder . . . ?"

"Are you thinking what I'm thinking?" she asked.

"I think so."

Logan frowned. "Wait a minute." He glanced from one to the other. "Are you suggesting that one of you could drink from Cassie and somehow track Alric?"

"I've already taken Cassie's blood since Alric bit her," Giovanni said. "I drank from her before you rescued us."

"Why didn't you say so before?" Mara asked. "Have you tried to locate Alric?"

"No. I had other things on my mind."

"Well, it's worth a try, don't you think? Unless you've got a better idea."

Giovanni shook his head. Closing his eyes, he summoned Alric's image. Concentrating, he tried to connect the blood bond he shared with Cassie to the one Alric had with her. "Nothing," he muttered after several moments.

"Maybe if you drink from her again it would strengthen the bond," Logan suggested.

Giovanni grunted softly. "Maybe." Although he was afraid he might have to take more blood than she could spare to accomplish it. "This isn't getting us anywhere," he said, getting to his feet. "I think I'll turn in while there's still a few hours of daylight left."

"We'll get him," Mara said.

"One way or another," Logan added.

Giovanni nodded, praying they were right.

He found Cassie in the guest room, sound asleep, her cheek pillowed on her hand, her hair spread over her shoulder like a river of sun-kissed silk. After removing his sweatpants, he slid under the covers and gathered her in his arms, sighed as her familiar scent enveloped him.

Closing his eyes, he whispered, "He won't get his hands on you again," as he surrendered to the Dark Sleep.

Alric swore every vile oath he knew in several languages as he stared at the open door. He didn't have to go inside to know the woman and the priest were gone, or that Mara had once again thwarted him. How? How had she found this place? He had warded it himself, using his own powers and that of a Black Witch, and yet Mara had breached both.

He swore again, hating her for making him feel incompetent. He was a Master Vampire. He had caused pain and suffering throughout the world. Others of his kind feared him, mortals trembled in his presence. And yet Mara and the priest viewed him with nothing but contempt.

Filled with rage, he transported himself to the next town where he vented his anger and frustration on the first mortal who had the misfortune to cross his path.

Chapter 40

Cassie woke with a start. The room was pitch-black and for a moment, she thought she was still trapped in that dreadful place, at Alric's mercy. Then she realized the windows were covered with blackout curtains, the bed beneath her soft and warm, and Johnny rested beside her.

The clock on the bedside table read 12:35 P.M. Cassie frowned as she realized she'd been asleep since late yesterday afternoon. Why had Johnny let her sleep so long? Not that she was complaining. After the events of yesterday, she had been exhausted mentally and physically.

Rolling onto her side, Cassie spent several minutes just looking at him, her heart swelling with love for the amazing man who had turned her life upside down and showed her a world she had never dreamed existed. Yes, there was fear and danger and pain in that world, but also wonder and laughter and the most amazing man she had ever known. He had taught her the meaning of love, given her renewed purpose, made her feel that anything was possible.

If she had never met Johnny, she would still be schlepping drinks at the Winchester Lounge, living in that squalid apartment, with no real hope of a better future. Now, she had a man who loved her and a chance of achieving her dream of becoming a hairstylist and maybe one day owning her own salon. It might not be as grand an ambition as finding a cure for cancer or saving the world, but it was something she had dreamed of ever since she was a little girl. She remembered the day when her mother—sober for a change—had taken her to the beauty shop with her. Cassie had been fascinated as she watched a pretty young woman cut and style her mother's hair, transforming a thick mass of unruly dishwater blond curls into gentle golden-blond waves.

Slipping quietly out of bed, Cassie tiptoed into the bathroom to shower and dress, then padded into the living room. The drapes were drawn against the sun's light, the house as quiet as a tomb.

An unfortunate choice of words, she thought, yet totally apropos, as three vampires rested within its walls.

Her stomach growled, reminding her that she hadn't eaten since Alric had abducted her. Wondering what the chances were of finding food in Mara's house, she wandered into the kitchen. There was a note on the refrigerator.

Cassie, there's food in the fridge and the cupboard. Make yourself at home.

Cassie grinned. Whatever else Mara might be, she was a thoughtful hostess. Rummaging through the cupboards, she found a jar of instant coffee, strawberry jam, and a loaf of bread. The refrigerator yielded butter, eggs, and bacon, as well as sandwich makings.

She quickly fixed something to eat, then sat at the

kitchen table, gazing out the sliding glass door. The backyard was lush and green, the hill thick with pine trees. Her wedding day had come and gone, she thought morosely, and wondered if anyone had notified Mara's family or the minister at the church.

She liked the women she had met at the shower. None of them seemed to regret being changed, not even the ones who hadn't had a choice in the matter. Frowning, she wondered what the circumstances had been that caused their husbands to turn them. She was curious to know what they missed the most, and if the ones who had made the decision to be turned would make the same choice again. So many questions she needed answers to before she reached the age when her own choice would have to be made.

So many questions—most importantly, where was Alric? Just his name sent an icy chill down her spine.

And no answers, she thought, as she tidied up the kitchen.

In the living room, Cassie drew back the heavy drapes from the balcony door. Hours until nightfall. What was she going to do until then?

She perused the bookshelves. Numerous volumes on ancient history and Egypt. Current novels. Books on evolution, geology, physics, reincarnation, ghosts and ghost towns, science, numerology. The variety was astounding.

She thumbed through a book on ancient Egypt, wondering how much of its history Mara had seen firsthand. Returning the book to the shelf, Cassie reached for the latest novel by C. S. Harris, who was one of her favorite authors.

Carrying the book out onto the balcony, she sat in one

of the deck chairs and lost herself in the latest adventures of Viscount Devlin, one of her favorite literary heroes.

"Enjoying the book?"

Cassie glanced up, startled, at the sound of Mara's voice. "Yes, very much."

Mara stepped onto the deck, pulled a chair into the shade and sat down across from her. "How are you feeling?"

"Much better." Closing the book, Cassie set it on the wrought-iron table beside her chair. "Can I ask you something?"

"If you like."

"Johnny told me silver left scars on vampire flesh, yet when he drank from you, the burns healed without a trace."

"Ordinarily, it does leave a nasty reminder. But my blood is old and powerful, as is his. The combination is potent. I wasn't sure it would erase the scars, but I knew it would heal his body and ease his pain."

"I'm glad you're his friend. It hurt me to watch him suffer."

"You do love him, don't you?"

"Yes, very much. He's the most wonderful man I've ever known."

"He has his moments," Mara said, smiling. "The family sends its regrets over the postponement of your wedding. Are you going to reschedule it?"

"I don't know."

The vampire arched one delicate brow. "Have you changed your mind?"

"No. But I think I'd like to wait until this trouble with Alric is settled one way or another."

"I see. Well, I guess I can't blame you." Mara stared out over the balcony. "I should have destroyed him years ago."

"Why didn't you?"

"I guess maybe I felt a little guilty for killing his woman," Mara replied with a shrug. "Not that she didn't deserve it. She betrayed both of us. I tried to tell him the truth but he wouldn't listen. If he would put his hatred aside for five minutes and remember what actually happened, he would be thanking me."

"What *did* happen?"

"I first met Alric in Transylvania hundreds of years ago. It was a chance encounter. We hunted together one night and then parted. I ran into him again decades later in Istanbul. He was madly in love with some exotic dancer he'd met. I warned him not to trust her. There was something off about Calidora, though I couldn't put my finger on it. Alric and I had rented a small house. He must have told her where we rested during the day, most likely while sharing her bed. As it turned out, the love of his life gave our location to a hunter who just happened to be her husband. Alric took off like the coward he is while I dispatched the hunter. I found Calidora waiting for her husband outside."

Cassie swallowed. "And you killed her?"

"Indeed. With a great deal of pleasure."

"And that's what this feud is all about?"

"More or less. He also has some minor issues with Giovanni. Speak of the devil," she murmured, "and he appears."

Cassie glanced up as Johnny stepped outside, felt her insides melt when he smiled at her. Hard to believe he had been bruised and battered only hours before.

Leaning down, he kissed her cheek. "Looks like you had a good night's sleep, love."

She nodded, conscious of Mara watching them, a slight smile curving her lips.

"I'll leave you two young lovers alone," Mara said. "I think I hear Logan calling my name." Rising, she glanced from Giovanni to Cassie, her expression inscrutable. "Be good to each other."

Cassie stared after the vampire. She was a fascinating woman, even if she was a little scary. What would it be like, to be that old, to have such power?

"Everything okay?" Johnny asked, taking Mara's chair.

"She was telling me about Alric and why he's so angry."

"Ah. I heard you tell Mara that you don't want to set a new date for the wedding."

"Then you must have heard my answer."

"I guess I can't blame you."

"But you're disappointed?"

"A little." He reached for her hand and gave it a squeeze. "But I understand. As long as the trouble with Alric is the only reason."

She glanced down at the ring on her finger. "What else would it be?"

"I don't know." His gaze searched hers. "You tell me."

"It's all just happened so fast," she said, the words pouring out of her. "I was terrified when Alric took me to that place and then he bit me and I was so afraid he was going to turn me and then I saw what he'd done to you, how he'd hurt you, and I thought he was going to kill you and . . ." Unable to help herself, she burst into tears.

"Cassie, Cassie." He lifted her from her chair onto his lap and held her tight, one hand stroking her back while she sobbed. What had he done to her? Every tear she shed was like acid in his soul. "Cassie," he begged, "please don't cry."

"I . . . I can't help it."

"I know." Resting his chin on the top of her head, he stared into the distance. He could erase her memories, starting from the night they'd met, with no more than a thought. She would forget him, forget every fear, everything Alric had done to her.

He looked up when he sensed Mara standing in the doorway.

She shook her head at him. *Don't do anything rash, Giovanni,* she warned. *Once erased, you cannot replace her memories, and they're not all bad. Be sure before you do something you'll regret.*

Meeting her gaze, he nodded that he understood.

When Cassie's sobs subsided, he dried her eyes with a towel that had been thrown over the back of a chair.

"I didn't mean to cry all over you," she said, sniffing. "Your shirt's all wet."

"It will dry soon enough." He paused to collect his thoughts. "Cassie, are you sorry we met?"

"What? Of course not! Is that what you think?"

"I don't know what to think. If you could wipe away the last few months, would you?"

She stared at him, her brow furrowed. "What are you saying?"

He raked his fingers through his hair. "I can make you forget we ever met. Make you forget everything, if that's what you want."

"You can do that?"

"Yes. If you want me to."

Cassie's gaze slid away from his. Was that what she

wanted? To forget she'd ever met him? She thought of how he had come to her defense in the park, walked her home nights to be sure she was safe. He had killed Lynx and his friends to protect her, offered her the hospitality of his home, given her a chance to fulfill her childhood dream. Made her feel loved, cherished, important. Did she want to throw all that away because some dumb vampire carried a grudge?

She looked into his eyes, beautiful hazel eyes filled with soul-deep sadness as he waited for her answer, and knew she could never leave him. He needed her.

And she needed him.

"No, Johnny," she said quietly. "I don't want to forget anything."

"Cassie!" His arms tightened around her as he buried his face against her shoulder.

She stroked his hair, her heart aching when she felt his tears against her skin. "I love you," she murmured. "Nothing Alric or anyone else can do will ever change that."

Clearing his throat, he said, "You're a brave woman, Cassie Douglas."

"I don't know about that."

"I do."

"When can we go home?"

He blew out a sigh. With all that had happened, he'd never gotten around to telling her that the house was gone.

"Johnny?"

"Alric burned it down."

"What? When?"

"The night you were abducted."

Cassie stared at him. The house was gone—and with it, everything she owned. She thought of all the lovely nightgowns she had received, the few new clothes she'd bought since moving in with Johnny. Her beautiful wedding gown. It wasn't much, to be sure, and none of it had probably cost as much as the black velvet pantsuit Mara had lent her to wear today. Still, it was everything she owned in the world.

"No wonder everybody hates him," she muttered. "Well, he can add my name to the top of the list!"

Chapter 41

"The girl has spunk," Mara said. "I like her."

"You do seem to have a soft spot for her."

Lying face down on their bed, she purred as Logan's hands moved over her back in long, lazy strokes. "That feels so good."

Bending forward, he ran his tongue along her spine. "I can think of something that will make you feel even better."

"I'll bet you can, but for now, I'd rather have those clever hands right where they are."

Logan grunted softly. "Why do you really think Alric hasn't come here? It's been a while since Sheree told him where we live."

"I told you—he's a coward. He doesn't have the guts to come here and face me on my own turf."

"Then why did he want to know where to find you?"

Frowning, she rolled onto her side. "I think that once he knew where I was, what little courage he had deserted him. It's one thing to strut around thinking you're the top dog when there's no one to challenge you. He knows I can beat him. Or maybe he intends to burn me out, the way he did Giovanni."

Logan sat on the edge of the bed, his fingers sifting through the wealth of her hair. "I guess the ball's in his court. He knows where you live. He's taken Cassie's blood, so he can track her whereabouts anytime he feels like it. I don't know what kind of game he's playing, but I'm ready to end it."

"Maybe we need to set a trap."

He snorted. "With Cassie as the bait? What makes you think the good Father will let you put the love of his life in harm's way?"

"I'm not sure that I'll tell him."

"What nasty little plan are you hatching inside that pretty head of yours?" he asked, tugging on a lock of her hair.

"Rane and Savannah have gone to Italy on vacation. They'll be away a month or so. What if we sent Cassie and Giovanni to stay at their place? The ranch house is sur-rounded by miles of open country where you and the rest of the family can hide. It'll be easy enough to make it look like Cassie's alone at night while Giovanni is supposedly out hunting. Once Alric goes into the house, you and the others will mask your presence and surround the place. We have enough power among us to keep him inside."

"What's to stop Alric from simply transporting out of there and taking Cassie with him?"

"She won't be alone. Giovanni will be there."

"It'll never work. Alric might be a coward but he isn't stupid."

"I know. It's a risk. But I still think it's a good plan."

* * *

After spending three days and nights at Mara's place, Cassie was ready to go home, even though they had nowhere to go. Mara and Logan were great company, the house was beautiful, but it wasn't home. And she didn't feel comfortable sleeping with Johnny under Mara's roof. It was disconcerting knowing Logan and the Queen of the Vampires could easily overhear everything they said. Or did. Plus, the days were long and boring. She had been forbidden to leave the safety of the house and honestly, how many books or movies could anyone read or watch in a day?

Standing on the balcony, gazing out over the city, she wondered where she and Johnny would live once Alric was no longer a threat. They couldn't stay here forever. And if Alric was after Mara, wouldn't they be safer somewhere else? Then again, maybe not, since he apparently had a grudge against Johnny, too.

The thought brought her up short. Alric had taken her blood. That meant he could track her. And since she was here with Johnny and Mara . . . she was putting them in danger, too.

For a moment, she considered running away, but that would be utterly foolhardy. Alric had used her as bait once before. He wouldn't hesitate to do it again.

So, what if Johnny used her as bait to trap Alric?

It was a scary thought, but what if it was the only way?

"Forget it," Johnny said when she suggested it that night. "It's too dangerous."

"We have to do something," Cassie said, pacing the bedroom floor. "How else are you going to find him? I might as well be in prison, for all the freedom I have here.

You go out in search of prey but I'm trapped inside all day and all night. I'm going stir-crazy!"

He snagged her arm as she passed by the bed and drew her down on his lap. "I know you're bored and frustrated, love, but I don't know what I'd do if I lost you."

Sighing, she rested her head on his shoulder. "Maybe we could go shopping tonight. I don't have anything to wear except what Mara lends me. You need some clothes, too."

"Yeah." It was Friday night. They should be safe enough inside a busy mall. He could transport them there and back. Even Alric wasn't foolish enough to make a scene in public.

"We'll go with you," Mara said when Giovanni informed her that he and Cassie were going out for the evening.

He glared at her. "Thanks, but I don't need a babysitter."

"I never said you did. But there's safety in numbers. You won't even know we're there."

"Would it do me any good to tell you to stay home?"

She smiled at him. "What do *you* think?"

Mara was as good as her word. If she'd followed them into the department store in the mall, Giovanni couldn't sense her presence, or Logan's either.

He stayed close to Cassie as she selected several pairs of jeans and T-shirts. He tried to look nonchalant as he followed her through the lingerie department, where she added a nightgown and robe, as well as a couple of lacy

bras and bikini panties to her inventory. He stood behind
her chair as she tried on shoes and boots.

Cassie looked up at him, eyes wide, at the cash register.
"What was I thinking? I can't pay for all this. I lost my
purse when Alric kidnapped me." She shook her head. She
had been so caught up in everything else, she hadn't even
missed her phone.

"It's okay, *cara,* it's on me." He pulled a credit card from
his wallet and handed it to the clerk.

"I'm going to have to get a new driver's license," Cassie
muttered. "And I should have reported that my credit cards
were lost days ago."

He grunted softly, thinking he needed to contact the
company that insured his house. "You can take care of all
that when we get back to Mara's."

"Damn Alric. Going to the DMV is a pain in the butt."

Their next stop was the men's department. It took
Johnny far less time to pick out jeans, shirts, and underwear.

Their last stop was the jewelry department, where he
told her to pick out a new crucifix, one with an extra heavy
silver chain. She put it on while he paid for it.

When he heard Cassie's stomach growl, he insisted on
getting her something to eat. Loaded down with several
bags, they made their way to the food court on the second
floor.

"What are you in the mood for?" he asked.

"A double cheeseburger with everything on it, fries, and
a strawberry shake."

They had just found a vacant table when Giovanni
sensed they were being watched. He turned his head slowly
from side to side. Expecting it to be Mara, he swore under

his breath when he spied Alric standing half-hidden behind a large potted plant.

The minute he made eye contact with the vampire, Alric vanished.

"What's the matter?" Cassie asked, noting the sudden tension in his jaw.

Giovanni shook his head. "It's a little unnerving, all these beating hearts in one place," he lied.

"We can go if you like. I can take this with me and eat it at Mara's."

"It's all right. Take your time."

When they returned to Mara's, Cassie headed to the guest room to take a shower and get ready for bed.

Giovanni strolled onto the balcony, where he stood looking out over the city, his hands wrapped around the rail, his knuckles white.

"We saw him, too," Mara said, coming to stand beside him.

"When we get him, just remember he's mine."

He had expected an argument, but she merely nodded. "I don't have a problem with that."

"I just wish I knew what he's thinking," Giovanni muttered. "Alric knows how to find Cassie. Why hasn't he done anything? What's he waiting for?"

"Trying to find his nerve, no doubt," Mara said. "Or maybe he knows that the waiting is making us all a little crazy."

Giovanni grunted. "If that's his game, it's working. I heard you talking to Logan about taking Cassie to Rane's place." He grinned when she arched one brow. "You're not the only one who eavesdrops now and then. I think it might work."

"The only problem is, you might have to stay there for an indefinite amount of time," Mara said, her brow furrowed thoughtfully. "There's no way of knowing if he'll even go looking for her. Or when."

Giovanni scrubbed a hand over his jaw. "Do you trust Angelica?"

"Most of the time. Why?"

"I think she once had feelings for Alric."

"What makes you say that?"

"Just a hunch. Something in the way she said his name."

"Alric asked her where to find me a while back but she refused to tell him," Mara said, her brow furrowed thoughtfully. "Probably because she's more afraid of me than of him."

"What if you meet her for drinks and let it slip that Savannah and Rane are out of town and I'm taking Cassie to the ranch for a few days. Do you think she'd tell him?"

"She might, but what's the point? He's taken Cassie's blood. He can easily track her."

"I know, but he wants me, too. Maybe knowing Cassie and I are alone out in the middle of nowhere will bring him to us."

"It might work," Mara said, green eyes glittering.

"And if it doesn't, Cassie and I will have a nice vacation."

Mara grinned at him. "And if it doesn't, we'll think of something else."

"And we'll keep thinking," Giovanni said, his voice little more than a growl, "until I take his head and his heart and burn what's left."

* * *

The next night, Mara sent a group text to Derek, Nick, Rafe, Roshan, Vince, Pearl and Edna Mae. She filled them in on what was happening with Alric and asked them to meet her at the Cordova ranch the following Saturday night. They should plan to stay there as long as necessary and pack accordingly.

"Do you really think we'll need the whole family to take him down?" Giovanni asked.

"Yes, because I don't think he'll come alone. No matter what Angelica tells him, he'll likely suspect a trap of some sort and bring his minions to spring it. He may not be smart or brave, but he's as cunning as the devil himself. I'll get in touch with Angelica in the morning," Mara said, thinking out loud. "The family will meet you at the ranch next Saturday. If you leave tomorrow night, you'll have a week to settle in and get the lay of the land," she said briskly. "The rest is up to you."

Giovanni grunted. All he had to do was convince Cassie that going to stay at Rane's place in Northern California was the smart thing to do. It shouldn't be too hard, he thought. After all, she had offered to be bait not long ago.

He just hoped she hadn't changed her mind.

Cassie felt her heart skip a beat when she saw Johnny sitting on the bed beside the nightgown she had laid out. She clutched the towel wrapped around her. Although they had made love before, she felt awkward—and a little shy—standing there practically naked while he was fully dressed.

"You smell good," he said, getting to his feet.

"Like blood?" she asked warily.

Laughing softly, he took her in his arms. "No. Like fresh air and sunshine."

She rested her head on his chest. Being in his embrace made her feel safe, as though nothing could ever harm her again.

His lips moved in her hair, and then he said, "I've missed holding you close, making love to you."

"Me, too." She looked up at him. "Do you think we'll ever be alone again?"

The perfect opening, he thought. "What would you think of going to the Cordova ranch up in Northern California?"

"Is it safe?"

"As safe as anywhere else," he said.

"But Alric drank from me. Doesn't that mean he can track me?"

"Yeah, depending on how strong the link is between you. I've taken your blood, too, so there's a chance it's weakened your connection to him. There's no way to know."

"So, this is a trap?"

"Hopefully one that will work. The ranch is a long way from here. The house sits on ten acres of land surrounded by timbered hills. There are no neighbors nearby. I can ward the house against intruders. I doubt if he'll try anything during the day. And if he gets close, I should be able to sense his presence." *He hoped.*

Cassie bit down on her lower lip. Now that Johnny had taken her up on her offer to bait a trap, she wasn't sure she had the courage to go through with it.

She thought it over for several moments, then nodded. She liked Mara. She liked Logan.

But it was unsettling, being in the midst of so much power day and night. "How soon do you want to leave?"

"Tomorrow night as soon as the sun goes down."

Chapter 42

Pearl stared at Edna, then shook her head. "But I don't want to go to Northern California," she said adamantly. "I don't want to get anywhere near Alric again! I don't care what Mara says."

"Shh!" Edna glanced around as if expecting to see the Queen of the Vampires eavesdropping from the shadows. "I don't want to go near Alric, either. But I'd rather face him than have Mara mad at us."

"I know, dear, but . . ."

"There is no but," Edna Mae said, her voice sharp. "You do what you want, but I intend to stay on her good side."

"Oh, I guess you're right," Pearl muttered irritably. "I just hope we don't live to regret it."

"It's not the best reason to go to the ranch," Abbey Marie said, "but I do love it there. Plus, it's been a long time since I went riding."

"We're not going there on vacation," Nick said. "I'm pretty sure there will be death and destruction involved."

"Well, that's right up your alley, isn't it? I don't care why we're going. It's been too long since the last time I was home." The ranch held some of her happiest memories. "I wonder if Freckles will remember me." It had been a couple of years since she'd ridden the Appaloosa mare.

"I'm sure she will." Pulling Abbey into his arms, Nick kissed her until her toes curled. "How could anyone forget you?"

Derek frowned at his mother's text. It had been a long time since the clan had been together. Whoever their target was, he must be a dangerous character indeed if she needed help to defeat him. He flexed his shoulders. Lots of open space on the ranch, he thought, smiling in anticipation. A good place for the werewolf to run when the moon was full.

Vince Cordova tossed his phone on the bed, then strolled into the bathroom, where Cara was taking a shower. Knocking on the stall door, he said, "Mara wants us all at Rane's place next Saturday night."

"Doesn't she know they're out of town?"

"Of course, she knows," he retorted. "The woman knows everything." He laughed softly as his lovely wife muttered a very unladylike reply.

* * *

"We've never been to the ranch," Brenna said when Roshan told her about Mara's text. "It might be fun."

"Somehow I doubt it," he said, ruefully. "I think we'll be more likely to encounter murder and mayhem." He tugged on her ear. "Your witchy powers just might come in handy."

Chapter 43

Cassie was packed and reluctantly ready to go when Johnny rose the next night. Between them, they managed to hold on to their suitcases and each other. She closed her eyes as he whisked her through time and space. When she opened them again, she found herself standing in the middle of a large living room.

"It's lovely," she murmured. The walls were a pale gray, the carpet a deeper shade. Heavy drapes in a gray-and-white print covered the front windows. A dark leather, high-backed sofa, a love seat, and a pair of matching chairs were grouped around a mahogany coffee table in front of a white stone fireplace.

"Do you want to look around?"

With a nod, she dropped her suitcase next to his. A door to the left led to a kitchen. She was surprised and relieved to discover it came with all the regular appliances. A round oak table sat in front of a window that looked out on a side yard; dark granite covered a long counter. A washer and dryer could be seen through an open doorway.

A narrow hallway led from the living room to a den, what appeared to be a guest room, and a bathroom.

Back in the living room, Giovanni picked up their suitcases and led the way upstairs. Four bedrooms lined either side of a wide, carpeted hallway. The door to a fifth bedroom stood open at the end of the hall.

Cassie peeked into each of the rooms. Three of them were furnished with double beds, small desks, a chair, and a chest of drawers, the only differences being the wood finishes and the colors of the walls and bedspreads, one being beige, one sky blue, one sea green. The fourth room, larger than the others, had obviously belonged to a family member. It held a few high school mementos, a shelf of well-worn books, a photograph of a lovely young woman with dark brown hair astride an Appaloosa mare, and a pillow embroidered with the words, *I Love New York*.

"This must be Abbey Marie's old room," Giovanni said.

"Abbey Marie? Oh, right, I met her at Mara's the night of the shower."

He nodded.

The last room was the master bedroom. Cassie shook her head. "I think we should use one of the other ones."

"I'm sure Rane wouldn't mind."

"No, but his wife might. Bedrooms are intimate spaces, you know."

"Whatever you think best, *cara*. Pick one."

"The blue one, I guess. It has a nice view."

Giovanni carried their bags into the blue bedroom, set Cassie's on the floor at the foot of the bed, then started down the hall to the next room.

"Hey, where do you think you're going?" Cassie asked, following him into the hallway.

Pausing, he glanced over his shoulder. "I didn't know what you . . . if you . . . ?"

"I don't want to sleep alone if that's what you're wondering."

"I didn't want to make the decision for you."

Cassie shook her head. "Honestly, Johnny, how many times do I have to seduce you?"

Between one breath and the next, he dropped his suitcase, gathered her into his arms, and carried her into the blue bedroom. A whisper of power flooded the room and the next thing she knew, she was lying naked on the bed next to an equally naked, blatantly aroused male.

Lips twitching, she said, "One more time, I guess," and then gasped as he rose over her, eyes blazing with barely bridled desire as he captured her mouth with his.

She was drifting, floating on a calm sea after a hurricane, her whole body throbbing from the storm that had engulfed her. A storm named Johnny. Always before, he had been gentle, almost tentative. But not tonight. Tonight, he had made her his in a way no words, no wedding ceremony, could have done.

Eyes closed, she smiled when he kissed her cheek.

"Are you all right?" he asked, his voice husky.

"Hmm. More than all right." She looked up at him through heavy-lidded eyes.

His gaze searched hers. "I was afraid I'd hurt you."

"Oh, I hurt all right," she said, her eyes sparkling with merriment. "I can't wait for you to hurt me again."

* * *

It was long after midnight when Giovanni left the blue bedroom. Not wanting to wake Cassie, he went to take a shower in the downstairs bathroom. He couldn't stop smiling as the hot water sluiced down his back. They had made love before and it had always been amazing, but tonight . . . He shook his head. Tonight was beyond anything he had ever imagined.

After stepping out of the shower, he grabbed a towel, wrapped it around his waist, then strolled out onto the veranda. Overhead, millions of stars shared the night sky with a bright yellow moon. An indrawn breath carried the scents of grass and hay, sage and pine—and the faint stink of a dead animal. A slight movement caught his eyes. Glancing to the right, he saw a gray wolf slinking through the shadows. The wolf stopped. Hackles raised, it let out a low growl when it saw Giovanni. For an endless moment, his gaze met the wolf's—two predators, he thought with a wry grin, and wondered what the lobo would do if man suddenly became wolf. Would they fight, or run through the night together? Had he not been afraid of leaving Cassie alone in the house, he might have shape-shifted to satisfy his curiosity.

The wolf whined low in its throat, then lifted its head and howled at the moon. A half-dozen others answered his mournful cry before the animal melted into the shadows.

After taking a last look around, Giovanni returned to the house. Making sure that the doors and windows were locked, he warded the house against all comers, then willed himself upstairs and crawled into bed beside Cassie.

She made a soft, contented sound as he drew her body against his, her back to his front, his nose buried in the flowery fragrance of her hair.

Sighing her name, he tumbled into oblivion, one hand cupping her breast, a smile of contentment on his face.

Cassie woke with a start, wondering what had roused her. She frowned when she heard the unfamiliar noise again. Was that a horse? She grinned, thinking she shouldn't have been so surprised. They were at a ranch, after all. She had seen the barn from the bedroom window. Still, she hadn't expected to find any animals since the owners were on vacation. Of course, it was likely they had hired someone to look after the place in their absence.

Careful not to disturb Johnny, she slipped out of bed and took a quick shower, then grabbed her robe and went downstairs, hoping to find something to eat.

A note on the refrigerator informed her that there was food in the fridge and the cupboards. She smiled at Johnny's thoughtfulness, even as she wondered when he'd had time to shop.

With a shrug, she looked out the kitchen window while waiting for a pot of water to heat for coffee. In addition to the barn, there were a couple of corrals. A dozen or so chickens wandered around, clucking and pecking at the ground. Trees and rolling hills stretched away as far as the eye could see. And over all, a clear blue sky dotted with puffy, white clouds.

The whinny of a horse drew Cassie's gaze to the barn again. She was sorely tempted to go have a look but the memory of being at Alric's mercy was enough to keep her inside. Maybe when Johnny woke up, they could go outside and have a look around.

She was about to turn away from the window when she

saw a dark-haired man dressed in faded jeans and a plaid shirt come around the far corner of the barn.

Fear coalesced in the pit of her stomach as she ducked out of sight. Was it Alric? What was he doing in the barn? She had a sudden image of him setting the place on fire, burning the horses alive.

She was about to go upstairs and wake Johnny when the man came outside leading three horses. After unlatching the corral gate, he turned the animals loose inside, closed the gate, then climbed on the rail to watch them run and kick up their heels.

Relief washed through her, leaving her knees weak. Just a hired hand, she thought, here to look after the stock.

Cassie smiled as she watched the horses—a bay, a chestnut and an Appaloosa—gallop around the corral, snorting, bucking and kicking up their heels. She had loved horses ever since she was a little girl, although she'd never had occasion to ride one.

Cassie was about to turn away from the window when the man glanced over his shoulder. When she met his gaze, she felt a cold chill run down her spine. Telling herself it was just her imagination, she moved away from the window, then went through the house, making sure all the doors and windows were locked.

When she looked outside later that morning, he was gone.

Thinking Cassie might be bored or maybe uneasy at being alone, Giovanni rose several hours before sundown. He pulled on a pair of jeans and a T-shirt before heading downstairs.

He found her in the kitchen, washing her dinner dishes. "How was your day?"

She spun around, one hand pressed to her heart, the other clutching her crucifix. "Oh, it's you."

"Were you expecting someone else?"

"No. No, of course not, but . . ." She blew out a shaky breath. "It's nothing."

"It looks like something to me. What happened?"

"There was a man outside this morning. I wasn't expecting to see anyone. He gave me a start, that's all."

"What man?"

She shrugged. "Someone who's looking after the ranch, I guess. He turned the horses out in the corral so they could get some exercise. When I looked outside later, he was gone. I never saw him again after that."

Giovanni nodded. He knew Rane had hired someone to keep an eye on things while he and Savannah were gone. Yet he couldn't shake off a sense of unease.

They spent the evening playing cards. He beat her at poker, lost at gin rummy, a game he had never played before.

Later, after Cassie had gone upstairs to get ready for bed, Giovanni strolled down to the barn to have a look around. He hoped Cassie was right and that the man who had been there earlier did, indeed, work for Rane and Savannah. He walked around the barn and the house, but found no hint that Alric or anyone associated with him had been there.

Deciding to widen his search, he headed toward the pasture. He'd hadn't gone far when he caught the faint scent of blood.

Human blood.

He found the body partially hidden beneath a pile of

leaves. The man's throat had been cut. From the look and the smell of the corpse, Giovanni figured he'd been dead more than twelve hours—too long for it to be the man Cassie had seen. A search of the man's pockets turned up a wallet that was empty of cash but held a driver's license issued to George A. Carlson with an address in Auburn, California.

"Carlson," he muttered. The guy Rane had hired to look after the stock while he was in Italy.

So, who had Cassie seen sitting on the fence that morning?

Pulling his cell phone from his pocket, he called Mara.

She answered almost before the phone rang. "What's wrong?"

He quickly told her about finding the body.

"I guess Angelica passed the word to him," she said, her voice thoughtful. "Either that or he tracked Cassie. Either way, he knows where you are."

The thought tied Giovanni's stomach in knots.

"Did the man make any attempt to contact her?"

"No. She said he turned some horses loose in the corral and when she looked again, he was gone."

"I'll send someone to pick up the body."

"Thanks."

"Be careful," Mara said. "Alric might be closer than we think."

"I didn't sense his presence."

"I don't think that matters. Don't forget, he's got a witch working for him, and I think this one is stronger and more devious than Angelica."

Giovanni grunted softly.

"I'm going to call the family and tell them to be there before sundown tomorrow instead of Saturday."

"Probably a good idea."

She paused a moment, then said, "I'm going to have Derek leave immediately. He can guard the perimeter. He'll stay in wolf form until the rest of us get there."

"Thanks."

"If you need us sooner, call me. Is everything else okay?"

"As far as I know."

"You'd better warn Cassie."

"I will. See you tomorrow evening."

"Be careful, Giovanni."

"Right."

He stood there a long while, staring into the distance, before returning to the house.

Cassie looked up from the sofa when Johnny materialized in the room. "Where'd you go?"

He shrugged. "I just went out to have a look around. I thought you were going to bed?"

"I'm not as tired as I thought I was." She paused a moment, her gaze searching his. "What's wrong?"

Johnny settled down beside her, one arm draped around her shoulders. "I found a body in the pasture."

"What?"

"Yeah. It's the Cordova's hired man."

She stared at him for a breathless moment as his words registered. "Then that man I saw this morning . . ."

"Was likely sent by Alric to keep an eye on us."

Cassie felt the blood drain from her face. He'd found them already.

"The family will be here tomorrow before dark. In the meantime, Derek's going to patrol the property."

She bit down on her lower lip, wondering if Johnny could hear the fearful pounding of her heart. What if Alric came tonight? She went cold at the thought, and then hoped he would. She was tired of running, tired of being afraid. *Let him come,* she thought, her fingers wrapping around her crucifix. Better to have it out once and for all. So, he was a vampire. He wasn't indestructible. He might be Undead, but that didn't mean he couldn't be destroyed.

Giovanni grinned as he read her tumultuous thoughts, amused by her bravado and yet proud at the same time. She might be afraid, but there was no shame in that. He was afraid, too, not of dying, but of losing her.

"What are you smiling about?" she asked.

"Just thinking I'm lucky to have you at my back."

She frowned at him. "I can't imagine why."

"It doesn't matter. I brought you something."

"A present?"

"Not exactly." Rising, he made his way upstairs, only to return moments later carrying a small canvas sack.

She eyed it dubiously. "What's in there?"

Sitting on the edge of the coffee table, he handed her the bag. "Take a look."

She opened it warily, then took out the contents one by one—three sharp, twelve-inch wooden stakes, a clear glass bottle labeled Holy Water, a silver-bladed knife in a leather sheath, and a lighter like the one she used to ignite the wood in the fireplace at home. The last item in the sack was a small pistol.

Brows raised, she looked at Johnny. "Just what I always wanted. A vampire-killing kit. How did you know?"

"Keep those handy."

"I will," she said, her expression solemn as she laid the pistol aside. "Is it loaded with silver bullets?"

"It's not for Alric. It's for any mortals he might bring with him."

She stared at him, then shook her head. It was one thing to destroy a vampire trying to kill her, but an ordinary mortal? How could she?

"I know what you're thinking, but any mortals with Alric will be under his spell. You won't be able to reason with them. Have you ever handled a gun before?"

"Of course not."

He spent the next half hour teaching her how to hold it in a two-handed grip and how to load it, then had her dry-fire it a couple of times. "Just point and shoot," he said.

Cassie nodded, though she doubted she would ever find the courage to pull the trigger. "It's really going to happen, isn't it? He's going to come here."

"I'm afraid so. And probably not alone."

Cassie snuggled close to Johnny in bed that night. She tried not to think that their days together might be numbered, that Alric might win the coming battle, that they might never marry. She told herself she was being too pessimistic, that there was nothing to worry about. They had Mara and her family on their side. How could Alric possibly win?

She sighed when she felt Johnny's fingers massage her neck.

"Stop worrying," he said. "It doesn't do any good."

"I know, but . . ." She rolled over to face him. "Make love to me."

Enfolding her in his arms, he murmured, "Always my pleasure," as, with a word, her nightgown and the pajama bottoms he'd taken to wearing to bed disappeared.

"Mine, too," she whispered, and pressed her lips to his.

Giovanni moaned softly as her hands moved over him. If they spent a thousand years together, he would never get enough of the exquisite pleasure of her touch, or the wonder of knowing that she loved him in spite of everything.

Whatever the future held, he would always be grateful for this woman, this moment.

He gasped her name as he buried himself in her velvety softness, felt his heart swell with emotion as the warmth of her love poured over him.

In the morning, Cassie slid carefully out of bed, tiptoed into the bathroom, quietly closed the door, and turned on the water in the shower. When it was hot, she stepped inside and shut the door. Closing her eyes, she sighed as the water sprayed over her back and shoulders. It was nerve-racking, waiting and wondering when Alric would strike next. The thought of being in his clutches again made her blood run cold.

She let out a shriek when someone touched her arm. Whirling around, she drove her fist into the intruder's face two seconds before she realized who it was. "Johnny!" she exclaimed as he recoiled. "You scared the crap out of me! What are you doing out of bed so early?"

"I didn't want you to be alone today."

"Oh. Did I hurt you?"

"Are you kidding?" he asked, drawing her dripping body into his arms. "I've been tortured by experts."

Going up on her tiptoes, she kissed his cheek. "I'm sorry."

"Is that the best you can do?"

Slipping her arms around his neck, Cassie pulled his head down and kissed him again.

And the next thing she knew, she was soaking wet in bed beneath a fully aroused, equally wet male with only one thing on his mind.

And that was okay, because she wanted him just as desperately.

After a short nap, Giovanni rose when Cassie did. Knowing one of Alric's goons had been at the ranch the day before, he didn't want to be upstairs, dead to the world, if something happened. They showered together, then dressed.

"I think I'll go out and have a look around while you're having breakfast," he said, following her down the stairs and into the kitchen.

"Be careful."

"Stay inside." He kissed her cheek, then dissolved into mist and left the house, heading toward the barn.

Hearing sounds from within, he peered round the edge of the door. A man was in there, forking hay to the horses. Giovanni drifted up behind him. Resuming his own form, he wrapped his arm around the man's neck and shoved him up against the stall door. "Did Alric send you?"

"I don't know . . . anybody . . . by that name," the stranger gasped, digging his fingers into the arm that was cutting off his breath.

"Lie to me again and I'll break your neck."

"All right! All right! I know him."

Giovanni turned the man around, his hand locked around his throat. "Where is he?"

"I don't know."

"When is he coming here?"

"I don't know."

Giovanni tightened his hold on the intruder's neck. "You sure about that?"

"He didn't tell me, I swear it. He just told me to keep an eye out and let him know when somebody showed up."

Giovanni grunted thoughtfully. He was thirsty. Cassie was having breakfast up at the house. He would dine in the barn.

"Oh, shit," the guy muttered as Giovanni's eyes went red. "You're one of them."

"Right the first time," Giovanni said, grinning wolfishly before he buried his fangs in the man's neck.

Giovanni found Cassie sitting at the kitchen table, sipping a cup of coffee, when he returned to the house.

Looking up, she tapped a finger to the corner of her mouth. "There's blood on your lip."

He wiped it away with a swipe of his hand.

"Whose is it?"

Taking the seat across from her, he said, "Alric's stooge."

"Oh. Did you . . . is he . . . ?"

"Dead? No. I sent him away. He won't be back. I imagine Alric will show up soon. But not to worry. The family will be here before sundown."

"I've been thinking. If we win . . ."

"Not if," he chided softly. "When."

"When we win, where are we going to live?"

"I found a place I think you'll like."

"When did you have time to look?"

"Actually, it was the night our house burned down. I'd

been hunting in a new town when I saw it. If it's still for sale when we get back home, I'll show it to you."

"I've been meaning to ask, what happened to the Mustang? I left it in the parking lot at the Winchester. Did you find it?"

"It's parked behind my lair, protected from sight by a bit of vampire magic."

"Good. I'm glad you didn't lose that, too."

Leaning across the table, he took her hands in his and kissed her lightly. "All I worry about losing is you."

"You won't," she promised. "You won't."

The day passed quietly but Cassie's nerves grew tighter with every tick of the clock. Mara and her family would be here in a few hours. What did that mean, exactly? She assumed they had a plan of some kind to capture Alric. She knew she was the bait, but that was all. And if they caught him, what then? Would they just kill him in cold blood? She told herself she didn't care; he was cruel, evil. And yet . . .

She tried not to think about it. He was a vampire and Giovanni and Mara's family would have to deal with him.

But no matter how she tried, she couldn't put it out of her mind.

Giovanni was well aware of her troubled thoughts. He considered and rejected a dozen ways to explain vampire justice, but they all sounded barbaric, which they were. Still, Alric was a danger to all of their kind. He killed indiscriminately, left bodies where they could be found, which drew attention to the vampire community, something that was expressively forbidden. Giovanni wasn't foolish enough to believe Alric would change his ways.

He glanced at Cassie. She sat at the other end of the sofa, a book in her hands, but she wasn't reading. Instead, she was staring out the window at the setting sun, her expression pensive.

He was about to reach for her when he felt a rush of power and Mara materialized in the room.

Cassie gasped, the book tumbling from her hands.

"Sorry," Mara said. "I didn't mean to startle you."

"Oh, that's all right," Cassie said, one hand pressed to her heart.

"I take it things have been quiet here," Mara said.

"So far. Any sign of Alric out there?"

"No, but we have to assume he's on his way if he isn't already here. The family has the house surrounded. Not too close, of course. As soon as it's dark, I want you and Cassie to go to the front door. You give her a hug and tell her you're going hunting and you'll be back as soon as you can."

"What will you be doing?"

"I'll be upstairs."

"I'm not leaving Cassie."

"Once you've dissolved into mist, you can join me upstairs. He can't sense our presence if we're not in physical form."

"How long do we wait for him?"

"As long as it takes. Cassie, you stay downstairs with the lights on." Mara glanced around the room. "Sit in that chair in front of the window."

"You must be expecting him to bring someone with him," Giovanni remarked. "He can't cross the threshold himself."

"I imagine he'll bring the witch."

"I don't like it." Giovanni shook his head. "It sounded like a good plan back at your place. Now I'm not so sure."

"If you've got a better idea, I'm listening."

He shook his head. "Cassie, keep that sack I gave you close at hand."

"I will," she said, her heart pounding so hard she thought she might faint. It hadn't been so long ago she'd told herself she was tired of running, tired of being afraid. Told herself she was eager to get this over with. But now she wasn't so anxious. In fact, running seemed like a darn good idea.

"All right," Mara said. "It's time." Transforming herself into mist, she floated up the stairs.

"It'll be all right," Johnny said. "We've got him out-numbered."

Unless he brought an army with him, Cassie thought. She forced a smile as she followed him to the front door.

He winked at her as he opened it. Then, speaking a little louder than usual, he said, "I'm sorry, Cassie, but I need to feed. I shouldn't be gone long. Keep the door locked and don't let anyone in."

Unable to speak past the lump in her throat, Cassie nodded, then lifted her face for his kiss.

And then he was gone.

Chapter 44

Cassie paced the living room floor for several minutes, her heart in her throat. Then, remembering Mara's instructions, she picked up the book, together with the sack Johnny had given her, and sank down on the rocking chair by the front window, the gun heavy in her lap.

It was full dark now, the night eerily quiet.

Was Alric prowling around out there, lurking in the shadows? Was he watching her, even now, plotting how to get past the wards that surrounded the house?

Vampires weren't supposed to be able to cross a home's threshold without an invitation. But one of Alric's goons could easily break down the door.

Was Johnny upstairs with Mara? She closed her eyes and tried to find the bond between herself and Johnny, but it didn't work. And then she recalled Mara saying Alric couldn't sense their presence when they were invisible. If the vampires couldn't do it, what chance did she have?

Cassie. Come to me.

Her head snapped up at the sound of her name. "Johnny?" she whispered tremulously, then went cold all over as she recognized Alric's voice in her mind.

She had no sooner said Johnny's name than he appeared beside her. "What's wrong?" His gaze darted around the room before returning to her.

"I heard Alric's voice in my head, calling my name, telling me to come to him."

"So, he's here." Staring out the window, Giovanni tried to connect with the link that bound Cassie to the other vampire. At first there was nothing and then he found it—weak and flickering, like the flame of a candle.

There was a shimmer in the room as Mara materialized beside him. "What's happened?"

"He's here."

Mara's phone beeped. She answered it, her brow furrowing as she said, "Right," and hung up.

"That was Brenna. She's detected the signature of another witch in the area." Mara glanced at her phone again when she received a group text message.

A moment later, Giovanni received the same text. He swore softly as he read it.

"What is it?" Cassie asked anxiously. "What's going on?"

"A number of revenants have been seen around the ranch. Vince encountered one. So did Nick and Abbey. And Edna." He swore softly. "It sounds like Alric's got an army out there."

Sheree clutched Derek's arm as a full moon rose over the distant mountains. "Are you all right?"

He grinned at her. "The wolf wants to go vampire hunting."

"Do you think that's a good idea?"

"I can smell him. He's not far away."

"But . . . Derek, behind you!"

He spun around, his body contorting, shifting, his clothes shredding as a revenant lunged at him, a sharp wooden stake clutched in his hand.

Caught up in Alric's spell, the revenant made no move to run or defend himself as the werewolf slammed him to the ground. One quick bite ripped out the man's throat, ending his life.

"Be careful," Sheree called, as the wolf bounded into the night.

Pearl's gaze darted restlessly from side to side. "How many of those creatures do you think he's made?"

Monroe shook his head. "Beats the hell out of me."

"Edna killed one."

"Good for her."

"It doesn't seem right," Pearl remarked. "Killing those poor men. They don't even know what they're doing."

"It's them or us, darlin'. Whatever happens to them is Alric's . . . Look out!"

Pearl let out a shriek as Monroe slammed into her, driving her out of harm's way. She screamed in denial as the stake meant for her back sank into Monroe's chest.

Springing to her feet, she buried her fangs in the revenant's neck, piercing his jugular. Tossing the body aside, she fell to her knees beside Monroe. "Don't be dead," she begged, shaking his shoulder. "Please don't be dead."

Tears welled in her eyes as she sobbed his name over and over again.

Brenna ghosted through the dark, Roshan at her heels, as she followed the faint signature of the other witch. It led in a roundabout way toward the ranch house, meandering through a corner of the pasture, weaving through trees and shrubs toward the back door.

Brenna came to an abrupt halt when she saw movement a few yards away.

"She's with Alric," Roshan whispered. "I wish I could hear what they're saying."

"Should we rush them?"

He shook his head. "He'll just vanish and we'll have to find him all over again."

"So, what are we going to do?"

"Wait and see what he does next. In the meantime, I'll tell Mara they're close to the kitchen door."

Fading back into the shadows, he sent a message to Mara's mind, warning her that Alric was nearby.

"He's closing in," Mara said. "We should go back up-stairs. There's a good chance he doesn't know we're here."

Giovanni shook his head. "I'm not leaving Cassie alone."

"He can't get in. If anyone else does, we can be down here in a heartbeat."

"I'll be all right," Cassie said. "Let's get it over with." Her bravado faded as soon as the two vampires dissolved into mist and drifted up the stairway. Palms damp, mouth dry, she stared out the window, only to leap to her feet when there was a growl from outside, followed by a hideous shriek as the front door exploded inward and flew across the room.

A moment later, a figure clad all in black stepped over the threshold.

Fear spurred Cassie to action and before she realized

what she was doing, she grabbed the pistol and pulled the trigger again and again and again.

Johnny appeared beside her. "That's enough, love. She's dead."

Cassie looked at him in horror. "Dead?" She dropped the pistol, then burst into tears.

Mara and Logan appeared moments later.

Mara stood over the body, then, in a singsong voice, she said, "Ding dong, the witch is dead. And I say, good riddance, whoever she is—or was. Logan, would you please take out the trash?"

He had no sooner carried the body out the front door when a big, black wolf trotted into the living room from the direction of the kitchen, a strip of bloody cloth dangling from its mouth.

With a wordless cry, Cassie shrank back against Johnny.

"It's all right," he said, drawing her into his arms. "He's one of us."

"He . . . he is?"

"It's Sheree's husband, Derek."

She vaguely recalled Johnny telling her that Mara's son was both werewolf and vampire.

Giovanni glanced at Mara. "What happened out there?"

"I guess we'll have to wait for Derek to shift to find out."

Knowing that when werewolves resumed their own shape, their clothes didn't magically reappear, Giovanni suggested Derek go into the guest room to shift.

Cassie breathed a sigh of relief when the wolf trotted out of the room. She clutched Johnny's arm when a howl echoed through the house.

"It's okay," Johnny said. "It's a painful transformation, shifting from human to wolf or wolf to human."

Sometime later, Derek returned to the living room, a blanket wrapped around his waist.

Mara smiled at her son as he dropped down on the sofa. "So, what happened?" She sat beside him, one hand resting on his shoulder.

"I found the witch and the vampire huddled together at the side of the house. The witch ran one way and he went another. I followed Alric." He gestured at the bloody scrap of cloth on the floor. "I almost had him."

"How did he get away?" Rafe asked.

"One of those revenants threw himself at me and tripped me up. By the time I regained my feet and tossed him out of the way, Alric was gone. I know vampires heal quickly, but the bite of a werewolf is almost as painful as silver. He'll be hurting for a while."

Mara smiled at him. "We'll get him next time."

All eyes turned toward the front door when Pearl staggered in, closely followed by Edna. James came in a moment later cradling Monroe's body in his arms.

The rest of the family filed in behind him, their expressions solemn.

James glanced around the room. Then, at a gesture from Giovanni, he carried the body down the hallway to the guest room.

Sobbing, eyes red and swollen, Pearl followed him.

"I'll go stay with her," Edna said.

Mara nodded.

"The revenants are all dead," Nick remarked quietly.

"The family killed them all?" Mara asked.

He shook his head. "We killed some of them. The rest just collapsed and died."

"I guess Alric had no further use for them," Giovanni

remarked. He didn't say what they were all thinking—
Alric could easily make more, if needed.

"So," Nick asked, "what's our next move?"

"We need to lay Monroe to rest before we do anything
else," Mara said.

"Where are we going to bury him?" Vince asked.

"I'm not sure." Mara glanced around the room. "Ideas?"

"There's an old cemetery a few miles from here," Rafe
said. "It hasn't been used in the last fifty years or so. We
can bury him there. The witch, too."

"No," Mara said adamantly. "We'll cremate the witch."

An hour later, the family gathered at the cemetery. It
was a small place, surrounded by a rusty, wrought-iron
fence. Wildflowers and weeds grew in scattered clumps
between the headstones.

Cassie shivered as she watched Derek and Logan dig
the grave. James interred the body, and Johnny prayed over
the remains.

They dug another hole outside the cemetery, dropped
the witch inside, and set the body on fire. Cassie turned
away, sickened by the smell of burning hair and flesh.

When the flames died out, Vince and Nick filled the
grave.

Silence fell around them.

"We should go," Mara suggested after a time.

Pearl shook her head. "I'm staying with Monroe," she
said, dabbing at her eyes. "I can't leave him here alone."

James and Edna exchanged glances as Pearl returned
to Monroe's grave. "You all go on," Edna said. "We'll look
after her."

One by one, the family hugged Pearl, then moved away from the cemetery.

"The rest of you might as well go home," Mara said. "It's unlikely Alric will try anything else tonight. His witch is dead and he's badly hurt."

"Keep in touch," Nick said, taking Abbey Marie by the hand. "He's killed one of our own now. We can't let him get away with it."

Two by two, they took their leave, until only Cassie, Giovanni, Mara, and Logan remained.

"Giovanni, why don't you and Cassie go stay at our place in Hollywood?" Mara suggested. "Logan and I are going to remain at the ranch for a day or two. We need to repair the front door and find someone to look after the stock until Rane and Savannah get back."

"All right, thanks. Talk to you soon."

Holding tight to Cassie, he transported the two of them to the house in the hills.

Cassie sat on the edge of the bed, hands tightly clasped in her lap, while Johnny ran water in the tub. She felt numb, empty. Guilty. She had killed someone. She avoided killing spiders or squashing bugs, yet she had taken a human life.

"Cassie?"

She looked up at him, her eyes haunted.

Without a word, he picked her up and carried her into the bathroom. Setting her on her feet, he undressed her, then lifted her into the tub. Removing his own clothes, he stepped in behind her and slipped his arms around her waist. "Relax, love. Try not to think about it now."

"I killed her," she said dully.

"Shh. You did the right thing, and probably saved lives doing it. No telling what kind of havoc Alric and the witch could have caused tonight." He massaged her back and shoulders until he felt the tension slowly seep out of her. When the water grew cool, he lifted her from the tub and dried her off. She stood like a mannequin as he slipped one of Mara's nightgowns over her head and tugged it down over her hips. After putting her to bed, he crawled in beside her, holding her close while she cried herself to sleep.

She was trapped in a room with no windows, surrounded by revenants who stared at her, their faces void of expression. She let out a cry of denial as Alric appeared, his eyes glittering red with hunger and hatred as he buried his fangs deep in her throat. And then *she* was the vampire, her fangs embedded in his neck as she drank his blood. The scene changed abruptly and she was firing a gun loaded with silver bullets. She killed Alric. She killed his witch. And then she killed Johnny. . . .

Cassie woke to the sound of her own screams, her cheeks wet with tears.

"Hush, love." Johnny's voice, soft and soothing in her ear as his hand stroked her hair. "It was just a bad dream. There won't be any more. Go back to sleep."

Go back to sleep. Unable to resist the compulsion in his voice, she closed her eyes and slept.

Cassie sighed and rolled over. A glance at the window showed it was still dark outside. She glanced at Johnny, sleeping soundly beside her and then, in a rush, the events of the night before came rushing back and she began to shake.

She had killed someone. Someone she didn't even know. She had never seen the woman's face, didn't know her name, yet she had shot her dead without even knowing if the woman meant her any harm. Although it was highly likely, she thought, since the woman was a witch working for Alric. Still . . . there was blood on her hands.

"Cassie?" Johnny reached out to her, his voice heavy with sleep. "You did the right thing."

He sounded so loving, so compassionate, she burst into tears.

Turning onto his side, he gathered her into his arms. "I know how you feel," he said as he stroked her back, her hair. "It isn't easy, taking a life, even when it's to save your own. And that's what you did. I don't have a doubt in my mind that if Alric gets his hands on you again, he'll kill you. Or worse, he'll turn you."

His words rang true. She shuddered as she imagined being turned by Alric, being in his power for the rest of her life, compelled to do his bidding. It was a fate worse than death.

Wiping her eyes on a corner of the sheet, Cassie snuggled against Johnny, grateful for his presence, his comfort, his wisdom.

It was barely light outside when Giovanni awoke. Cassie stirred, a sleepy sound rising in her throat, but she didn't wake.

Rising, he strolled into the living room, then wandered outside to stand on the porch. He blinked against the light of the rising sun. Still, he stood there for several minutes.

It had been a long time since he'd seen the sun rise. It was a beautiful sight.

When the heat, though mild, caused his skin to tingle, he went back inside and closed the heavy drapes that blocked the sun's light.

Alric, that elusive coward, had escaped them yet again. How much more havoc would he cause before they destroyed him? Would they *ever* destroy him? He was beginning to doubt it. Damn the man. He had the devil's own luck.

Giovanni frowned. If he turned Cassie, Alric would no longer be able to find her. . . . Damn! What was he thinking?

He put the thought out of his mind, yet it crept in again. It would solve a number of problems—her blood would no longer be a temptation. She would be better equipped to resist Alric. And she would be strong, even as a fledgling, because his blood was old and powerful, and even more so because Mara's blood was mixed with his.

He dragged a hand across his jaw. He knew Cassie had been thinking about it. What would her reaction be if he suggested it? Horror? Curiosity? Fear? She had accepted him for what he was readily enough. He knew being with the family made her nervous, but she didn't seem to be afraid of any of them, except maybe Derek, which was understandable. In his werewolf form, Mara's son was easily three times larger than any normal wolf, and scary as hell.

Feeling the pull of the Dark Sleep, he padded silently back to bed.

Chapter 45

Alric cursed Mara as he took refuge in the first dark, uninhabited place he could find–some dilapidated old shack in the middle of nowhere. The werewolf had bitten him in his right thigh, both arms, and his left shoulder. He had suffered numerous injuries in his life, but nothing as painful as this. Where the hell had they found a werewolf? His wounds, which usually healed rapidly, were still leaking blood and burned like hell's own fires.

He groaned low in his throat as he curled up in a ball. He needed to feed, but he was too weak and in too much pain to hunt.

He closed his eyes, thoughts of vengeance crowding his mind as he tumbled into the healing power of the Dark Sleep.

Chapter 46

When nothing suspicious happened during the next two weeks, Giovanni decided it was time to stop hiding and get back to living. Mara's house was nice. It was safe. But he knew Cassie was uncomfortable there. He had put aside his idea of talking to Cassie about becoming a vampire, at least for the time being.

"What do you say we get out of here and find a place of our own?" he asked her when he rose one night.

She looked up at him from the sofa. "I think it's a wonderful idea."

"Will you marry me?"

"Didn't I already say yes?"

"I mean in Las Vegas as soon as we can get a reservation at one of the chapels. I already went online and filled out a pre-application." It was good for sixty days, but he didn't want to wait that long.

"Seriously?"

"Seriously. There's no waiting period, no blood tests. Just pay for the license, find a church or maybe a chapel, and say 'I do.'"

She was about to agree when the memory of what had

happened at the ranch rushed to the forefront of her mind, and with it the memory of being kidnapped by Alric and everything that had happened since. Worst of all, she had taken a human life. If she married Johnny, would their future be one, long continuous battle for survival? Would she always be running, always looking over her shoulder?

"Cassie?" He swore inwardly as his mind brushed hers. She was having second thoughts again—and who could blame her? He had brought her nothing but trouble since the night they'd met. "Never mind, love," he said quietly. "We'll leave here tonight. I'll find you an apartment and make sure you're safe. Don't worry about paying for your schooling. I'll take care of it. And your rent, too, for as long as necessary."

And when she had her license and was making enough to take care of herself, he would wipe his memory from her mind, leaving her free to live a normal life with no bad memories to cause her nightmares or regrets.

Cassie stared at him. Out of everything he'd said, the only part she'd heard was that he was leaving her. Why wasn't she relieved? No more vampires. No move revenants or witches. No more Alric.

And no more Johnny.

"Just like that?" she said, blinking up at him.

"Just like that."

He'd given her the perfect out. No muss, no fuss. So why did she feel like crying?

Was that what she wanted, to just walk away? Sure, she'd been through hell a couple of times, but did she want to trade what she shared with Johnny for a life without him? She gazed into her future—a future without him— and saw nothing there. True, she might fall in love again, but it would be a pale shadow of what she felt for Johnny.

No other man would ever love her, or need her, the way he did.

"Get your things together while I tell Mara what's going on."

Suddenly, instead of being relieved, she was angry. Slapping her hand on the sofa cushion, she said, "So, you're going to leave me, just like that?"

Confused, he frowned at her. "I'm just trying to help. I don't want to bring you any more grief than I already have."

She blew out a deep breath. "And I don't want to live without you." Whatever the future held, she wanted Johnny to be part of it.

His gaze searched hers. "Are you sure?"

Rising, she put her arms around his waist and rested her head on his chest, then grinned as the words *for better or worse* ran through her mind. "I'm sure. One hundred and ten percent."

Wrapping his arms around her, he crushed her body to his.

"Am I interrupting something?" Mara asked from the doorway.

"We're getting married!" Giovanni said, smiling at Cassie. "Just as soon as we can find a venue."

"Well, congratulations."

"Notify the family, will you?" he asked. "We're leaving for Vegas tonight. I'll text you when we have a date and time."

Nodding, Mara went to find Logan and tell him the news.

"Are you sure all we need is a license?" Cassie asked, dropping down on the sofa.

"And a photo ID."

"That's going to be a problem," she said, frowning. "I

lost my wallet and everything in my purse when Alric abducted me, remember, and I still haven't applied for a new driver's license."

"Not to worry. Do you remember the number on the old one?"

"I think so."

"I'll take care of it. Are you ready to go?"

"Wait! What about a dress?" The one she'd bought had burned in the fire, along with everything else.

"We'll buy a new one when we get there, and anything else you need."

Cassie stared up at him, overwhelmed by the suddenness of it all. But one look at his face, the love shining in his eyes, drove the last of her doubts away. For a day or a lifetime, she was his and he was hers.

Smiling, she stood and reached for his hand. "Let's go!"

He wrapped her in his arms and the next thing she knew, they were standing on a busy sidewalk on the Las Vegas Strip. Cassie blinked in astonishment. It was dark out, yet it seemed as bright as day. There were lights everywhere in a myriad of colors—solid and blinking. And people—she had never seen so many people in her life, and they were all in a hurry. Men in shorts, sandals, and Hawaiian shirts. Women in cocktail dresses and heels, or jeans and tank tops. A young mother sat on a bench, nursing a baby. A man carrying a ferret on his shoulder. A woman in a sari, a man in a tuxedo. A wall of noise rose all around her—people shouting, laughing, the screech of tires and horns blaring as taxis wove in and out of the traffic. How did anyone get used to it?

She held tight to Johnny's arm as they made their way down the street to a hotel that was lit up like a Christmas tree.

Cassie glanced left and right as they made their way to the desk. It was almost as noisy in here as it was outside—the clinking of ice, the whir of a wheel, bells and whistles from numerous slot machines, exuberant shouts from the gaming tables.

Johnny grinned at her. "It's a bit much, isn't it?"

"Kind of exhilarating, though." She glanced at the people gambling only a few feet away. "Do you think we could try our luck?"

"Anything you want to do is fine with me," he said after they had checked in and collected their key cards. "Just name your poison."

Giovanni watched with amusement as Cassie moved from the craps table, where she won a hundred dollars on one roll of the dice, to the roulette wheel, where she lost half of her winnings. Their next stop was the blackjack table. He stood behind her, unable to stop grinning as she won hand after hand. This was her game, he thought, novice or not.

Cassie glanced at him over her shoulder as she raked in her winnings. "I've got more than enough for a new dress," she said, grinning. "And shoes to match."

"Keep it up and you'll have enough for the first payment on our new house."

She stared at him, eyes wide. "You bought a house?"

"You remember that one I told you about? I made an offer over the phone last week and they accepted it." He winked at her. "It's your wedding present."

"Oh, Johnny!" she squealed. Sliding off her chair, she threw her arms around him.

"Hey, lady," the dealer called. "You playing this hand or not?"

"What? Oh, yes. I can't stop now." She kissed Johnny on the cheek before turning back to the game.

When she called it quits an hour later, she'd won over nine hundred dollars.

"I had no idea you were such a gambler," Johnny remarked as they headed for their room.

"Beginner's luck," she said, shaking her head. "I've never played blackjack—or anything else—before."

Their room was located on the fourth floor at the end of the hall. Cassie gasped as she followed Johnny inside. "It's beautiful!"

It should be, he thought, considering what it cost. The walls were papered in a subdued gray and blue stripe. A luxurious carpet covered the floor. A pair of sofas were placed in front of a big screen TV; a small table and two chairs occupied a corner of the room.

"This must have cost a fortune," Cassie murmured.

"More than you won tonight," he said.

"No way!"

Sweeping her into his arms, he carried her into the bedroom. "Alone at last," he said, setting her on her feet.

Cassie flushed under his heated gaze. They had only made love a couple of times while staying at Mara's, and she was eager to be in his arms again.

She shivered in anticipation as he lifted her sweater over her head, reached behind her to unfasten her bra, then lifted her onto the bed. Kneeling, he removed her shoes, then unfastened her jeans. Excitement thrummed through her as he slowly peeled them down her hips, then tossed the Levi's aside.

She stretched out on the bed and watched him undress, and then he was lying beside her, his hand absently caressing her thigh.

"While you were breaking the bank at the blackjack table," he said, "I made reservations at the Sunnyside Garden Chapel for us for tomorrow night at nine."

"But I still don't have a dress."

"We'll look for one tomorrow. Okay?"

"Yes," she murmured, and then he was kissing her and she forgot everything else but the wonder of being in his arms, of loving and being loved in return.

The sun was shining brightly when Cassie awoke in the morning. Turning her head, she let her gaze move over Johnny. She never tired of looking at him. Even now, knowing they were going to be married that night, she couldn't believe it was true, that he loved her, that he wanted her as much as she wanted him.

Almost as much as she wanted breakfast, she thought, as her stomach reminded her she hadn't eaten since yesterday.

"Sounds like my lady is in need of nourishment," Giovanni remarked, rolling onto his side.

"I'm starving," she admitted.

"So am I."

Cassie felt her heart skip a beat when his gaze slid to the pulse throbbing in the hollow of her throat. It had been a while since he'd drunk from her, and though she hated to admit it, she missed the intimacy. Her pulse raced in anticipation as she pushed her hair out of the way.

"Are you sure, love?"

More than sure, she thought, remembering the first time he'd bitten her. He had warned her then that she would want him to do it again and when she'd asked how he could be so sure, he had grinned and said, *Because you liked it the first time.* He had been right on both counts.

He rained featherlike kisses on her cheeks, her brow, her lips, then ran his tongue along the side of her neck. Every touch inflamed her senses. His bite, when it came, filled her with a wave of sensual pleasure, almost as if he was making love to her.

She moaned in protest when he lifted his head, but the best was yet to come. Rising over her, he claimed her lips with his as he made slow, sweet love to her until she lay sated and content in the circle of his arms.

It was midday before she finally made it to the hotel dining room.

Giovanni rose a little after three. He showered and dressed, and then he and Cassie went shopping at one of the department stores on the Strip.

"Seems as if we just did this," Cassie muttered. She hadn't wanted to go back to the ranch, not even long enough to pack their clothes, so Mara and Logan had generously shared their wardrobes once again.

Cassie strolled through the ladies' department, picking up jeans, T-shirts, a couple of skirts, and a light jacket. She had decided to save the best—finding a wedding dress—for last.

He grunted softly. Until Cassie, he had never shopped so often, or spent so much time being awake during the day. He supposed he should be grateful he was able to be out and about with her when the sun was up, but it was wearing on him. He could feel the hot Vegas sun draining his strength.

When she'd bought everything she needed, he made a

quick trip through the men's department and then they went up to the third floor in search of a wedding dress. Giovanni found a place to sit and left Cassie to it.

An hour later she hurried toward him, a smile on her face, a garment bag over her arm.

"I guess you found one you liked."

"It's dreamy! I can't wait to wear it."

He waggled his eyebrows at her. "I can't wait to see you in it. Next stop, city hall."

Cassie blew out a sigh as they left city hall, marriage license in hand. Looking up at Johnny, she said, "Just think, in a few hours we'll be married. Can you believe it?"

"Not really," he said, chuckling. "I keep waiting to wake up in my old lair and discover that meeting you was nothing more than a dream."

"Except vampires don't dream," she reminded him. "So I must be real."

His gaze caressed her as he murmured, "Thank the good Lord."

Back at the hotel, Cassie called room service and ordered steak and lobster for dinner. While waiting, she took a long, hot shower. It was really happening. She was going to marry Johnny. She felt as if she was smiling inside and out.

She turned off the water, stepped out of the stall to dry off, then slipped into one of the fluffy hotel bathrobes and padded into the other room.

Johnny kissed her as he passed her on his way into the bathroom. "Your dinner is here."

She ate while he showered, wondering if the whole family would show up for the wedding on such short notice. Of course, traveling a few hundred miles was no hardship for Mara and the others. All they had to do was think themselves wherever they wanted to be and *voilà!* They were there. No doubt they saved tons of money on gas and airfare, she mused with a grin.

Thinking of Mara and the family brought Alric to mind. He really was a monster. Had he been cruel and inhuman before he was turned? If she let Johnny turn her one day in the future, would she still be Cassie? Or would she be transformed into a vile creature like Johnny's sire?

After setting her plate on the side table, she went to look out the window. She knew Johnny had killed people. Mara certainly had. What about the others?

She smiled as Johnny came up behind her. Slipping his arms around her waist, he nuzzled her neck. "What are you thinking?"

"Nothing important."

"That's not the feeling I'm getting."

"I was thinking about vampires."

He grunted softly. "What about them?"

"Did it change you?"

"What do you mean?"

She turned to face him. "When people are turned, do they change? I don't mean just the transformation from human to vampire. I mean, does it change who they are."

"Generally speaking, no."

"So, Alric was a horrible person before he became a vampire?"

"I didn't know him before, but I would venture to say yes. Although even vampires change. Mara has certainly mellowed since I first met her. Granted, most vampires take a life at some point or other, usually to defend themselves or someone they love. There are those few people who are turned and can't handle the transformation. Some become drunk with power. Some destroy themselves. But on the whole, people stay true to what they were before—good or bad." He chuckled softly. "This is a heck of a conversation to be having on our wedding night."

"I know but . . . it's something I need to know."

"I can understand that." He glanced at the window. "Shouldn't you be getting ready? It's almost time to go."

"You're right. I love you, Johnny."

"And I love you. Now scoot, love. We don't want to be late!"

Chapter 47

Cassie stood in the bride's dressing room, attended by Mara and Brenna. Standing in front of a full-length mirror, she could only stare at her reflection. For the first time in her life, she felt beautiful. She had chosen an off-the-shoulder gown of silk and lace, with a fitted bodice and a long skirt that flared at the bottom. The matching veil trailed behind her.

"Your face is practically glowing," Mara remarked.

"It's Johnny," Cassie said, smiling. "He makes me happy."

"And he's crazy about you," Brenna said. "Anyone can see that."

"It's time," Mara said. "Are you ready?"

Suddenly too nervous to speak, Cassie nodded.

Brenna went to get Derek.

A moment later, he poked his head in the door. "Everybody ready?"

"Let's go," Mara said, leading the way to the chapel.

It was a lovely room. The walls and chairs were white, the floor dark oak. Wrought-iron sconces adorned the walls. Two steps led to the altar. Trees and greenery were visible through the four windows behind the altar.

The family sat in front—Abbey Marie, Nick, Sheree, Brenna, Roshan, Vince, and Cara on one side of the aisle, Rafe, Kathy, Pearl, Edna Mae, and James on the other. Even Rane and Savannah were there, having come home early from Italy for the occasion. Cassie smiled, thinking it was nice that some of their guests had chosen to sit on the bride's side, since she had no family of her own there. She was surprised—and touched—to see Edna Mae sitting next to Pearl. It couldn't be easy for Edna attending a wedding after so recently losing her own husband.

Johnny and Logan stood to the right of the alter, both looking extremely handsome in black Hugo Boss suits.

As the music started, Mara, clad in an exquisite floor-length, green silk gown, started down the aisle.

Johnny winked at Cassie when he saw her.

Heart pounding with excitement, she winked back.

Butterflies took wing in the pit of her stomach as she placed her hand on Derek's arm and followed Mara down the aisle. When Derek placed her hand in Johnny's, Cassie forgot anyone else was in the room. Tears of joy stung her eyes as Johnny repeated the vows that made him her husband.

Her voice trembled as she repeated her own vows. Johnny smiled at her, his hands squeezing hers as she promised to love him for as long as they lived.

"Cassandra and Giovanni, I now pronounce you husband and wife," the minister intoned. "Mr. Lanzoni, you may kiss your bride."

"Everlastingly mine," Johnny murmured as he lifted her veil and took her in his arms. His kiss was gentle, almost reverent, filled with the promise of forever.

The family crowded around afterward, exchanging hugs and kisses and congratulations.

They had decided to forego any kind of reception and celebrate at the casino in their hotel. Two limos awaited them outside—one for the bride and groom, and a stretch limo for the guests.

Johnny reached for Cassie as soon as the driver closed the door. Taking her in his arms, he murmured, "Come here, Mrs. Lanzoni."

She lifted her face for his kiss, one hand sliding around his neck, her fingers delving into his hair.

He nibbled on her earlobe, then slid his hand under her skirt to skim her thigh. "What do you say we skip drinks at the casino and go straight to our room?"

"That would be terribly rude, wouldn't it?" she asked breathlessly.

"I think they'll understand." His gaze burned into hers as he lowered her onto the seat, his hands cupping her cheeks as he covered her mouth with his in a searing kiss that made her toes curl in anticipation.

Mara laughed softly. "I'm afraid the bride and groom aren't going to make the party."

"Are you surprised?" Logan asked. "The looks he was giving her at the altar were so hot, I thought the chapel might go up in flames."

"She'll be good for him," Brenna predicted.

"And he for her," Roshan said. "Like you are for me."

"Well, I'm happy for them," Vince said, hugging Cara. "I just hope they'll be as happy as we are."

"As I was," Pearl said, blinking back her tears.

Edna Mae gave her friend's hand a sympathetic squeeze. "We all wish Monroe was here."

"I don't mean to spoil the party," Derek said, drawing Abbey Marie against his side. "But Alric's in town."

Mara's gaze snapped to her son. "How do you know?"

"Trust me, I know. The werewolf never forgets a scent. Or a taste."

"Is he alone?" Logan asked.

"As far as I can tell. He has a talisman of some kind to shield his presence."

"Then how do you know he's here?" Abbey Marie asked, frowning.

"Whatever the magic is that he's using, it doesn't work on werewolves."

"I hope he is here," Pearl said. "I won't rest until my Monroe has been avenged."

Mara shook her head as she stared out the window. "That's what started this whole mess in the first place," she reminded them. "Alric's need for vengeance."

"You avenged yourself on the man who turned you," Pearl said, her voice sharp. "Don't tell me you didn't enjoy it."

"And I'd do it again," Mara said, her voice icy. "I'm just saying the stakes are higher this time. It isn't just a fight between Alric and myself. It involves the whole family now."

"Are you saying we should give up?" Pearl asked. "Just quit and let him win?"

"He hasn't won yet," Logan reminded her.

"And he won't." Mara's voice was quiet, but it held a layer of steel underneath. "I have a plan to end this once and for all. Brenna, Derek, this is what we're going to do."

Chapter 48

Cassie's heart pounded with excitement as they entered the hotel. Several people smiled at them as they crossed the lobby, a few called out their congratulations. She laughed as an older man simply shook his head.

Hand in hand, they took the elevator up to the fourth floor. Cassie let out a startled gasp when Johnny swung her up into his arms and carried her down the hallway. Holding her close, he unlocked the door and carried her inside. Still holding her in his arms, he rained kisses on her cheeks, her brow, her lips, before setting her on her feet.

Stifling a grin, Cassie said, "So, Mr. Lanzoni, what would you like to do now?"

He frowned at her a moment, and then he laughed. "I'm not sure, Mrs. Lanzoni. What would *you* like to do now?"

She faked a yawn behind her hand. "I'm awfully tired. Maybe we should just go to bed."

"I think that's the best idea you've ever had," he agreed with a roguish grin.

And the next thing Cassie knew, she was naked in bed in Johnny's arms.

"Do you have any idea how much I love you?" he murmured as his hand feathered up and down her thigh.

"Show me," she whispered.

Giovanni's gaze bored into hers. "This is the happiest night of my life, Cassie," he whispered fervently. "Thank you for loving me."

"Oh, Johnny, I love you, too! More than I can say."

Lowering his head, he nuzzled the side of her neck as his hands moved lightly over her body, exploring every hill and hidden valley, lingering on her breasts. He watched the play of emotions on Cassie's face as he aroused her, still amazed at the wonder and beauty of making love to her. His for now and, hopefully, for always.

Cassie responded in kind, her eager hands performing an in-depth study of their own. His body was hard and unyielding where hers was soft, and she gloried it in. She loved caressing him, hearing him gasp with pleasure at the touch of her hands. He was hers now, only hers. And she was his. The thought filled her with a sweet sense of belonging. Of coming home.

His eyes were hot, tinged with red, when he rose over her. "Mine," he whispered softly as his body melded with hers.

Smiling up at him, she touched his cheek as her body welcomed his. "Mine."

Alric sat at the roulette table, easily winning time and again as he mentally manipulated the wheel's outcome. He had tracked the woman, Cassie, to the hotel. He wasn't worried about the vampires as long as he stayed out of their sight, since his scent was masked by a talisman given to him by the witch they had killed. It was time to end this farce once and for all.

His fledgling might think himself safe in the suite upstairs, but a hotel room was not a home and the threshold had no power to repel him. He would bide his time until the priest and the woman were asleep and then, at last, he would have at least some measure of revenge. And if he was lucky, he might avenge himself on Mara, as well.

He smiled as his number came up yet again. Whatever happened, he was going to leave here a wealthy man.

It was an hour before dawn when Giovanni slipped quietly out of bed. After pulling on a pair of trousers, he padded into the living room, only to pause when he saw Mara and the family. "What the hell are you all doing here?"

"Hopefully setting a trap for Alric," Mara replied.

"He's here?"

"Derek caught his scent."

Giovanni glanced at the wolf sitting beside her. The rest of the family perched on the sofa and chairs or made themselves at home on the floor. They were all here, still wearing the clothes they'd worn to the wedding. "So, what's the plan?"

"You're going to go downstairs and wander around, pull the slots, whatever. Just be sure he sees you. If he comes upstairs, as we think he will, I'll call you."

Giovanni shook his head. "Even if you're right and he comes here after Cassie, once he catches sight of you, he'll grab her and transport himself out of here before you can stop him. You know that."

"That's where Brenna comes in. She has a spell that will prevent him from leaving once he's inside the room."

"How do you know it will work?"

"Try it."

Giovanni summoned his power and attempted to vanish from the room. When he couldn't leave, he tried to dissolve into mist, but that, too, failed. "That's damned impressive." He smiled at the witch. "I'm glad you're on our side."

"It's taken me years to perfect. I always knew it would come in handy one day."

"There's just one other thing. He's bound to sense you're all in here, waiting for him."

Roshan smiled at his wife. "Brenna's taken care of that, too," he said, his voice laced with pride. "We'll be outside, on the balcony. He'll never know we're there."

"What about Cassie?" Giovanni asked. "We should tell her what's going on."

Mara shook her head. "Not a good idea. There's too great a chance of Alric reading her mind and discovering what we're up to."

"I don't like it," Giovanni muttered. But Mara was right.

"This will be a battle to the death," Logan remarked. "And it might be our last, best chance to take him out."

"Just remember he's mine," Giovanni said flatly. "Don't get in my way."

Mara nodded. "Don't worry. We're just here for backup. If you can't defeat him, it will be my turn."

"And if she fails, the rest of us will take him out," Nick said, his expression grim.

"One way or another," Mara said. "Alric dies tonight."

* * *

Giovanni strolled through the casino. He had no sense of Alric's presence, but he knew he was being watched. He played a couple hands of blackjack, spent a few minutes at the craps table. He'd just taken a seat in front of a slot machine when the feeling disappeared.

Moments later, he heard Mara's voice in his mind. *He's at the door.*

I'm on my way. Not caring whether anyone saw him or not, he transported himself to the fourth floor in less than a heartbeat. Dissolving into mist, Giovanni arrived in the hallway just in time to see Alric transform himself into mist and slip under the narrow crack at the bottom of the door.

Resuming his own shape, Giovanni pushed the door open and stepped inside. The spell that masked Alric's scent didn't prevent him from being seen.

Alric spun around to face Giovanni. "Just the man I was looking for," he said, hands clenching and unclenching at his sides.

"Let's finish this. Now." Without giving Alric time to respond, Giovanni sprang forward, his hands reaching for the other vampire's throat.

But Alric was quick. Avoiding Giovanni's grasp, he darted past him, turned on his heel, and slammed his locked fists into the base of Giovanni's neck.

Giovanni stumbled forward, his thigh connecting with a table as he whirled around.

Alric sneered at him. "You're dead."

Giovanni snorted. "So are you, but I intend to make it permanent in your case."

Alric flew across the room, arms outstretched, hands like claws. Giovanni met him halfway. Grappling for purchase, they rocked back and forth until Giovanni twisted out of Alric's grip and drove his fist into the other vampire's face.

Alric reared back just as Cassie, clad in a short robe, stepped out of the bedroom. Before she realized what was going on, Alric sprang forward, grabbed a fistful of her hair with one hand and wrapped his other hand around her throat.

Giovanni let out a roar as Alric held her in front of him like a shield.

"Say good-bye to the pretty lady," his master said.

"Let her go, you coward!" Giovanni snarled. "This is between you and me."

"The spoils of war," Alric gloated. "Tonight, she'll be mine."

"Damn you!" Giovanni took a step forward, only to stop when Alric bared his fangs and leaned over Cassie's neck. "Do you want to watch?"

"Let her go," Giovanni said. "Take my life if that's what you want. I won't fight you. Just let her go."

"Johnny, no!"

"It's all right, *cara*. What do you say, Alric? Me for her."

"It's tempting," the vampire said. "But I think not. Once she's turned, I'll come back for you. Bye, now." Power flooded the room as he tried to transport himself and Cassie out of the building.

But nothing happened.

"What is this?" Alric glanced around the room.

"Magic. You know about magic, don't you?"

Alric took a step back, dragging Cassie with him. "I

guess you want to watch," he said, and buried his fangs in Cassie's throat. He drank quickly, greedily.

Eyes blazing, Giovanni took an involuntary step forward.

"Another step and I'll kill her."

"Go ahead. You can't get out of here. If you kill her, you're dead."

Alric snorted. "You and I both know her life is more important to you than my death."

"Maybe. But is it more important to you?"

"I'm willing to gamble with her life if you are," Alric countered, running his tongue along Cassie's neck.

Giovanni swore under his breath.

"Last chance, Priest. She's almost gone. Now open the damn door."

"All right, you win." For a moment Giovanni considered calling Mara into the room, but he quickly dismissed that idea. One look at Mara might drive Alric over the edge. Knowing he couldn't get away, knowing Mara could easily defeat him, he would likely kill Cassie out of hand. "Let her go."

"I don't think so. She's my insurance."

Mara, tell Brenna to open the door and be quick about it.

Are you sure that's wise?

He'll kill her. My life's no good without her.

Very well. It might take a minute or two.

"I've contacted the witch," Giovanni said. "It'll take a few minutes to revoke the spell."

"Take as long as you want," Alric said, and again lowered his head to Cassie's neck.

Dammit, Mara, tell Brenna to hurry! He's feeding on her. Hands fisted at his sides, he watched the color fade from Cassie's cheeks, listened as her heartbeat slowed and grew sluggish.

She's done.

"It's open now," Giovanni said through clenched teeth.

Holding Cassie tightly, Alric dragged her toward the door.

Hoping she could hear him, Giovanni found his link to Cassie. *Fall down when he opens it!*

She went limp in the vampire's arms, causing him to stumble as he opened the door.

Giovanni darted forward and scooped Cassie into his arms as Mara materialized in the doorway, blocking Alric's escape.

A surge of power whispered through the room as Brenna refreshed the spell.

Alric backed away from Mara, his gaze darting left and right.

"It ends here," she told him. "You should have quit when you had the chance."

"Go to hell!"

She laughed softly, then glanced at Giovanni. "Shall I finish him, or do you want to try again?"

"He's mine. Take Cassie for me. Whatever happens, promise me you'll look after her."

Nodding, Mara took Cassie in her arms and carried her into the bedroom.

Alric licked Cassie's blood from his lips. "A tasty morsel. One I can't wait to sample again."

"That was the last you'll ever have."

Giovanni stalked toward Alric, the rage inside him growing with each step. He watched Alric's eyes go red, knew his looked the same. He bared his fangs, then sprang forward, oblivious to the blows and bites he received as he savaged Alric's throat and clawed long, bloody furrows down his arms and chest.

Alric fought back, but he was no match for Giovanni's fury.

When the vampire stumbled and went down, Giovanni pinned him to the floor, then sank his fangs into his throat once more. The blood was vile, but he didn't care. Nothing mattered but destroying the creature who had hurt Cassie.

Weak from the loss of blood, Alric stropped struggling.

Giovanni was about to break his neck when, from some deep, desperate instinct to survive, Alric found the strength to wrest his way free. Frantic to escape, he hobbled across the floor toward the sliding glass door.

Watching from the balcony and sensing his intent, Brenna hastily removed the spell keeping him in the room.

When Alric saw Giovanni coming after him, he opened the balcony door, staggered outside, and let out an exultant cry as he climbed over the rail.

A cry that swiftly turned to a shrill scream of agony as the rising sun turned his flesh into ash.

Giovanni grunted softly as he watched what was left of his sire drift away on the wind. Drained nearly dry, his strength almost gone, the vampire had lacked the power to endure the sun's light.

"Giovanni," Mara called. "You'd better get in here."

He ran into the bedroom, skidded to a stop beside the bed. "Is she . . . ?"

"Not yet. But the only way to save her now is to turn her. She's too far gone for anything else."

He shook his head. "I can't. I promised her I would never do that."

"Then I'll leave you to tell her good-bye, although I'm not sure she'll hear you."

Taking Cassie's hand in his, Giovanni sank to his knees beside the bed. "Cassie, can you hear me?"

She didn't move, didn't answer. He stared at the savage wounds in her throat, the bright red blood that stained the collar of her robe. Her face was deathly pale, her heartbeat weak and unsteady.

"I can't lose you, *cara mia,*" he murmured. "I know you trusted me to keep my promise, but I can't let you go. Not now. Not ever." He blinked the tears from his eyes. "I'd rather live with your hatred than without you." *Cassie, I love you.*

I . . . love . . . you.

Forgive me.

He kissed her cheek, and then he turned her head to the side, gently sank his fangs into her throat and drank what little blood she had left.

Mara's head jerked up. "He's done it," she said, her voice almost reverent. "He's made Cassie one of us." She glanced at the family, who had all gathered in her room. Although the sun was up, it was dark enough inside that even those few who generally had to rest during the day were able to be awake, though not for much longer.

They all turned to stare at her, their faces reflecting surprise, shock, or disbelief.

"She was dying," Mara said.

"What else was he going to do?" Logan asked. "He couldn't let her go."

Derek smiled at Sheree. "I understand his motives completely."

"I think we all do," Nick said. Reaching across the table, he squeezed Abbey hand.

Vince grunted softly. "I wonder how she'll react?"

"Hard to tell," Mara said. "The fact that she made him promise he would never give her the Dark Gift makes it more complicated."

Roshan shrugged. "She might feel differently about it when she realizes what the consequences would be if he hadn't."

Edna and Pearl turned mildly accusing eyes on Rafe, who grinned back at them.

"We hated you for a long time for turning us against our will, didn't we, Pearl?"

Forcing a smile, Pearl said, "Yes, dear," in a voice still thick with grief.

All eyes swung toward the door when it opened and Giovanni stepped inside.

"Is she all right?" Sheree asked.

"She's resting."

"You look like you've been through hell and back," Mara said, eyes narrowed with concern. "Are *you* all right?"

"At least until she wakes up tomorrow night," Giovanni replied with a rueful grin.

Chapter 49

"Well," Edna said after they transported themselves to Mara's home in Northern California. "Where do we go from here? The café is gone and our lair with it. And while this place is nice, we can't stay here forever."

"You once said something about going back to Texas," James remarked. "I've never been there but it sounds like a great place to start over."

"What do you say, Pearl?" Edna Mae asked.

She shook her head. "I don't care what the two of you do."

"Hey, I don't want to hear you talking like that," Edna Mae said sharply. "We've been friends for a long time, you and I. We've been through hell and back together. I know losing Monroe is hard, but I'm not going to let you crawl into a hole and pine away. You're my family. *Our* family," she said, taking Pearl's hand. "Together through thick and thin, remember? We've faced vampires and werewolves and Mara's wrath. If we can survive all that, we can survive anything. So, what do you say? Light out for Texas?"

"We're not going anywhere without you," James said,

taking Pearl's other hand in his. "So, you might as well say yes."

Pearl smiled faintly. "I guess tomorrow night we're going to Texas." She glanced from Edna to James to the sliding glass doors. "The sun's up. How can we still be awake?"

Mara stretched out on the bed beside Logan, her head pillowed on his shoulder. "All's well that ends well."

"You think so?"

"Yes. Don't you?"

"I suppose it depends on how Cassie handles the change."

"She'll be fine," Mara said with a dismissive wave of her hand.

"You sure about that?" he asked, somewhat skeptically

"Of course. She's alive and in love. And I can't think of anyone better than our favorite priest to see her safely through her fledgling year." She ran her fingernails over his bare chest. "It was nice, having the whole family together for a while, don't you think?"

He grunted softly. "Who *are* you and where's my wife?"

She bit him playfully. "It *was* nice. We've been lucky."

"How so?"

"Well, except for Monroe, all the people we care about have survived, although tonight was a close call. Alric was obviously out of his head to jump off the balcony like that with the sun coming up."

"Giovanni must have bled him almost dry." He shuddered. "I can't think of a worse way to go."

"No more than he deserved. He was a nasty piece of work."

"We're lucky the sun didn't get any of our people,"

Logan remarked. And then frowned. "Not all of them are able to be awake during the day."

She made a *tsk*ing sound. "Did you think I wouldn't take care of them?"

Brow furrowed, he met her gaze. "What do you mean?"

"I protected them, of course."

"How?"

"I shielded them with my preternatural energy, enough to last until they were all safely home."

"Is there anything you *can't* do?" He'd known her for centuries, Logan thought, yet he was still amazed at the seemingly unlimited power she possessed.

"I don't know," she murmured, tracing his lower lip with her fingers. "I guess only time will tell."

A low growl rumbled in his throat as he rose over her, his eyes smoky with desire. "Enough about the family," he muttered. "It's time you paid attention to me."

"Always my pleasure," she purred, throwing her arms out wide. "Do with me what you will."

Chapter 50

Cassie woke abruptly. One minute she had been locked in thick darkness and the next she was wide-awake and aware of everything around her. The room was pitch-black, yet she saw everything clearly, including the small brown spider crawling across the ceiling. She frowned as she heard footsteps in the hallway outside the suite, the cacophony of laughter, voices, bells, and whistles from the casino floor below, honking horns from the street. Why could she hear these things now when she couldn't last night? How was it even possible? And why did she feel so strange, as if she was inhabiting someone else's body? She seemed to vibrate with energy and a sense of strength and power she had never felt before.

Frowning, she sat up, her mind replaying the horror of being in Alric's grasp, the pain of his fangs at her throat as he drank and drank. The black abyss that had swallowed her whole.

Horrified, she realized he must have turned her. That was the only explanation. She was his now. The reality of her fate drove every other thought out of her mind. Was he here? She tried to sense his odious presence but she couldn't concentrate, couldn't think past the horror of what had happened.

And then she shuddered as a new thought crossed her mind. If Alric had turned her, then Johnny must be dead.

Before she had time to process her loss, she heard the sound of footsteps on the other side of the door.

Alric!

She sprang out of bed, her heart in her throat, as the door swung open. Only, it wasn't Alric silhouetted in the doorway. It was Johnny. How could that be?

"Cassie?"

"Oh, Johnny," she cried, throwing herself into his arms. "I'm so glad to see you! Tell me it was all a nightmare. Tell me Alric didn't turn me!" She stared up at him, feeling a sudden, sinking feeling in her heart. "What's wrong?" she asked, seeing the sadness in his eyes. "Why are you looking at me like that?

"He didn't turn you," he said, his voice little more than a whisper. "I did."

She backed away from him, her eyes dark with accusation. "You promised me," she said flatly. "You promised me you would never do that. And I believed you. I trusted you!"

"Cassie, listen. I had no other choice. You were dying," he said quietly. "I couldn't let you go, not if there was a chance I could save you. Hate me if you must. Hit me. Yell at me. Drive a stake in my heart. I can live with your hatred, but I don't want to live without you."

She glared at him. How could she hate him? His words, filled with love and regret, torn from the very depths of his soul, brought tears to her eyes. "I could never hate you, Johnny."

His gaze, filled with hope, burned into hers. "You're not angry?"

"Oh, I'm angry!" she exclaimed, thinking that didn't begin to describe how she felt. And then she blew out a sigh as she realized it could be worse. "But . . . well, I guess I'd rather be alive and a vampire than not be alive at all. And far better for you to be my master than Alric."

He drew her into his arms, holding her so tightly, he likely would have crushed the ribs of an ordinary mortal. "I love you, Cassie. Now and forever," he murmured.

"And I love you."

His gaze caressed her, and then he lowered his head and claimed her lips with his in a kiss she hoped would never end.

She was about to pull him down on the bed when a sharp pain unlike anything she had ever known threatened to send her to her knees. Gasping, she pulled away from him, wrapping her arms around her middle as she doubled over. Was she dying? It certainly felt like it.

"Cassie, it's okay," he said, his voice calm and reassuring. "Don't panic."

"Okay?" she croaked as her stomach clenched. "Are you kidding?"

"You're a new vampire," he said, slipping one arm around her shoulders. "You need to feed, that's all."

Feed. Hunt for prey. Drink blood. How could she have forgotten that part? Her head snapped up as she felt an ache in her gums and realized she had fangs. Fangs that were very sharp against her tongue.

"Let's get dressed," Johnny said, "and I'll take you hunting."

Even though she could see clearly in the dark, Cassie turned on the lights. Grabbing a change of clothes, she padded into the bathroom—and got her second big shock of the night. Looking in the mirror over the sink, she saw only the wall behind her. She stared at it for a long time. Reached out to touch the glass as a cold chill settled in the pit of her stomach. She remembered asking Johnny how he'd felt when he realized he had no reflection. "Invisible," had been his reply. And that was how she felt.

Feeling numb, she took a long, hot shower as she tried to come to terms with what she was. No more worrying about what to eat, she thought glumly. From now on, she would survive on a warm, liquid diet and an occasional glass of red wine. No more decadent chocolate desserts, no more pasta or burgers or pizza. No more waffles or scrambled eggs and bacon. Or freshly baked bread.

Just someone else's warm, red blood.

No more sunbathing. No more dreams. She blinked rapidly as tears stung her eyes. Had her hopes of becoming a hairdresser died with her humanity? Maybe not. Maybe she could find a salon that opened after dark, one that was willing to let her work nights.

Stepping out of the shower, she fisted the tears from her eyes. No use crying over spilled milk. So, there were things she couldn't do, she thought as she pulled on her underwear. Lots of people had handicaps and limitations and they survived. And so would she. She was alive and Johnny loved her. And that was all that really mattered.

She groaned softly as her stomach tightened. It was time to hunt, she thought, grimacing with pain.

Like it or not.

Giovanni paced the bedroom floor. He had felt Cassie's dismay as she looked in the mirror. He well remembered what that was like—the shock, the disbelief, the sudden sense of having disappeared from the face of the earth. It had taken a long time to get over it. Probably harder for a woman, he thought. Most of them spent an inordinate amount of time in front of a mirror every day, doing their hair, applying makeup, checking their appearance.

He dragged his hand across his jaw. Though he would do it again, he couldn't help feeling guilty for stealing her life. He knew it would take time for her to come to terms with what she'd become, but she was a strong woman, stronger than she knew.

And she had a whole family of vampires, including the Queen of them all, to help her get through it.

He found part of that family waiting for him in the living room. "Mara. I should have known you'd show up sooner or later."

"It's nice to see you, too, Giovanni," she said dryly. "Is Cassie all right?"

"She will be."

Gliding toward the window, Mara drew back the drapes and looked out at the neon lights. "I scarcely remember what being a fledgling was like. I only recall being angry and filled with rage and I took it out on everyone I met. Except Logan." She smiled at the memory. The attraction between them had burned brighter than the sun itself. His power, even when first turned, had been stronger than that of any of the others she had turned. Perhaps it was because he had been arrogant, self-confident, and incredibly strong-willed, even as a mortal.

Mara turned to face Giovanni, who leaned against the back of the sofa, arms folded across his chest. "Cassie should adjust to her new life quickly. After all, she has your blood in her veins, and since you have mine . . ." She shrugged. "She'll be strong and resilient once the initial shock wears off."

Giovanni nodded. Because of that blood, Cassie would likely be able to be awake a few hours each day, and then for longer periods of time as she grew stronger, something most vampires accomplished as they aged.

"Since all is well here," Mara said, "I think Logan and I will go home. Perhaps take a trip to Egypt. A honeymoon of sorts," she said with a smile. "That's where we met, you know." She closed the distance between them and caressed his cheek. "You're an amazing man, Father. Take good care of yourself. And Cassie, too."

"I will. You take care of you. I don't know what the family would do without you."

"Hopefully, you'll never find out."

"Good," he said with a grin. "I'm getting used to having you meddle in my affairs."

She laughed softly and then, with an airy wave of her hand, she was gone.

"Was that Mara's voice I heard?" Cassie asked, emerging from the bedroom.

"Yeah. She came by to see how you were doing." His gaze moved over her. "How are you doing, love?"

"I'm so hungry!"

"Let's go."

Cassie looked at Johnny, dressed in ubiquitous black, and then down at her green sweater and jeans. "I guess I'll have to buy *more* new clothes," she said ruefully. "Something in black that won't show the bloodstains."

* * *

There was no shortage of prey in Las Vegas, Giovanni thought as they strolled down the sidewalk. The streets and walkways were thronged with people. The trick was finding someone alone.

And it couldn't be just anyone, not for Cassie's first hunt. It had to be a young man, one who looked good and smelled good. In desperate times, he had fed on drunks and addicts and an occasional lady of the evening, and there were plenty of those around in the city's dark underbelly. But not for Cassie.

He finally spied a well-dressed man in his early thirties coming out of a sports bar.

Taking Cassie by the hand, they followed the man to his car, which happened to be parked on the side of a building, out of sight of passersby. Dropping her hand, Giovanni walked up behind the man and tapped him lightly on the shoulder.

The fellow whirled around, eyes wide. A bit of preternatural power kept him from bolting down the street, and then Giovanni spoke to his mind, telling him to relax, assuring him that he was in no danger.

Giovanni looked at Cassie over the man's shoulder. "The rest is up to you."

She glanced at the stranger, at Johnny, and back at the stranger. "What do I do?"

"What do you *want* to do?"

"Nothing."

"Cassie."

"All right. I want to sink my teeth into him and bleed him dry! How sick is that!"

He laughed softly. "It's pretty normal, actually. Forget your human revulsion and let the vampire within you take over. Just follow your instincts."

"I have vampire instincts now?" she asked, wide-eyed.

"It won't be unpleasant," he said, amused by her response.

"Will it be like drinking from you?"

"No. Vampire blood has a kind of kick that can be addictive for mortals. But this man's blood will be sweet. He's young and healthy and he hasn't been drinking too much or smoking pot."

"What happens if you drink from someone who's got the flu or is diseased or . . . ?"

"Nothing. The blood might taste bad, but it won't hurt you. Unless it's poisoned. That might make you sick for a while." He winked at her. "Stop stalling, *cara mia*. We can't stand here all night."

Cassie nodded as she moved slowly toward the man, and then she hesitated. He looked like a nice guy. Was he married? A father? What if she accidentally took too much and killed him? Shaking her head, she took a step back. "I don't think I can do this."

"Yes, you can." Bending down, Giovanni bit the man below his ear, just enough to draw blood. And then he grinned as Cassie's eyes took on a faint reddish glow.

Cassie took a deep breath, and then, unable to believe what she was doing, she sank her fangs into his throat. Ambrosia. The nectar of the gods. Better than dark chocolate. She closed her eyes as warmth and strength spread through every fiber of her being, easing the awful pain in her gut. Caught up in the moment, she thought nothing had ever tasted so good. Nothing except Johnny.

He laid his hand on her shoulder. "Enough."

Lifting her head, she snarled at him and then, embarrassed,

she turned her back to him. "It's not funny," she exclaimed when he laughed. "I'm turning into a monster!"

Still laughing, Johnny pulled her into his arms. A quiet word released the man from his thrall and sent him on his way.

"It's not funny," she said again, her voice muffled against his chest.

"But not unexpected." Putting his finger under her chin, he raised her head. "None of us want to quit the first time. In the beginning, you need to learn to feed from many to satisfy your thirst instead of just one. That way you don't have to worry about taking too much from any of them."

She supposed that made sense. "I guess you can't learn everything you need to know just by living with a vampire," she said, ruefully. "I'm glad I have you to teach me the ropes. I don't know how you ever survived on your own."

"I was just lucky."

"I don't think so. I think you've always been a kind and decent man. Becoming a vampire didn't change that." She smiled up at him. "Aren't you the one who told me good people stay that way?"

"I guess so. Let's get out of here."

Hand in hand, they walked back to the hotel.

"What happened to Alric? I sort of forgot about him with everything else that's happened."

"That's understandable."

"I'm guessing he must be dead, since the family went home."

"You might say he met an unfortunate end."

"Does that mean you killed him?"

"In a way. He took a nosedive over the balcony."

"I don't understand. Why didn't he just land on his feet?"

"He might have except for one thing—the sun was coming up at the time."

She frowned. "I still don't understand."

"I think he was a little out of his mind at the time and not thinking straight. He'd lost a lot of blood during our battle. It left him weak and vulnerable." He saw no need to go into the grisly details. "I'm glad he's gone once and for all."

Cassie grimaced. What a horrible way to die. Quick, she supposed, but gruesome. "Will you teach me all the things you know? Like how to turn into mist and think myself where I want to go? And how to mesmerize people, and leap tall buildings in a single bound, and . . ."

"You're thinking of Superman now," he chided gently.

"No, I'm not. You're better than he is. Stronger. Sexier."

"Sexier?" He lifted one brow. "You think I'm sexy?"

"Don't you believe me?"

"Well, no one's ever called me that before."

"Maybe I was mistaken," she said with mock disappointment.

"Let's go up to our room," he suggested with a leer, "and I'll see if I can live up to your expectations."

Chapter 51

Angelica watched Giovanni and the woman enter the hotel. Unbeknownst to Alric, she had followed him to Vegas. She had been outside the hotel when he died. She'd tried to save him, but it had all happened so fast, he had disintegrated before she could summon her magic.

She blinked back her tears as she recalled the night she'd met him to inform him of Giovanni's whereabouts. It had led to hours of reminiscing about the past. They had talked of old times and old friends, about the five years they had spent together in Spain. In those days, she had seen a side of him that few people knew—a less angry side that he rarely showed. It had reminded her of how much she had once loved him. When they'd parted that night, they had made plans to meet again.

And now he was gone.

And it was all Giovanni's fault.

No doubt the priest thought he was going to live happily ever after with his woman, Angelica mused, but it was never going to happen.

Because she had other ideas.

Chapter 52

Cassie let out a whoop as her slot machine hit a jackpot, the bells and whistles adding to the cacophony of sound that filled the casino. "Twelve hundred dollars!" she crowed. "I can't believe it!"

Giovanni smiled, not because of the money but because she seemed so happy and carefree. He had worried that she would start to regret being turned, that she would resent him for it. Of course, that might still happen, since she'd only been a vampire for a few days. Once the danger had passed, Cassie decided she wanted to stay in Vegas for a while. Not that he could blame her. In addition to gambling, there were shows and concerts and lots of elite shops. He grinned, thinking she would be able to go on quite a shopping spree with all that cash.

Seeing the growing agitation in Cassie's eyes, he suggested they collect her winnings and leave the casino. He remembered what it was like to be a fledgling, knew how overwhelming the noise, the bright lights, and the crush of people—not to mention the constant temptation of so many beating hearts—could be.

"I can't believe I won a jackpot!" Cassie exclaimed as they made their way down the street.

"You've got the devil's own luck," he said. "I think you've walked away a winner from every game you played tonight."

Cassie grinned at him. "The *devil's* own luck?" she teased.

"It's just an old saying, love. I don't mean that *you're* the devil."

"Where shall we go now?"

"I think maybe we should go hunting. Your eyes are looking a little red and not because you're tired."

"Will I always need to hunt every night?"

"For a while. In time, you can feed less often."

"Hmm." He had told her that he fed every night because he liked it, not because it was necessary. "Will you show me how to dissolve into mist?"

"After you feed, if you like."

Cassie had just released her chosen prey from her thrall when Johnny laid a hand on her arm.

"Did I do something wrong?" she asked.

"No." Raising his head, he drew in a deep breath. "I thought . . ." Not wanting to worry her, he shrugged it off. Maybe he'd been imagining things.

Cassie glanced around. "What is it?"

He shrugged. "Nothing. Are you ready?"

"I guess so."

"It's a little scary the first time. It takes a lot of concentration. You have to picture yourself with no physical form—weightless. Think of how you felt when you looked in the mirror right after you were turned and there was nothing there. Focus on that feeling of nothingness."

Cassie did as Johnny had suggested. She concentrated on how it felt to have no reflection, that horrible sense of being invisible to the world, of being nonexistent.

"Cassie?"

She tried to speak and couldn't. It took her a moment to realize she was floating above Johnny's head. She felt a moment of exhilaration. She'd done it! Swiftly followed by a sense of panic. What if she couldn't resume her physical body? What if the wind blew and swept her away and Johnny couldn't find her? What if . . . ?

"Cassie, calm down. I'm right here. You're doing fine. Imagine your feet planted on the ground. Feel the weight of your body, the pull of gravity. That's it. Relax into yourself."

She concentrated on his voice, grabbed his arm with a sigh of relief when she felt the sidewalk beneath her. "I'm not sure I ever want to try that again."

Giovanni laughed softly. "Sure you will. It gets easier, with practice." He felt it again, that subtle sense of being watched. "Give it another try. This time, propel yourself toward the hotel. I'll be right behind you."

It *was* easier this time. Cassie floated above the ground, wondering how it was possible to see where she was going without having a physical form. Drifting over the crowded street below was almost like flying. The hotel was just ahead. She couldn't just materialize on the sidewalk where people would see her, she thought, glancing around. She floated onward until she found a dark spot between two parked cars. Taking on her own shape, she saw Johnny standing beside her.

"It's all so weird," she remarked. "I mean, where do our

clothes go when we're mist and how do we get them back?"

"I don't have the slightest idea," he said with a shrug. "Mara's been doing this a lot longer than I have. Maybe she knows. It is odd, though. I know when Derek shifts to werewolf, he has to undress first or the change shreds his clothes. Just one of life's mysteries, I guess," he said, taking her hand. "Speaking of mysteries, you still have a few I haven't discovered."

"Oh?" A shiver of anticipation raced up her spine at the thought of being in his arms again.

"I've been wanting to make love to you all night," he said, his voice whiskey-rough. "I can't wait any longer."

"Why didn't you say something earlier?"

"You were having such a good time in the casino, I didn't want to stop you."

She stared at him, wide-eyed. "Do you really think I'd rather gamble than be in bed with you?"

"I hope not."

Before she could reply, they were standing in the middle of their hotel room. A smile played over Cassie's lips as she slid his jacket off his shoulders and tossed it aside, then lifted his T-shirt over his head and threw it on top of his jacket. He wasn't wearing an undershirt. "Is this what you had in mind?" she purred.

"More like this." He reached around her and slowly unzipped her dress.

She stepped out of her heels, then kicked her dress out of the way. Clad in nothing but a bright pink bra and matching bikini panties, she said, "My turn." She removed his belt, waited while he toed off his boots before unzipping his trousers to reveal a pair of black bikini briefs that left little to the imagination.

Cradling her in his arms, Giovanni headed for the bedroom. "I can't believe you're really mine," he murmured, raining kisses over her cheeks, her brow, her breasts. "I keep thinking I must be dreaming, but I know that's impossible."

"I'm really here." She ran her hands over his back and shoulders. "Feel me touching you."

"Don't stop," he growled as he rose over her. "Don't ever stop."

Angelica swore softly as she prowled the dark streets searching for prey. Giovanni and the woman had disappeared, but it didn't matter.

She knew where to find them.

Cassie woke abruptly, wondering if she would ever get used to the sudden shift from nothingness to full awareness of the world around her.

"About time you woke up," Johnny murmured.

"How long have you been awake?"

"Not long." He skimmed his fingers across her lips, then kissed her, slow and sweet. "I love having you beside me when I wake up."

"Will I ever be able to wake up as early as you?"

"Soon. What would you like to do tonight?"

Cassie pursed her lips thoughtfully. "I'd like to go see Cirque Du Soleil. I hear it's amazing."

"Whatever my lady wants."

* * *

He managed to get tickets to the last show. And it was just as breathtaking and amazing as she'd heard.

Later, they strolled hand in hand down the sidewalk, stopping at one casino or another to try their hand at black-jack and roulette.

"Looks like your luck's changed," Johnny remarked when she lost four hands in a row at the blackjack table.

"At least in this casino," she agreed. "But I'm still over a thousand dollars to the good. Why don't you play?"

"It's not much of a challenge when I can read people's minds and learn what cards they're holding."

"Oh! I've never tried that."

"It doesn't take much concentration. Slot machines are really the only challenge," he said with a grin. "Of course, I can manipulate them without much trouble."

"Being a vampire is kind of like being a magician, isn't it?"

"I never thought of it like that, but, yeah, I guess it is. Do you want to try your luck somewhere else?"

"Okay," she said, then grimaced as her body clenched with need, her veins tightening painfully.

"I think maybe you need to hunt first."

"I guess so," Cassie agreed. *I'm living on human blood.* It should have grossed her out, but instead, it filled her with anticipation.

It was near three A.M. when they headed for a residential area on the west side.

"Do you think we'll find anyone out and about at this time of the morning?" Cassie asked.

"Bound to be someone coming home from work or

getting ready to go," Johnny said. And sure enough, five minutes later, he spied a man walking out the front door to his car. "Told you so," he said, grinning. "All you have to do is call him."

Cassie stuck her tongue out at Johnny, then, concentrating, she called the man to her. It still surprised her that she could mesmerize people and make them do her bidding. After calming the man's fears, she bit him as gently as she could, even though it was tempting to sink her fangs into his neck and drink and drink. She wouldn't, of course. She didn't want to kill anyone. But the temptation was always there.

When she finished, she licked her lips and sent the man on his way. "I like that way too much," she muttered, which made Johnny laugh.

"You're a vampire now, love. You're supposed to like it."

"It's a good thing I have you with me," Cassie remarked, reaching for his hand. "Otherwise there might be bodies everywhere."

He laughed again as he drew her into his arms. "I think that's Mara's blood talking."

"Mara? What does she have to do with it?"

"Her blood runs in my veins, remember? And mine runs in yours."

Cassie wasn't sure she liked that idea. From what she'd heard, the Queen of the Vampires had once killed indiscriminately. Maybe she still did.

"Come on," Johnny said. "We'd better get back to the hotel. The sun will be rising soon and believe me, you don't want to be caught outside when it does."

* * *

They were nearing their hotel when Giovanni paused. Head lifted, he scented the air. It took a moment to sort the witch's scent from that of the dozens of other people on the street.

"What is it?" Cassie asked.

"Angelica is here."

"Who?"

"She's a vampire and a witch. I'm not sure what she's doing here, but I don't think it's a coincidence that she's outside our hotel."

Cassie glanced around, her gaze searching the darkness. There! A flicker of movement behind a stone pillar. Grabbing Johnny's arm, she whispered, "I see her, too."

"Don't stare. I don't want her to know we've seen her. Look at me as we walk that way."

Johnny kept his focus on Cassie as they strolled in the witch's direction. He wasn't sure what his next move would be, but as they neared the pillar, Angelica made the decision for him.

Screaming, "You killed him!" she sprang forward, the long, wooden stake in her hand arrowing toward Giovanni's heart.

With a cry of her own, Cassie threw herself in front of the witch, her arm deflecting the blow meant for Johnny's chest. The stake skidded across her forearm, opening a shallow gash.

With lightning speed, Giovanni grabbed the witch by the neck and gave it a sharp twist. She went limp in his grasp. Tossing the body aside, he glared at Cassie. "What the hell were you thinking, jumping in front of me like that? You could have been killed."

"What did you expect me to do?" Cassie retorted, eyes flashing fire. "Just stand there and watch her destroy you?"

"Damn right. Better me than you."

Arms akimbo, she glared back at him. "Is that right? Well, I don't think so!"

With a shake of his head, he leaned forward and kissed her cheek. "How's your arm?"

"What?" She glanced at the wound, which had already healed. "Fine. I didn't even feel it."

"You're one hell of a woman, Cassandra Douglas Lanzoni. I'm glad you're on my side."

"Is she dead?" Cassie asked, and wondered why she wasn't more horrified by what had just happened. Johnny could have been killed. She could have been killed. But she felt nothing for Angelica. Maybe she was more like Mara than she thought.

"Not yet." Bending down, he picked up the stake and drove it into the witch's heart.

"What are we going to do with the body?" Cassie asked, grimacing.

"Leave it here."

"Seriously?"

"Either someone will find it and report it to the police, or it might turn to ash when the sun comes up. I'm not sure what the effects of the sun are on witches who are vampires. If she doesn't turn to ash, the city will bury her if they can't find any next of kin."

When he jerked the stake from the witch's chest, a thin trickle of black blood oozed from the wound.

Laughing with morbid humor, Cassie remarked, "I guess what happens in Vegas really *does* stay in Vegas."

* * *

When they returned to their hotel room, Cassie sank down on the edge of the mattress. She tried to feel sorry for the witch, but the woman had wanted to kill Johnny, so what little sympathy she had was short-lived and quickly forgotten.

Kicking off her shoes, she said, "I don't know about you, but I'm ready to leave Sin City. In fact, I think it's time I got to see my wedding present, don't you?"

"You have but to ask."

It took only minutes to pack their few belongings.

"How about if you carry our bags," he said, "and I carry you?"

He had already paid for the room, so after leaving their key cards on the dresser, Giovanni slipped his arm around Cassie's waist and transported the two of them to their new home.

When they reached the front porch, a wave of his hand unlocked the door. Taking their luggage from Cassie, he set it on the porch. "Welcome to your new home, Mrs. Lanzoni," he said, lifting her into his arms.

Cassie clasped her hands behind Johnny's neck as he carried her over the threshold. A new life in a new home with the man she adored, she thought, happily. Who could ask for more?

"Oh, Johnny," she murmured as she glanced around the living room. "It's lovely."

"I hoped you'd like it," he said, setting her on her feet. "Of course, you can change anything you don't care for."

She followed him through the house, imagining how she would furnish it. The electricity hadn't been turned on, but one of the perks of being a vampire was that she didn't need artificial light. The carpets were the color of oatmeal, the walls a light tan. That was the first thing she would change, she thought. No neutral colors. Maybe a pale mauve, or a light turquoise blue. The dining room was paneled in cherrywood; the kitchen held all the modern appliances—none of which they were likely to use, she thought with momentary regret. She visualized a vase of artificial flowers on a corner of the counter, maybe a colorful teapot to set on the stove and a picture or two on the walls just to make the kitchen look lived-in.

Upstairs were the bedrooms—a master and two smaller ones, each with a walk-in closet and its own bath.

Returning to the master bedroom, Cassie made a slow circle in the middle of the floor. The carpet was the same oatmeal color as downstairs, but the walls were a pale robin's egg blue. In her mind's eye she pictured the room done in blue and white with yellow accents.

"What do you think?" Johnny asked.

Grinning, she said, "I think we definitely need a bed."

"Later. You haven't seen the backyard yet." Taking her in his arms, he transported the two of them outside. Overhead, a million twinkling stars smiled down on them.

"Oh, Johnny, it's beautiful! I've never seen anything like it." She gazed around, wide-eyed. The grass looked like green velvet. There were flowers and shrubs, and a swimming pool that reflected the light of the full moon. "I love it!" she exclaimed. "It looks like the Garden of Eden."

"And you're my Eve," he murmured as he sank down on the grass. He stretched out, drawing her body close to his as his gaze caressed her. "No regrets?"

"No. You?"

"Are you kidding?" He cupped her face in his palms and kissed her lightly. "You've made my life complete, *cara mia,* given me everything I ever wanted and more." He rained kisses on her cheek, her brow, the tip of her nose before claiming her lips with his. Lifting his head, he gazed into her eyes. "Still think we need a bed?" he asked with a grin.

"A bed of grass is just fine for our first time in our new house," she said, eyes sparkling with anticipation. Now that she was a vampire, the blood link they shared made their lovemaking even more intimate.

"But by no means our last," he murmured as he gathered her into his arms and swept her away into a wondrous world all their own.

Connect with

Visit us online at
KensingtonBooks.com
to read more from your favorite authors, see books
by series, view reading group guides, and more.

for sneak peeks, chances to win books and prize packs,
and to share your thoughts with other readers.

facebook.com/kensingtonpublishing
twitter.com/kensingtonbooks

Tell us what you think!

To share your thoughts, submit a review,
or sign up for our eNewsletters, please visit:
KensingtonBooks.com/TellUs.